DANGEROUSLY HIS

ANNA J. STEWART

Harlequin

ROMANTIC SUSPENSE

Harlequin®
ROMANTIC SUSPENSE™

ISBN-13: 978-1-335-47197-0

Dangerously His

Recycling programs
for this product may
not exist in your area.

Harlequin Enterprises ULC
22 Adelaide St. West, 41st Floor
Toronto, Ontario M5H 4E3, Canada
www.Harlequin.com

HarperCollins Publishers
Macken House, 39/40 Mayor Street Upper,
Dublin 1, D01 C9W8, Ireland
www.HarperCollins.com

Printed in Lithuania

1 2 3 4 5 6 7 8 9 10 LIT 28 27 26 25

Anna J. Stewart is an award-winning national and *USA TODAY* bestselling author of over sixty romances ranging from heartfelt to suspenseful. Her stories focus on love, family and building large circles of friends. When not writing or editing, she's usually cooking, binge-watching favorite shows or being supervised by her cats, Rosie and Sherlock.

Books by Anna J. Stewart

Harlequin Romantic Suspense

The McKenna Code

Arctic Pursuit
Under the Marshal's Protection
Dangerously His

The Coltons of Roaring Springs

Colton on the Run

Colton 911: Chicago

Undercover Heat

The Coltons of Owl Creek

Hunting Colton's Witness

Visit the Author Profile page
at Harlequin.com for more titles.

For Mikayla and Liam as you live happily ever after.

Prologue

"Something's wrong." Undercover ATF Agent Regan McKenna pressed her hand against the cabin wall of the outdated twin-prop cargo plane as it banked heavily to the left. From less than ten thousand feet up, she looked through the grimy window as the ground tilted away from her view. They were an hour out of Campeche, Mexico. They should have at least caught a glimpse of southern Texas by now. Their planned arrival was set for an abandoned airfield near Brownsville, where backup would be waiting to take the cargo, and everyone else on board, into custody.

Yet the creeping feeling they were not where they were supposed to be prickled the back of Regan's neck. Yeah… She inwardly flinched. Something was definitely wrong.

"Don't ignore your gut," she murmured to herself. It was one of the many McKenna family mantras. She swallowed hard. There was no indication of any towns, no power grids, and definitely no ATF backup waiting for their arrival. Never-ending canyons stretched into the horizon, eroding her remaining hope of reaching the Rio Grande.

Regan shifted slightly. The heavy stench of jet fuel made her stomach churn. The sidearm wedged into the back of her jeans dug deeper into her lower spine as she slid her gaze toward her ATF partner sitting beside her. His eyes dropped to her mouth when she said, "We're not crossing the border."

Special Agent Javi Perez checked his tactical watch before casting a quick glance at the guard sitting at the back of the plane. When he met her eyes once more, she saw resignation and agreement in the dark depths before he slipped his arm around her shoulders and offered a confirming squeeze. She shifted on the narrow wooden bench along one side of the fuselage; a bench that had not been built for comfort but to ensure maximum storage capacity for the illegal drugs being run in and out of the US. Even the emergency parachutes were in short supply, stashed beneath the bench where the guard sat next to the only exit door held shut by one simple, quivering lever.

The cargo container strapped in across from them held a fraction of the amount of narcotics the cartel they'd infiltrated was capable of producing. The plan was to get at least some of the supply back to the States and document the route. That could be enough to make the case against the cartel and maybe, if they were lucky, seriously weaken the foundation of one of the biggest active smuggling operations.

Years of training allowed her some control over the unease that descended when a case took an unexpected turn. She and Javi had been partners for less than six months and, however ill-advised, romantically involved for half that time. There was something temptingly dangerous about trusting her partner not only with her life and career, but also her heart.

A trust that had been tested to the limits since they'd infiltrated this particular organization only weeks before. Their investigation required they pose as corrupt married cartel intermediaries looking for a quick payday. Roles Javi jokingly teased they'd been born to play. She would bet he wasn't laughing now, though.

Alarm bells rang in the back of Regan's mind as she smoothed a finger over the face of her own watch. She looked to the armed guard as he tightened his grip on the compact semiautomatic weapon resting on his lap. The dead-eyed expression in the man's eyes when he met her gaze told her their return to the States was going to be anything but smooth.

It was hard to figure the particulars, but she silently ran through them nonetheless. It could be that she and Javi were about to be eliminated simply to save the money they were due for locking in the deal. Or there could have been a change of plans and the cargo was going to be air-dropped for later retrieval by a third party hired by the cartel. Or…

Or her and Javi's cover had been blown and they were about to find themselves chucked out of the plane for an unexpected sunrise skydive. Good thing they were ready for multiple contingencies.

"I think I'd like to see things from up front." Regan lifted a hand to Javi's chest before she stood up.

The guard at the back sat up straighter.

Regan pretended not to notice him watching her as she turned and steadied herself against the cargo crate. Strapped in as tightly as it was, it didn't budge so she couldn't confirm just how heavy it was. They could only hope the drugs were still in there and this entire flight wasn't a ruse to get rid of them.

She stumbled her way to the cockpit as the plane rode out turbulent currents like a tugboat caught in a storm. The metal of the ancient plane rattled and strained. She'd always teased her FBI sister about her fear of flying, but Regan was beginning to see Wren's side of things. It really was like being trapped in a flying tin can.

Regan heard Javi's voice echo through the cabin as she slid into the empty copilot's seat.

"Hi. *Hola.*" She offered the middle-aged, rotund man a smile as she pointed to the anemic control panel. Duct tape stretched across parts of the console. "I've always wanted to learn how to fly," she told him and earned a furrowed brow of confusion. *"¿Hablas ingles?"*

He shook his head, waved toward the cargo hold as if she were a pesky fly at a picnic, but she stayed where she was.

"Me encantaria aprender a volar." She pretended to fly the plane. *"Es divertido.* Fun!"

"Sí," he grumbled and looked back over his shoulder as if searching for help.

Regan kept her attention straight ahead, trusting Javi to follow their plan and divide and conquer. Covering both ends of the aircraft was the best way to deal with whatever was about to happen.

"Detener!" Stop!

Regan twisted around and she saw Javi reach for the crate's latch, about to pop it open. The guard launched at Javi, catching him against the side of the head with his weapon before following up by plowing the butt of his weapon into Javi's stomach. Javi, still choosing to rest rather than fight back, doubled over and dropped to his knees, his shoulder crashing hard into the container of drugs. Their pilot turned the yoke all the way to the left. The plane banked hard and began to circle.

Regan straightened her legs, her feet pushing hard against the floor as the force of the plane brought her out of her seat. When the pilot leveled the plane once more, she saw blood trickling down the side of Javi's face as he tried to push himself upright.

Her partner seemed to be struggling to catch his breath, but when he looked over his shoulder at her, there was determination on his face. And more than a glint of anger. She shoved herself out of the cockpit, reaching behind her to wrap her hand around the butt of her gun.

The guard advanced past Javi, his weapon now trained on her. *"No te muevus!" Don't move!*

It didn't matter how long she'd been an agent. Staring down the barrel of a gun always made her question her life choices. The white noise of the plane helped to clear her mind and her focus returned. Her fingers flexed before she raised her arms in surrender.

She stared at the man's finger pressing against the side of the trigger. "I'm not moving. See?" She lifted her hands higher. "Javi? You okay?"

"Sure." Javi pulled himself forward as the guard took another step in Regan's direction. "Almost there."

"Mas alto, hora!" the guard yelled. *Stand straight!*

Regan waved her arms, her ears popping as the plane climbed higher. The roar of the straining engines nearly stopped her heart. Javi took advantage of the guard's hesitation about what to do next and elbowed him hard behind the knees.

The world shifted into slow motion. Regan barely blinked before the guard's finger tightened on the trigger as he pitched forward. She dived down as a bullet whizzed past her head. It plowed through the cockpit wall and straight into the pilot's back. The second bullet went high. She twisted around as it shattered the inner layer of the windshield with a violent crack. A third shot sounded muffled, followed by an exchange of fists hitting flesh.

Cold air whipped around her, stinging her face, making her eyes water. The cockpit filled with the telltale whistle of pressure and whining. The cabin was silent otherwise.

The pilot slumped forward against the yoke.

The plane nose-dived into an instant free fall.

Regan tumbled back into the cockpit. She landed hard, the back of her head bouncing off the edge of the control panel. She scrambled to grab hold of the pilot, fingers slipping and sliding against the blood-slicked metal of his harness. The click of release was barely audible over the wind rushing through the cockpit.

Papers and maps cycloned around her. She used the deadweight of the pilot to pull herself up and once she was upright, dragged him out of the seat. She climbed over him, ignoring the spattering of blood against the control panel as she slid in to take the now-dead pilot's place. The spiderwebbed windshield was mostly fractured and reminded her of the kaleidoscope she had when she was a kid.

Regan wrapped sticky, blood-soaked hands around the yoke and planted her feet on the rudder pedals. Her biceps strained as she pulled, tipping the nose of the plane back up as the ground suddenly loomed too close. She lifted up out of the seat slightly, legs locking hard. Her lungs burned against the frigid air.

She jumped at the sound of another shot, curled in on herself as if bracing for another bullet, but instead she heard the dull sound of a body hitting the floor.

"Javi?" She couldn't even let herself consider he was dead. Keeping her left hand on the yoke, she reached out with her right to try to clear the blood off the instrument readings.

"I'm here." Javi poked his head into the cockpit, looked down at the pilot before hauling him into the cabin. "Guess we won't be getting these two to flip on their bosses." He threw himself into the copilot's seat. "You okay?"

"Peachy." She pushed her left foot, then her right, to stabilize their direction. After another dip that had Javi grabbing for his own harness, she got the plane flying correctly. "What?" she demanded when he laughed.

"I was just thinking about how I gave you a bad time about taking flying lessons."

"Two." She actually held up two fingers. "I've had two lessons!"

"That's two more than me." He leaned over and let out a hiss of breath that rivaled the whistling wind. "Ah. This isn't great."

"What?" Regan saw him press a hand to his side. He drew back fingers covered in blood. She swore, tightened her grip on the yoke. Ignoring her racing heart, she concentrated on what to do next: get them on the ground.

"Sorry about that. It's a through and through." He grimaced, shook his head and briefly felt his back. "Seriously thought he missed."

"What did you do? Walk into one of his bullets?" She twisted around for another look at the guard. He was still, lying face down, his gun on the floor halfway across the plane. "You sure he's dead?"

"I'm sure," he replied, sounding annoyed with the outcome. "Any idea how far off course we are?"

"Far enough to know we should land as soon as we can." She let out a slow breath. "Start looking for a place to set down." Regan jerked her chin toward the smooth terrain in the distance.

He leaned forward, wincing, and peered out the windshield, his left hand pressed hard against his side.

Her fingers ached from clutching the yoke. Her arms burned. She tried to relax, just like her flight instructor said, but lessons with a licensed pilot were a far cry from being eight thousand feet up in the air with only her wounded partner and two dead guys for company.

She turned the plane to the right, hoping this was their original course. "Heading east toward Texas. Not sure what this…" She reached out and pressed a lever up, then down. "Okay, flaps work. What do you see?"

"You mean other than the very hard ground?"

His reliance on humor as a pressure release only served to further shred her already frayed nerves. Airspeed was ninety knots. That was good. Nice and steady. She adjusted her hold, focused on the readouts on the console and keeping the aircraft from bouncing around too much. It felt like hours before she spotted the distinctive meandering curve of the Rio Grande coming into view in the distance.

"Finally. Got my bearings." She snatched up the mic off the radio. "See that dial there?" She pointed to the instrument panel. "Turn it until it reads one hundred twenty-one point five."

"On it." Javi groaned as he shifted forward and twisted the knob until it clicked into place. "What is it?"

"Emergency frequency. Closest air traffic control will pick us up." She waited until the readout was clear before she depressed the side button on the mic. "Mayday, Mayday, Mayday. This is ATF Agent Regan McKenna declaring an emergency. Pilot is down." She clicked off for a second when Javi slumped in his seat. "Don't you die on me, Javi. Not up here."

"Not dying." He squeezed his eyes shut. "Just hurting."

Static erupted for a second over the radio before a voice could be heard. "This is Laramie Air Traffic Control to unknown aircraft," said a female voice that echoed through the cockpit. "Please respond and confirm identity."

She had to stop herself from yelling in response. "Say again, this is ATF agent Regan McKenna. Badge number 792465. I'm carrying cartel narcotics, two cartel members and wounded personnel. Request assistance. Minimal flying experience." Massive overstatement. "Need help getting us on the ground. Damage to the windshield and possibly some controls. Requesting law enforcement detail upon arrival."

"Copy, Agent McKenna. Need your altitude and approach vector."

"Right." Regan again swiped her hand across the blood-covered dash. "Uh…" She rattled off the information, giving thanks that her instructor had been so meticulous about her learning the console.

It seemed an age before she received a response. "Copy, Agent McKenna. We've got you on radar. We're going to talk you through landing once you're on the other side of the Grande."

"Copy that." She reached out and nudged Javi's arm. "Hey! You still awake?"

"You think I'd miss this?"

That smirk of his was her Achilles' heel. But it wasn't something she was comfortable admitting even to herself.

The plane shuddered as she reduced pressure on the throttle gradually. They began their descent. No more than five hundred feet per minute, she muttered as a reminder. Slow and steady.

"Continue your airspeed between eighty and one hundred knots," the voice over the radio said. "You should see wide-open space in a few minutes. Keep coming down nice and easy."

"Copy that." What she wouldn't give for a headset. "Javi? Take this. I need both hands." She passed the mic to him.

"What's that?" Javi pointed far out ahead of them as they continued to drop lower. The terrain evened out and opened up, giving her a clear area to land in. "Are those lights or am I hallucinating?"

She sat up slightly, saw what he did. Patrol cars. A lot of them circling around before breaking out in different directions. She would have felt reassured if they hadn't still been riding out the turbulence. She wouldn't be able to relax one bit until the plane was on the ground.

"I see them," she assured Javi and winced at his sigh of relief. He was usually so controlled, hearing him slipping into uncertainty and doubt raised new alarms she didn't have the luxury of addressing.

She was freezing. Her hands were about to go numb. She flexed her fingers again. There wasn't a part of her body that didn't ache. Almost there.

"Okay, landing gear is…" She hit the switch that lowered the wheels. No warning lights went on so she assumed it had worked. They'd find out soon enough.

"Level up with the ground," the controller told her. "Keep your altimeter even."

"Right." As if the woman could hear her.

"Reduce the throttle," the voice came again. "Take it down to seventy. Extend your flaps."

Regan pushed that lever again, tilted the nose slightly up. The ground was coming at them far too fast for her liking, but all she could think about was getting them out of the air.

"Stay calm. Just gently tap down and let the wheels take the brunt," the controller said. "You're going to bounce. Just go with it. Foot pedals will keep you straight, apply pressure equally."

"Uh-huh. Javi?"

"Hmm." He sounded sluggish now, as if he were running out of steam.

"Hey! Stay with me! You can't go anywhere just yet," she yelled. "You keep promising to take me to the beach, remember? Tropical paradise. Just the two of us. Sun, sand, surf and sex."

He chuckled. "Lots of sex."

"There you go. Hold on to that thought." That last

hundred feet flew up to meet them. She nearly clipped the top of the trio of local sheriff's cars below.

When the wheels hit the runway, she levitated out of her seat, her head just missed hitting the top of the plane by less than an inch. She pressed both feet down flat on the pedals, put all her weight into the yoke and reached for the hand lever that would slow their velocity.

Gravel and dirt crunched as they kept moving, taking far too long to come to a stop. When the plane was finally still, she couldn't quite believe it. She stayed frozen in her seat, waiting for her brain to catch up. The only thing she could hear now was her own labored breathing.

"Do I park this thing or what?" She almost laughed at the way she was looking for a gear shift. But her humor didn't last. One glance at a slumped over Javi, and within seconds, she was out of her seat. She shoved his hand away, replaced it with her own and pressed down on the wound. Hard.

He jolted, eyes going wide as he cried out.

"Sorry." She cringed as blood seeped between her fingers. "Just checking."

"Agent McKenna!" A loud voice came from outside the plane by her window. "You need to open the back door!"

"Right." She leaned in to press her lips against Javi's for one brief, necessary kiss. He might not have needed it, but she did. "I'll be right back."

"I'll be right here," he assured her as he reached up to touch her face. "Thanks for saving my life, partner."

This was not the time to get sappy. Affection and fear had surfaced, but she shoved them both down. *Not now.* "Well, it is my job." She took the extra moment to press her forehead to his, squeezed her eyes shut in a quick, silent prayer of thanks. "I'll make sure you get the chance to return the favor."

With that she turned and quickly made her way to the back door to let the authorities onto the plane.

Chapter 1

"I'm not going to make it without them."

Regan looked across the scarred faux wooden table and into the desperate eyes of her former college roommate. Dina Antius had lived a lot of life in the years since they'd last seen one another. Gone was the ebullient, optimistic young woman ready to take on the world, who Regan had known.

In her place sat a thinner, considerably sadder and far more desperate thirty-one-year old clinging to reality as tightly as she clung to her coffee-filled paper cup.

"My kids are the only thing I've got that mean anything, Regan," Dina whispered, glancing around the Colonial Grounds Café located a few miles outside the small Philadelphia suburb Dina had moved to after her divorce. "They're the only things that matter."

The air was filled with the intoxicating—and some would say addicting—aroma of fresh-brewed caffeine, accented with hot butter and fresh-baked pastry. The high walls gave way to narrow, long windows letting in the strained sunlight of an early-summer day that promised to be hotter than normal. Regan glanced at her second cup of coffee and gave serious consideration to setting up an IV drip to erase the exhaustion that threatened to drag her under the slightly wobbly table.

It had been a month since Regan had worked undercover on a long-term domestic terrorist operation that had ended less than ideally. Sure, they'd taken down a significant player in the ghost gun business, but the ATF and Regan herself had paid a disturbingly high price. So high that for the first time in her professional life, she'd agreed to take the leave she was offered. She needed the time to regroup, reevaluate and recharge. After weeks spent focusing on some self-care, that antsy, anxious buzz was pushing her to get back to work. In fact, she'd been about to call her supervisor when Dina's email popped up in her inbox, asking, pleading for an in-person meeting.

Less than a day later, Regan had stepped off a commercial flight from her home base in Baltimore to meet her old roommate. How she wished she could say she'd kept up with Dina via social media, but who was she kidding? The only reason Regan ever tapped open a social media app was if she was setting up an undercover identity or attempting to track and/or get information on a suspect.

"I know what you're going to say," Dina went on, and caught Regan's attention. "Three stints in rehab—"

Regan held up a hand, irritated with herself for having drifted off. Official case or not, someone had asked for her help and Dina deserved her concentration. "Are you sober today, Dina?"

"Yes." Dina sat up straighter, as if Regan's question bolstered her confidence. "I'm going to meetings, three, sometimes four days a week, and next week I'll get my year chip."

"Congratulations." Regan offered a practiced, encouraging smile. She'd done enough volunteer work at various support groups and mental health centers to know only today, only this moment, mattered. "Let me see them." She motioned to the cell phone sitting beside Dina's trembling hand. "Your kids."

Dina's smile widened. She ducked her head and tapped on her screen. In that brief moment, Regan tried again to find the student she'd roomed with, but between Dina's now unevenly dyed dark hair and strained features, all Regan could see was a ghost of her former friend.

She accepted the cell phone with a bit of a reverent touch. The image of the two kids brought a smile to her face. She could almost hear the laughter from when the picture was taken. Gangly and a bit on the tall side, nine-year-old Brandon kept a protective if not tight arm around six-year-old Avril. Regan nodded, seeing the friend she'd known once upon a time in the faces of Dina's children. The blond hair, bright brown eyes, crooked smiles. "They're gorgeous."

"They're my life. My light," Dina said. "I'll admit I didn't always—"

"Stop." Regan handed her back the phone. "I'm not here to discuss your mistakes, Dina. You're on the other side of them, aren't you?"

"I sure hope so." Dina clicked off her phone. "I'm trying to be."

"Okay, then." She reached a hand across the table and touched Dina's arm. "What's going on?"

"Their father is taking me back to court for full custody." Tears filled her sunken, light brown eyes. "He moved out permanently to California now that his import business has taken off. I've got a steady job as a receptionist and assistant at a real estate office while I study to get my license. The kids were in a good school and my parents help. They live only a few minutes away from our apartment. I've got a good life going for them. For all of us. Now…"

"Breathe, Dina." Regan squeezed her arm. "I'm not in any rush. What's his reason for suing for full custody?"

"He doesn't need a reason," Dina scoffed. "He's rich and I have what he wants. He just has to snap his fingers and people bow at his feet. I should know." She shifted in the squeaky upholstered seat. "That's how he got me. Power. Prestige. Fancy parties, clothes and friends. It was seductive and wonderful and a bit of a blur until Avril was born." She winced. "There were complications and a lot of pain afterward, completely different from when I had Brandon. Avril was perfect, thank goodness, but I was a mess. I needed…help."

"Painkillers," Regan commented without needing to ask.

"And postpartum. It got bad," Dina admitted. "Real bad and for a while, Marcus was right. It was dangerous for me to be around them, but I've worked hard. Even he admitted it when we agreed on shared custody. He assured me I'd earned the right to be in their lives again. I think that was more his new wife's influence, but it didn't last."

"And now that he's moved, he doesn't want his kids so far away." Regan wished she felt a bit more positive about the situation. It was obvious Dina was still a bit shaky; that wouldn't read well in front of a judge tasked with protecting the well-being of two young children. Not that she thought Dina didn't deserve the chance she'd earned, but talk about an uphill battle. "Dina—"

"He's their father," Dina cut her off. "But he's not their dad. He's not…hands on. He hired a nanny as soon as I had Brandon, and if the nanny wasn't stepping in to help me, it was Brigit, his head housekeeper." Dina's lips actually curved. "She reminds me of my gran. We got along really well and I could tell she didn't approve of a lot of Marcus's behavior. She sends me pictures and keeps me up-to-date. I don't think Marcus knows," she murmured absently. "Brigit is the one who convinced me that I needed to take the time and focus on me, so I could be the mom Avril and Brandon deserve. But when I got back from my first try at rehab, she told me Marcus hadn't spent more than a few hours at a time with either of the kids while I was away. He travels a lot. He's hardly ever home and when he is, it's all work. I don't understand why he even wants them."

Power. With the added bonus of causing Dina pain, Regan would bet. "How do the kids feel about it? About him?"

"They love him." Dina shrugged. "He's not cruel or abusive. Just…distant. They're always trying to get him to notice them, especially Brandon. He just wants to spend time with his dad, but Marcus just waves him off." She shook her head. "He doesn't need them, Regan. I do. They're the reason I finally got sober."

Regan bit her tongue. She knew for a fact few succeeded in staying sober for someone else but now was not the time to point that out. "I sympathize with you, Dina, but I'm not sure what you're hoping I can do."

"I need information. Ammunition," Dina whispered almost desperately. "I need something I can use against him in court so I can keep my kids. Something that's as damaging to him as my medical records are to me."

"He has your medical records?" Regan sat up straighter. "How did…? Right." She heaved a sigh. "Like you said. He's rich."

"And he paid for my first two stints in rehab," Dina confirmed. "Privacy laws aside, obviously, the facility apparently didn't have any issues sharing the files with him. When I told him that wasn't legal, he told me to fight him on that in court, because that would be the best way to get my history on the record. I lose no matter what."

"If he uses that against you, he's showing the court what kind of man he is." Not that that might go very far where a ruling was concerned.

Dina's eyes dimmed. "It'll also show he'll do whatever it takes to protect his kids from me. He'll spin it to say what he did was necessary. Nothing I say will matter, Regan."

Regan made a mental note to get the details on these facilities Dina had been a patient of, but she could only get so far unofficially. And officially? There really wasn't anything she could do. Frustration had her squirming in her seat. "Dina, I'm sorry, but—"

"Marcus and I were married for almost eight years," Dina went on as if Regan hadn't spoken. "I heard a lot of rumors over that time, nothing I can prove, of course." She frowned as if second-guessing herself. "He was one of the biggest real estate and construction moguls here in Philly for over a decade. It all happened so fast, his success. I'm sure you know the sketchy reputation that industry has. Now that he's a big name in imports…" She shrugged.

Regan bit the inside of her cheek. All that was true enough.

"There has to be something." Dina's voice dropped to a desperate whisper. "Something he's done that I can threaten to use against him in court."

Regan didn't know Marcus Antius, not even by reputation, but if half of what Dina had told her was true, that could be a potentially deadly move. "I don't think—"

"No, listen, Regan," Dina insisted. "He had a special safe in his office to store all the cash he kept on hand. He's always had a ton of cash. Like tens of thousands."

"Cash doesn't necessarily prove criminal activity." Except for possible tax evasion, and that wouldn't necessarily mean anything in a custody case, either. Regan really didn't want Dina getting her hopes up too high. "Dina—"

"I know how I sound," Dina went on. "But there's more. I did some research before I reached out to you. I didn't want to come empty-handed or without proof." She twisted to dig into her purse and then dropped a handful of folded-up pieces of paper onto the table. "I made a list of all the names I could remember from when we were married, then I checked them out online." She fumbled to smooth one of the crinkled slips of paper. "This guy. Here." She stabbed a finger into the paper, slid it toward Regan. "I remember seeing him frequently at the house."

Regan turned the paper around and felt the warmth drain from her body.

The grainy face in front of her was all too familiar and sent her careening into the past. Anger simmered low in her belly, familiar. Toxic. Distracting. She wasn't a vengeful person. The idea of revenge didn't complement the badge she carried, or any badge for that matter. That said?

Some individuals got what they deserved.

"You know who that is, don't you?" Dina whispered. "You recognize him."

"I do." Regan nodded slowly, giving her brain time to catch up with her pulse rate. "Edik Valeri." Not someone she'd dealt with personally, but she'd had a front-row seat to the substantial fallout to his being taken into custody a few years ago. Fallout that had ended up costing Regan everything—including the soul of a good man, along with the future she'd hoped to have with him.

Javi...

No. Regan pushed away the memories that surged. *No, I'm not doing this now.* She'd written Javier Perez out of her life as soon as he'd been dismissed from the ATF. Or at least she'd tried to. No matter how hard she strove to come to terms with his betrayal, it still didn't make sense. Chances were it never would. She hated to disappoint Dina, but Regan had to tell her the truth. The words almost got caught in her throat.

"Edik Valeri isn't going to be of any help to you. He was killed in prison last year." She wasn't surprised that Dina hadn't heard. The bureau of prisons had worked hard to keep Valeri's death under wraps.

"Oh." Dina frowned and Regan could all but see the

gears turning in her head. "But he was a bad guy, wasn't he? Even if he is dead, Marcus took a picture with him. They look like friends." Dina tapped a finger against the paper. "That proves Marcus is or at least has been involved with dangerous people. And I know, I *know* they were in business together," she said, pleading. "Marcus told me once that Edik made him nervous but that the profit margin cut through his concern." She sat back, swiped her hair out of her eyes. "No one will listen, or believe me, but if *you* could find proof they were working together, maybe…" A barely there glimmer of hope emerged in her watery eyes. "They'd believe you, Regan."

Regan pressed her lips together until they went numb. She could see the logic in Dina's argument, but that didn't mean she thought dragging the Valeri brothers into a custody dispute was a good idea. Besides, she recognized that tone in Dina's voice, the desperation in her friend's eyes. Regan had seen it before and knew from experience it wouldn't lead anywhere good. She would not let Dina step onto that same path. Not if it was possible for her to do something to prevent it.

Stomach clenched, she chose her words carefully. "I can make a couple of calls to try and confirm whether your ex-husband is being or has been investigated as an associate of Edik Valeri." She shrugged, feeling helpless. "But I can't say whether anything I uncover would be admissible in court."

"What about the court of public opinion?" Dina spoke so quietly Regan had to lean across the table to hear her. "I could go to the press. Show them that picture. Tell them what I know. Then the judge couldn't ignore it, right? He'd have to question whether Marcus is a suitable parent."

A chill raced down Regan's spine. "You do not want to do that, Dina."

A solitary tear plopped onto her cheek and she flailed a hand in the air. "What other option is there?"

"If you go to the media, you'll be putting a target on your back. Maybe even on your kids, as well." Not to mention that if Dina did go to the press, she could blow up any ongoing investigation into what was left of the Valeri organization. Regan couldn't afford to pull any punches when it came to Dina's threats and ideas. "You wouldn't only be outing your ex, you'd make an enemy of whoever he might be working with. And they could retaliate. I'm not trying to scare you, Dina, I'm just being honest."

Dina didn't appear convinced. "You don't think me being out in the open with all this would be a protection of sorts?"

"Guys like this don't tend to lead with reason." Then again, neither did women fighting for their kids.

"So I either let Marcus railroad me in court and I never see my kids again, or I take a chance and go to the press and see what happens." Dina gathered up the papers and the tears evaporated. "I have to do something, Regan. I have to fight back somehow. I'd rather be dead than have my kids think I just walked away from them without trying to get them back."

The tug-of-war between Regan's heart and brain was tearing her up inside. Logic and experience battled against emotion as she tried to figure out how to win this argument with Dina. But when it came to a mother trying to protect her children? Well. There wasn't a more powerful force on earth, was there?

Even as the warning bells chimed in her head, Regan took the papers and pictures from Dina, folded them up and shoved them into the back pocket of her jeans. She was probably going to regret this, but she couldn't walk away and let Dina believe she was on her own. It wasn't the McKenna way.

"Give me time to see if there's something we haven't thought of." It seemed the best way to make use of the last of her leave, especially if she could stop Dina from going to the media. "Where are Brandon and Avril now?"

Dina sagged in her seat like a deflated balloon. "They were supposed to be with my parents for the summer." A surprising edge sharpened Dina's voice. "But Marcus changed his mind at the last minute and sent them to some summer camp in Northern California instead."

Regan gnashed her back teeth. She really hoped Marcus Antius was as dirty as Dina purported him to be.

"You and I are going to make a deal." Regan finished off her coffee and held out her hand, palm up, for Dina to take. She wasn't surprised the other woman's fingers trembled when Regan squeezed. "You will give me some time to look into this. You are not going to go to the press. Not in any way, shape or form. And you won't call me every day to see what I've found out. You have to trust me that when I have news, I will let you know. I'm asking a lot of you, but if you want me to help you, that's the price. Understand?"

Dina nodded, but there was doubt on her face.

"I want you to focus on your new life so that when you get to court there's nothing to question," Regan went on.

"Don't give Marcus any more ammunition to use against you. When is your next AA meeting?" Regan steered her back to what was important: keeping her sobriety intact.

"This afternoon." Dina tightened her hold on Regan's hand before she pulled free. "My sponsor's going to be there."

"Good. Do you have the custody papers Marcus served you with?"

"Yes." Dina dug back into her purse. "There's a court date scheduled for the end of the month. I don't have the money to fly out to California and he knows it."

"Courts make allowances for video appearances these days." Sometimes. Two weeks. That should give her enough time to find something more than hearsay for Dina to use in court. Even if it was only confirmation that Marcus Antius was on law enforcement's radar. That could buy Dina more time with the court or maybe even delay the custody ruling.

Barring that, bank statements and business contracts weren't a bad idea. The question was, how did she get her hands on something like that? The ATF frowned on agents using their badges and authority for personal vendettas or investigations. But then there were times when it was better to ask for forgiveness than permission. "Who's your lawyer?"

Dina didn't answer.

"Dina?" Regan's stomach dropped. "Tell me you have a lawyer."

"I did have one for the divorce," Dina said. "But after the paperwork was signed he said he couldn't represent me any longer. I think going up against Marcus scared him. No lawyer I've spoken with since will take my case to keep custody. He still has a lot of friends here in town. And even more in California."

Regan's mind raced. Marcus probably put the word out he'd make trouble for any lawyer working for his ex-wife. "I've got friends here myself in Philly." She was already making a mental list. "There's one in particular who would enjoy the challenge. Her ex is a real estate developer. Could make it personal." And there she went using her friend's personal bias for her other friend's advantage.

She simply had to do better.

"Regan, I don't have the money—"

"She owes me a favor. A very big one, actually." Regan had been happy to keep that ace in her back pocket for the better part of a year, but she was willing to play it for a good cause. "I'll need time to lock things in place. You okay with me giving her your number?"

"Yes, yes. Of course. You are going to help me." Dina's eyes flooded with tears again. Only now her eyes glimmered with hope rather than despair. "I knew you would. Back in school, you were always the one we could depend on when we got into a mess. We always felt safer with you around."

It was, Regan thought with a quick quirk of her lips, the McKenna way. "Well, you're definitely in a mess now. But I want you to try to stop worrying, okay? Focus on the things you can control." Like staying sober. The worst thing Dina could do was ruin her sobriety. "I'm going to do everything I can to help."

Dina sobbed. "Thank you, Regan. Thank you so much."

Whatever thoughts Regan had a mere hour ago about

ending her leave early, vanished in a new wave of determination.

She was a McKenna. McKennas always, no matter what, stood up for what was right. Close friends or strangers, it didn't matter. Making sure that Dina kept her kids, permanently and forever, was definitely the right thing to do. No hesitation. No doubt.

California, here I come.

"You're going to want to think this through, kid." Not for the first time in his life—certainly not for the last—Javi Perez stared down the barrel of a loaded gun.

The fact that said weapon was only a few feet from his face really should have given Javi pause, but considering the hand holding the gun was shaking more than the San Andreas Fault on a bad day shifted his chances of getting shot to about thirty percent. Forty. Okay, fifty. Maybe. "Put the gun on the ground, turn and walk away."

His advice was ignored. Instead of following instructions, the young man with wide eyes and spiky dark hair straightened and widened his stance. His clothes hung off of his thin frame, as if he'd forgotten to eat for weeks. The panic remained in his light brown gaze, but that locked jaw told Javi he was on a mission.

And Javi had stepped right in his way.

Typical.

This was seriously the last thing he needed right now.

"See that?" Javi pointed behind him to the camera above the Miami club's rear door, which only opened from the inside. "That's one of a dozen security cameras they've got around this place, which means you have approximately three minutes before security takes you down." Javi held up both hands, making sure the motion revealed the Colt .45 he kept strapped at his hip. "Whatever it is you're planning to do—"

"I'm planning on killing him." The kid cocked the safety on the revolver that could very well be older than Javi.

"Him who?" Given the clientele of Club Mirage, the possibilities were endless. The owner, Tobias Sharpe, was rumored to be one of the biggest drug suppliers on both coasts. His club's patrons considered the place a safe haven for business deals on both sides of the law. Javi had no doubt the club was under constant surveillance by various law enforcement agencies, but Sharpe had long ago proved himself to be the new Teflon king, dodging and evading charges at every turn. "You're going to have to be more specific considering everyone who's inside."

The younger man's brow knit, as if he couldn't understand why he was being questioned by some random guy who happened to be in the wrong place at the wrong time.

Except Javi wasn't in the wrong place.

The meeting he'd set up with a low-level foot soldier in Sharpe's organization was supposed to give Javi a heads-up on the mystery guests attending an upcoming gathering that Javi's boss was hosting. Having the new head of the Valeri syndicate, and whoever he was bringing with him, was a big deal. Only now, thanks to this kid, Javi's contact had no doubt been spooked, which meant Javi had to talk this kid down before Sharpe's men came out with guns firing.

Was anything in this investigation ever going to go his way?

"Tell me who you're here to kill. More importantly..."

Javi took a step forward, eyes shifting between the kid's drawn, pale face and slightly trembling gun. "Tell me why he needs to die."

"She's dead. My girlfriend's dead." Tears exploded from the kid's eyes. "His poison killed her."

So it was Sharpe. Great. Javi reluctantly understood. "Tougher guys than you have tried to kill Tobias Sharpe," Javi said quietly. "They're all dead and gone. And their families will never know what happened to them." Javi inclined his head. "You got a family, kid?"

"Stop calling me *kid*!" The desperation in his voice told Javi not to push, but Javi dismissed it and stepped forward again.

It wouldn't require much to snatch the gun out of the young man's grip. The trick was doing it so the gun didn't go off. Given how this kid's finger was twitching, Javi's odds of success were quickly dwindling.

Javi's pulse rate kicked into overdrive. Every synapse in his brain was firing, trying to find the right words to disarm the boy before anything worse happened.

"Okay. Not kid. What's your name, then?"

He shook his head, hurt and anger shining brightly behind the tears. "Kevin."

"Kevin, do you have a family? Mom? Siblings?"

"I've got a brother." Kevin sniffled, wiped his nose with his free hand. "He's twelve. And a mom. Kind of."

Those last two words struck a deep chord Javi chose to ignore. He had something to work with at least. "Do you want your brother to have to deal with losing you, Kevin? Do you want him left alone in this world with your kind of a mom?"

Kevin's brows pinched again, as if he hadn't contemplated anything other than success. "He has me."

"He won't have you for long." Just one more step, Javi thought. His hands flexed as he lifted his foot, placed it slowly back on the ground. "Give me that gun before you ruin all our lives." Javi lifted his hand. "Give it to me, Kevin."

The back door slammed open.

Kevin jumped. The gun wobbled.

"I've got it!" Javi yelled to whoever it was who'd entered the scene as the vibrations in the alley turned deadly. "You've lost whatever window there was, Kevin." Javi lowered his voice. "Give me the gun. Sharpe will get what's coming to him. Not tonight. Maybe not for a while. But he will pay." Javi locked his gaze on Kevin's. "I promise."

He could see the struggle within the young man, the internal debate over whether to believe. Whether to trust.

Javi had been there. So many times. Before his life had shifted into one of purpose. It was, he thought sadly, a bit like looking into a mirror of the past.

"Give me the gun." Javi gently wrapped his hand around the barrel of the weapon, slipped it free from Kevin's grasp and reset the safety. "Don't move," he ordered a worried-looking Kevin. "You hear me?"

Kevin nodded, clearly unable to blink because of the terror.

"Everything's okay!" Javi yelled over his shoulder. He didn't bother looking behind him. It didn't matter if there were two or ten henchmen ready to take on the lone kid with a gun. What mattered was that Javi stood in their way. He held the weapon out to his side, barrel to the sky. "Tell Mr. Antius I'll be back in an hour." He stuffed Kevin's gun into his suit jacket pocket, grabbed the boy's shoulder, spun him away from Sharpe's men before they could get a good look at the kid's face. "Move it!" He shoved Kevin forward into the shadows of the alley. "Do what I say, exactly," Javi murmured as he pushed Kevin toward the rented sedan he'd parked hours ago. Footsteps echoed behind him. *Awesome. An audience.*

Javi popped the trunk with the remote. "Get in."

"Wh-what?" Kevin sputtered and gasped. "Wait, no, man, please!" He tried to fight Javi but Javi lifted him off the ground far too easily.

"Get in."

Kevin scrambled into the trunk, childlike eyes wide with horror. Javi had to blank out the image.

Javi stepped back, pulled out his own weapon and aimed it at Kevin.

"No! Please!" Kevin screamed.

Javi adjusted his aim at the last second, fired two shots point-blank into piles of garbage beside the car. He could feel the heat of the ricochet but the sounds were muted by the music blaring from the club.

Kevin slapped both hands over his mouth, his eyes staring in horror at Javi as he slammed the trunk shut. Javi turned, holstered his weapon as a trio of men headed toward him in the dim alley.

"You get a name?" the tallest of the three demanded. "Any idea who he was?"

"Junkie looking for a fix," Javi replied. "Said he planned to rob the place after it closed." It was the fastest and best fake explanation he could come up with on the fly. "There's a homeless encampment about two miles from here. I'll leave him there. It'll look like a drug deal went bad. Won't garner more than a cursory look by the cops."

Guy number two had dark eyes that glistened in the streetlamps. "You think?"

"I know," Javi told them without having to lie this time. "I grew up about ten blocks north. Trust me." Javi headed to the car. "No one will ever know or care that he was here." Even as Javi said the words, he tasted sour bile in his throat. "I'll be back to pick up Mr. Antius."

"Sure you don't want to change employers?" the third man called after him, his high-pitched voice bouncing along the midnight air. "Sharpe could use a guy like you."

"I'm good where I am," Javi called back. "Appreciate the offer, though." He waved before dropping into the driver's seat. He slammed the door and drove out of the alley, turning right before speeding off into the night.

He didn't stop for over a mile. Traffic was light. It was almost 1:00 a.m. Pulling into the vacant parking lot of an office building, he stopped the car, killed the lights and waited to a count of sixty just to make certain they hadn't been followed. He turned off the engine and climbed out.

When he popped the trunk again, Kevin shrank back into the darkness, hands over his tearstained face.

"I didn't save your butt just to kill you now." Javi reached in, helped him out, then pushed him onto the bumper of the car so the kid could sit and catch his breath. "How old are you, Kevin?"

"Nineteen." The way he was dragging in breath made Javi worry he'd start to hyperventilate.

Old enough to want revenge. Too young to understand the price it demanded.

"I get that someone you loved is gone," Javi said. "Believe me, I know what that feels like. But there are smarter methods to get what you want. Even if it's not Sharpe himself, there are others out there hurting people the way your girlfriend was hurt. The way you're hurt."

"What smarter methods?"

Javi took a deep breath, mentally kicking himself for opening the door. "You know the community center off Rosemeade and Fifth?"

"Sure." Kevin shrugged.

"You go there, ask for Father Simon. You tell him Javi Perez sent you and that you're looking for options for the future. Good options that will get you what you want."

"I don't know what I want."

"Sure you do." Because Javi had. Deep down. It had just taken Father Simon's thoughtful advice to help him make a plan. "You want a life of purpose. You want your brother to be safe and to have the life he wants. You don't do that with a gun in your hand." He pulled out the revolver. "At least not an illegal one. You want to take down the bad guys, there are legitimate ways. Better ways. You feel me?"

Kevin stared blankly for a moment before he nodded. "Yeah. Father Simon." He nodded again. "He'll help me?"

"It's what he does," Javi said. "You keep your head down. Stay away from the club and Tobias Sharpe. His men didn't see your face, but I'd rather you be safe than sorry." No telling what those cameras had picked up. "You put your brother first, but don't forget this feeling,

Kevin. And don't waste your second chance. Can you get home from here?"

Kevin indicated across the street. "Yeah, it's just a few blocks away."

"Good. Get going, then. When you get home, you go check on your brother. And you promise him you're going to do what it takes to make his life better. Most importantly, you keep that promise to stay on the right side of the law. Everything will be okay after that." Eventually.

"You sure?" Kevin asked with more than a little doubt in his voice.

"I'm sure." Javi rested a hand on Kevin's shoulder and squeezed. "Now go on home."

Javi watched as Kevin hustled away, his legs still shaky as he found his footing again. It wasn't until the kid turned the corner and vanished from sight that Javi relaxed.

"Okay, then." He took a calm, steeling breath. "Time to get back to it."

He climbed into the car and, after blinking the rest of the past from his mind, he started the engine and headed for the club.

Chapter 2

"Exactly where do you suggest I hide that?" Regan eyed the square silver compact her brother Aiden held out. "And since when does going undercover come with a makeup routine?"

"Since you're going in unauthorized, off book and without my on-site guidance." Aiden's patient, big brother tone reflected his many years of experience in law enforcement—first as a Secret Service agent and, since his retirement, as owner of Minotaur Security. Given his authoritative nature, he believed running one of the top private security firms in the country had left him with certain nonnegotiable expectations. "None of my people go undercover without protection and tech backup. That's doubly true for my sister."

At least he hadn't said *baby* sister. Regan's mouth twisted in an ironic smile.

Of the four McKenna siblings, Aiden stood head and shoulders above the rest. Figuratively, at least. Their US marshal brother, Howell, had a few inches on him.

It wasn't Aiden's jet-black hair and laser-beam-focused green eyes that gave him his intensity. It was about how he comported himself in a manner that, even to a new acquaintance, garnered respect. And maybe a little fear. Every cell of her big brother's being was a full-on advertisement of their family code: Honor. Duty. Family.

Aiden had been her first call after she'd met with Dina. Between the two of them, they'd run through their connections with every law enforcement agency in existence, asking about any active investigations into Marcus Antius.

The responses had ranged from quick and straightforward noes to crickets and nonresponses. Regan and Aiden's conclusion was that Dina was probably onto something where her ex was concerned, but there wasn't anything official on the books. Or nothing official that someone was willing to talk about.

And Regan had a lengthy discussion with Dina's new lawyer. Regan's longtime friend, who was a former federal attorney, had quickly agreed to take Dina's case. She also agreed with Regan's concern that Regan could very well be putting her career at risk by starting a secret investigation, but Regan was assured a work-around could be found should legalities be called into question. That was enough to ease Regan's worry and shortly after that meeting ended, she made the trip west to meet up with Aiden in a small one-bedroom apartment in a shabby part of downtown Los Angeles.

Given the time crunch—only ten days before the custody hearing would take place—Aiden put his staff to work creating her fake identity as Regan McKendrick, the newest employed member of the Antius household.

Regan hoped she wouldn't need her cover to last for long. The job was a live-in position and should give her enough access to make quick work of her "assignment." Find something Dina could use in court to balance the scales and get out fast.

In and out. A few days, maybe a week, tops.

Still.

Regan frowned at the intricate embossed design on the front of the metal compact she held. Aiden might be overreaching this time. "Domestics don't usually carry antiques on their person."

"You will." Aiden's voice left no room for debate. "Call it sentimentality if anyone asks. Plus, I need it field-tested." He clicked it open, turned it around and tapped the top mirror. A full-on digital display blinked to life. "Digital camera for photos, automatic upload to a dedicated cloud account I've set up for you. Tap here to focus." He demonstrated, aiming the compact at her. "Click the latch to capture the image. It'll distinguish between faces and documents, so if you find paperwork to support Dina's claims of criminal or suspicious activity, you can scan." He clicked the compact shut. "As soon as you close it, it'll automatically upload. It'll also work as an electronic surveillance detector to make sure you aren't being listened to."

"Okay, you've got me." She grinned and snatched it out of his hand, was tempted to play with the device. "That's pretty cool."

"Be careful with it," Aiden warned in that dubious tone he'd used for most of his thirty-eight years. "I know fancy equipment is new to you. It's not like they give you a lot of this kind of stuff at the ATF."

"They give me enough." She turned away before he could catch her gaze.

At thirty-one, Regan was old enough to recognize an oncoming sibling interrogation session when it was headed her way. Regan had no doubt Aiden meant well. She'd had a rough few months and, if she was honest with herself, helping Dina regain custody of her children was as much a distraction for Regan as it was a necessity for her friend. At some point Regan was going to have to come to terms with the fallout of her last case. But today was not that day.

Besides, it would be refreshing to work on something where she wasn't dealing with bombs, ghost guns or psychopathic criminals determined to go out in a blaze of glory.

Her jaw tensed as the past attempted to grab hold. In the back of her mind, she heard the explosion, the ear ringing before the raw screams set in. Before everything went silent. She blinked quickly, as if she could reset her brain and forget.

"Got your new ID, driver's license, passport just to be safe. Car registration." He gestured to the door. "Beige clunker parked outside. Old Garfield sticker in the back window. You can't miss it. Credit cards."

"Yeah?" She brightened.

"Hundred-dollar limit on each one," he warned. "You think of anything I missed, say the word."

She couldn't because as usual her brother had thought of everything. "You can turn down your worry monitor, Aiden." She tucked the compact into the large, worn fabric bag she'd picked up at a local thrift store. "I'm fine."

Or she would be.

Eventually.

Regan's smartwatch vibrated, alerting her to an incoming text. The second she saw who it was from, she grinned and dived into her purse for her phone.

"Hot date?" Aiden teased.

"Not unless I switch teams." Regan tapped open her message app and scanned the text. "Salina's going to be on the East Coast in a few weeks." She glanced up. "You remember Salina, don't you?"

"No one could forget Salina," Aiden said. "You and Wren convinced Mom and Dad to let her live with us while she finished high school. Two years ahead of you, if I remember correctly." His fake innocent look didn't fool her. "Two whole years. And aren't you the same age?"

"Shut up." Regan laughed. She wasn't offended by the reminder. Salina's high intelligence had helped her cope with her tough circumstances, which, as a child growing up in the foster system in Boston, had been challenging and difficult. From the second she and Salina met in eighth grade, they'd been inseparable. Their lives had diverged once Salina went to college at sixteen on a full academic scholarship, but they'd kept in touch and frequently got together for a girls' weekend. Usually in Vegas or Atlantic City. "I caught up to her, eventually."

"Uh-huh." Aiden didn't sound convinced. "Tell me, is Salina's juvie record still sealed or has she added to her criminal résumé?"

"Hey, now," Regan warned as she typed a response. "She did what she had to do to survive. And for your information, she put those pickpocket and math skills of hers to pretty good use. She's one of the most successful professional poker players in the world."

"Yeah, right." Aiden rolled his eyes.

"Considering the circles you work in, I'm surprised her name hasn't come up." It was all she could do not to go online and find Salina's résumé for him. "Hotels and casinos pay her obscene amounts of money to play in their tournaments, and what she makes joining in private games?" She shook her head in amazement and let out a low whistle.

"Oh, well," Aiden scoffed. "That sounds totally legit."

Regan waited until he met her pointed gaze before answering. "She makes more money than you do."

Aiden snorted. "Doubtful."

"Don't believe me? Check her out." But Regan let the subject drop. Aiden might have dedicated his life to justice and the law, but he didn't necessarily believe in redemption. First impressions usually lasted a lifetime for her oldest brother. Even when it came to someone the rest of the McKennas considered family.

Regan let Salina know she wouldn't be home for a few weeks, but that she'd touch base when she was done with this job. When she got a thumbs-up emoji in response, Regan set her phone down and returned to the suitcase she'd been packing with a puzzling array of clothes and belongings befitting a woman in flux.

Her daily office ATF wardrobe did not fit her assumed persona of the recently separated woman looking to start her life over with the help of her mother's friend, Brigit Sweeney. Not that Regan's closet was filled with designer clothes and accessories, either. To be honest, Regan couldn't recall what was in her closet back home. The truth was she didn't spend much time in her one-bedroom apartment these days, as evidenced by the stacks of boxes in her living room. After six months she probably should have unpacked…something.

"You'll be needing these, too."

Regan turned around and stared down at the jewelry box he cracked open.

"Jewelry from my brother." She planted a hand on her hip and pinned him with a look. "Just what I've always wanted."

He chuckled and plucked out a thin silver chain that held an overly large weathered locket and passed it to her. "Open it."

She found herself looking at a reduced image of one of their childhood dogs. "Aww." She felt a bit misty looking at that dusty mutt's face. "Donut." The McKenna family dog had gotten the name because of the white ring around his left eye.

"Exactly the reaction you should have for sentimentality," Aiden said. "Press his face."

"Okay, this is getting a little strange." But again, she did as she was told. Across the room, the open laptop on the kitchen table beeped. Her interest piqued. "Tracker?"

"Dormant unless you activate it," Aiden said. "But if we don't hear from you after a forty-eight hour-period, we'll remote ping it to get your location."

"Guess I'd best keep in touch, then." She flashed a smile that she suspected didn't quite reach her eyes. Undercover was always a risk. Underestimating the possible pitfalls was a surefire way to get herself killed. Hopefully, that wouldn't be the case, given this was essentially a custody issue. But if Marcus Antius was as connected to organized crime as Dina suggested…

Aiden nodded. "With me or your handler."

"My handler?" Regan frowned. This was the first she was hearing about that. "I thought you—"

"I've got a job I'll be working while you're sleuthing around the Antius estate. Howell would have been a good alternative now that he's out of the field and teaching, but—"

"He and Kara have that Brady Bunch trip." Regan recalled their brother's last email. "Their first run at seeing how his kids and Kara's kids get along for more than a weekend."

"A week at a beach house on the Jersey Shore with four preteens." Aiden shuddered yet grinned. "I'd rather go through counterassault training again."

Now it was Regan's turn to chuckle. The McKenna siblings had started falling like dominoes in the love department recently. First, their sister, Wren, finally saw what had been standing in front of her for the better part of a decade in the guise of her longtime FBI partner, Ty Savakis. Now Howell, who, if Regan's last conversation with him was any indication, had been doing serious jewelry shopping. That left her and Aiden as the remaining single McKenna siblings still standing. Romantically speaking. She'd be the last for sure. She'd lost her heart once. She wouldn't lose it again.

"So." Regan cleared her throat. "If you aren't playing overseer, who is?"

The cell phone in his pocket chimed. He pulled it out, checked the screen. "Speak of the devil." He texted something back, then nodded to the door. "Punctual as always."

Regan clasped the locket's chain around her neck, dropped the locket inside her shirt, and had just opened the apartment door when a very tall, rather intimidating man made his way up the exterior staircase. He met her gaze and quickly beelined for her, a duffel slung over his shoulder. Immediately, her mood lifted.

"Well, well. Slade Palmer." Regan stepped back, closed the door and immediately embraced the former FBI agent in a quick hug after he dropped his bag on the floor. "I haven't seen you in ages." She squeezed his tailor-suited arms and beamed up at him. "How are you?"

"Good." His smile made his eyes twinkle. With close-cropped blond hair and blue eyes, the man was a beautiful sight in more ways than one.

His physical stature had been of benefit to him during his years with the FBI and that intimidating factor had served him well on his own undercover assignments. Until the one that nearly got him killed. He'd had some of the tattoos required of him removed but she could still see ink poking out from beneath the collar of his T-shirt. Currently, he worked at Minotaur with Aiden on special projects.

"I didn't think you left Sacramento much these days," Regan said.

"I do when the Valeris are involved," Slade answered before Aiden did. "I spent two years of my life, most of that time in federal prison, infiltrating their organization. If what Aiden tells me is true, you working for Antius could help prevent the organization's attempted resurrection."

"I'm going in to help a friend get custody of her kids." Regan felt the need to explain. "That's the primary goal. Not blow up an organized crime outfit."

"Don't be so sure." Slade's eyes narrowed for a flash of an instant.

Regan glanced at her brother, then at Slade. "What was that look?"

"Nothing," Slade answered.

"It's never nothing with you," Aiden said. "Something bugging you?"

"Maybe." Slade hesitated but then said, "I got a call from an old contact in the justice department last night." He looked to Aiden. "He wanted to know why you've been asking around about Marcus Antius."

Regan pursed her lips in frustration. "I knew it." Too many people had issued too many denials. "They've got something going already, don't they? I'm walking into an active investigation."

"He wave us off?" Aiden asked.

"Not in so many words," Slade explained. "It was more like a warning that any curious parties should step carefully moving forward."

Regan knew how to interpret that comment. "Someone's already under."

"Maybe." Aiden paused. "Best be prepared for anything."

"Another one of our family mottoes," Regan said. She really did not need any complications this early on.

That said, she appreciated her brother's calm reaction. Aiden could have easily pulled the plug on this whole idea and she wouldn't have necessarily fought him on it. She'd take the warning to heart and tread with caution.

"How have you been, Regan?" Slade pivoted the conversation. "Everything okay?"

Irritation struck the second she saw the thinly masked

concern in his eyes. "I'm fine." Not that she expected either Slade or Aiden to believe her. No matter how many times she said it. "Yes, I had a close brush and yes, my last case didn't end well for anyone." That was the understatement of the decade. "But I'm good. I don't need a babysitter if that's why you're here."

"Babysitter, no," Slade agreed and quickly exchanged a fist bump with his boss. "Backup is another story. The Valeri syndicate isn't anything to play with, not even peripherally."

Doubt and regret squirmed inside her. Given the organization's ability to destroy every life it came into contact with, she couldn't argue with him. "This shouldn't take longer than a week," Regan admitted. "I'm sure you don't want to be away from Ashley and the baby for long."

"That baby is about to have his first birthday." The smile that spread across Slade's face lightened Regan's heart. He pulled out his cell phone, tapped the screen. "Just took these before I flew out this morning."

Regan moved in and gazed down at the beautiful image of Dr. Ashley McTavish, Slade's wife, and their very happy, very chubby son. The boy had Slade's bright, assessing eyes and Ashley's gorgeous round cheeks. "I'm sorry, I'm sure Aiden told me, but what's his name again?"

"Micah. Micah Javier Palmer." The pride in Slade's voice was all the proof Regan needed that he was more than content with how his life had shifted. But...

"Javier?" She glanced at her brother, who turned away far too quickly in her opinion. She went back to Slade. "That's an unusual choice."

"Javier Perez." He inclined his head. "You two were

partners for a while at the ATF, weren't you? Before he…left."

"We were." *Careful*, she told herself. "Are you still in touch with him?"

"No." But there was a certain sharpness in his gaze when she met his eyes. "I haven't heard from him in years. And before you ask, I'm aware of what the official record says about why he left the ATF. I know you probably don't want to talk about it—"

"No," she said firmly. "I don't."

"Fair enough." He nodded. "But just to get it out there, I don't believe that record for a second. The man saved my life when he didn't have to," Slade continued. "Mine and Ashley's. Without him, there wouldn't be a Micah. A man like that doesn't turn traitor all of a sudden. Nor does he take a bribe, or steal evidence or do anything else remotely corrupt." His features shifted, the shadows leaving his face. "He just doesn't."

The pressure of hope filled her chest. "You think he's innocent?"

"I think there's more to the story," Slade countered, gestured to Aiden. "So does he."

Regan waited to speak until Aiden glanced over his shoulder. "You do?" It didn't come as a complete surprise. Javi and her brother had a friendship that went back years. Their brief conversations about Javi's *situation* hadn't progressed past "I just don't understand."

Her brother sighed, shrugged and looked as flummoxed as she'd ever seen him. "Last time I was with him, he was…off. Not the guy I remembered."

"Being fired by the ATF will change a man," Regan countered. "When did you see him?"

He shrugged. "Little over two years ago. He was looking to go freelance, asked for help with some tech he wanted. And before you ask, no, I don't know what he's doing now, where he is or how he's getting by."

"I didn't ask." But she did wonder. More often than she should.

"Well, I hope one day Javi can meet his namesake." Other than Aiden, Slade was the first person she'd spoken with about Javi who hadn't automatically assumed her former partner was guilty.

There was an odd kind of relief in knowing she wasn't the only one who had doubts. Not that that changed anything.

Slade put his phone away. "Last I heard, Javi had his sights set on Caleb Flynn. But that was before… Well, before."

"Flynn's the turncoat FBI agent who worked for the Valeris," Aiden added, as if Regan didn't already know.

She'd gotten a jaded earful about Caleb Flynn in those months after Javi's undercover case with Slade ended.

Aiden continued. "Word is Flynn is the one behind the rebranding and rebuilding of the Valeri organization. It would make sense. He'd embrace keeping the name that carries a lot of power with it."

Figures, Regan thought. One thing Javier Perez carried better than anyone was a grudge.

"Javi never could shake the suspicion Caleb Flynn was the main contact for the human trafficking operation my cousin Georgiana got caught up in." Slade flinched as if the thought brought him pain. "Somehow he tracked her down, got her home safe."

Regan had heard some of that story. They'd become

partners shortly after Javi's return to full duty at the ATF, following the Valeri takedown.

"But since Javi left the job?" Slade claimed a chair and sat. "Nothing. Not a peep from him. I tell myself he's started over somewhere else. Somewhere far away." His voice dropped to a whisper. "It's better than thinking he's dead."

Or corrupt.

"Right," Regan murmured and ignored the glance Aiden had shot in her direction. Her stomach had knotted so hard she almost couldn't breathe. "Let's hope that last part's not true."

"Slade's going to be monitoring you until you take yourself out of the Antius household," Aiden told her. "We've put him in your background as your ex-convict, soon-to-be ex-husband, Patrick Callahan. That's what the ring's for." He gestured to the box she still held in her hand.

"Odd way to say *I do*." She grinned at Slade as she slipped the ring on her finger.

"FYI, Patrick can't keep a job," Aiden went on. "He's a little too fond of a six-pack and taking cars that aren't his. You need a place to stay now that he's kicked you out of this palace." Aiden gestured around the very brown, very grim decor of the sparsely furnished apartment. "Makes you seem a bit desperate going in as the interim live-in domestic."

"Sorry about all that," Slade teased as Regan shrugged. "I should have treated you better."

"I'm sorry we lived in such a dump," Regan shot back, enjoying the banter. "Clearly our relationship couldn't take the strain of this place." The one-bedroom apartment could barely be called livable with a blink-and-miss-it kitchenette, lumpy double bed and the constant smell of mildew and desperation.

"This is better than prison, I can tell you that," Slade countered. "And Patrick sounds like a charmer compared to some other aliases I've had." His gaze intensified. "You know what you're walking into with the Antiuses?"

"I do." She started to get the fidgets, something that always descended when she prepped for an assignment. Regan checked her watch, flexing her fingers against the tingling. She was due at the Antius estate in three hours. The biggest hurdle she foresaw was whether head housekeeper Brigit Sweeney could play her role effectively where Regan was concerned.

If Marcus Antius and his wife, Celeste, didn't buy Brigit and Regan's supposed connection, any hope of finding Dina the evidence she needed would be dead before Regan stepped onto the estate.

"I made sure to bump into Brigit yesterday while she was running errands," Regan told Slade. "We didn't have long to chat, but she's on board. She's going to recommend to Celeste that she take me on as her assistant since hers eloped recently."

"Good thing Brigit and Dina kept in touch," Aiden said. "Gave you the perfect in."

Regan agreed. Brigit was an older woman who had struck Regan as practical and straightforward. How that affected the woman's ability to sell a lie remained to be seen. "Aiden gave me a good history of Antius and his import business," Regan told Slade. "Along with as much personal information as he could gather in a short time. I have a pretty good idea of what to expect from the man." Distrust was always at the top of the list. Criminals weren't super successful if they weren't at least partially paranoid.

She knew a lot, like Marcus's college roommate's name, plus, what Marcus had called his first pet—Splash Gordon, a betta fish. And even that he'd been kicked off the high school debate team for bullying the opposition. He was a bully. That fit with what Dina had told her, so Regan definitely had a read on Marcus Antius.

The background info she had available as an ATF agent might have been considered thorough, but the deeper details Aiden had provided proved her brother had access to areas and information law enforcement agencies usually couldn't reach. It should bother her. Using whatever means to get what was needed. But…

She'd always feel more confident with extra information, rather than less. It didn't matter where it came from if it gave her an advantage or insight.

"Did you pick up a burner phone?" Aiden asked Slade.

"Before I left Sac." He retrieved his bag, dug around inside. "Not the most advanced. I'll get it banged up to make it look like you've had it a while," he told Regan.

"Main number will be Patrick's," Aiden said while Slade popped the phone out of its packaging and banged it on the rickety coffee table. "We'll get another one that's for your mom, which goes to a direct dedicated line at Minotaur Security, and a third that's a straight line to me under the name Craig Stoddard."

"As in my first boyfriend?" Regan marveled at his memory. "Wow, that's pulling from the past."

"And you knew how to define him," Aiden said. "Means you won't have to lie. If you can't get ahold of Slade, call either as backup." Again, his tone left no room for argument. "We'll have someone to you within thirty minutes."

"Got it." This was, for the most part, fairly routine. Hopefully her time with the Antiuses would be equally so.

"Make friends with the rest of the staff," Aiden suggested. "Would be nice for you to get some additional people on Dina's side if it's needed."

"I can win anyone over." She inclined her head toward the computer station Aiden had set up. "How about you run me and Slade through our communications setup."

"Before we do that." Slade was still trying to beat up her phone by banging it against a scarred dining table. "Who's your least favorite relative?"

"My…" Regan turned and frowned at him. "My what?"

"If you need to call and tell me things are ramping up but we haven't reached panic button stage, I want a code in place." Slade looked from her to Aiden. "Who would it be?"

Regan and Aiden glanced at each other. "Aunt Minnie," they said at the same time before they grinned.

"When this is over, I want to hear that story," Slade said before his eyes narrowed. "You get in trouble, you call and tell me you have to speak to Aunt Minnie. That'll alert me to get ready to haul in support."

Aiden nodded. "Good idea. Thanks. And Regan, you will have support standing by," he assured her. "Don't doubt that."

"With you? Never." She liked working with her big

brother. And at least with him as her partner, she didn't worry about whether or not she could trust him.

Nope. Not going there. Not now.

Javi Perez was in the past. Permanently.

Adrenaline surged through her system as that telltale sign that told her she was ready to get in and get started. In a matter of days, she would be able to put this case in her rearview mirror and move on.

The same way she'd moved on from Javi.

Chapter 3

After more than fifteen years of undercover assignments, Javi knew he should have acclimated to three hours of sleep a night by now. But this last week—which was bad even for a travel hound like his boss, Marcus Antius—was pushing it.

Marcus had taken the near miss of one of his associates being killed at the Florida club as a sign to keep on the move and far away from any kind of predictable schedule. Something that was starting to get to Javi and not in a good way. At least they were back on their home turf now.

Where Javi could exert some control.

Behind the wheel of the luxury SUV that came stocked with a small champagne fridge in the back—Celeste Antius did like her fancy French wine—Javi flexed his hands and rolled his shoulders to stave off exhaustion. Several four-hour-plus plane rides in the space of a day was not his idea of fun even if they had been in a private jet.

Must be age. Forty might be a few years away, but he could feel it barreling toward him like a brakeless

18-wheeler. Maybe the exhaustion came down to the fact that he was stuck in this case as if it were quicksand.

Real estate magnate turned importer Marcus Antius was Javi's best chance—perhaps his last chance—to put a final nail in the coffin of the Valeri crime organization.

And bring traitorous former FBI Agent Caleb Flynn to justice once and for all. But eighteen months undercover as Marcus Antius's personal bodyguard and chauffeur had taken its toll both mentally and physically on Javi.

"Sorry for the early return flight." Marcus Antius's voice carried that "I really should care more than I do about this" tone, which Javi was now very familiar with.

"Not a problem," Javi lied.

His boss was nothing if not easily appeased. On the surface, anyway. Marcus's aboveboard reputation, coupled with his duplicitous, in-the-shadows business practices, had made his DriftCore Global the perfect option when the Valeri syndicate had gone shopping for a new partner. One with extensive assets, like a network of warehouses and a fleet of vessels. The Valeri organization—even though the namesakes were long dead—needed solid connections in order to smuggle their trafficked goods, and humans, in and out of the country. And Marcus?

Well, Marcus couldn't resist the opportunity to increase his reputation, not to mention his financial portfolio.

"The meeting with Reggie Bogart we had scheduled for next week in LA got moved to tomorrow night," Marcus informed Javi, sounding displeased with the change of plans. "I've been asked to host a dinner for him and some of his associates. Bad timing, given this whole Brigit situation."

Javi frowned. "What Brigit situation?" Had he missed something? Had the head housekeeper been in an accident? Was she ill? "Is she all right?"

"Oh, she's fine." Irritation slid into Marcus's voice. "Just taking an unexpected vacation. Today's her last day for a while, hence our early return."

"I can't imagine Brigit taking anything resembling a vacation," Javi mused, feeling a bit shell-shocked. The longtime housekeeper kept the Antius estate running with military precision. The idea she was taking time off didn't particularly suit her.

"First time for everything," Marcus said under his breath. "Glad she managed to slide it in before the kids get back from summer camp."

Yes, Javi thought sourly. That was a very good thing. From what Javi had witnessed ever since his boss had gained temporary full custody of his children from his first marriage, neither Marcus nor his current wife had any particular interest in parenting Brandon and Avril. It was Brigit who oversaw most of the kids' daily routine and provided the affection they were in desperate need of.

What would happen to those poor kids if Javi did his job properly and sent their father to prison for his part in keeping the Valeri organization afloat?

An uneasy knot tightened his stomach. From what Javi had heard, the children's biological mother wasn't necessarily fit to parent, either. But… He swallowed the guilt attempting to rise. That wasn't his concern.

He'd banked on taking the next week to plan how he'd approach this meeting that could—hopefully and finally—lead him to Caleb Flynn. Javi had no clue as to his whereabouts. He might not even be in the country. Flynn had disappeared almost two years ago after being outed as a Valeri operative working deep in the FBI. It had taken Javi months and cost him nearly every favor he was owed to confirm Reggie Bogart, a known criminal intermediary with countless connections around the world, had been tasked with helping Flynn vanish.

The fact that Reggie Bogart had been the primary investor of capital to get DriftCore Global off the ground put Marcus on the ATF's overactive radar. That substantial investment explained why Marcus got to hopping when Reggie told him to jump.

Bogart was connected to Flynn and with Marcus partnered with him, that gave Javi a potential path to Flynn. The next few days would tell, he supposed.

Javi glanced in the rearview mirror when Marcus answered a phone call. As Javi hit the turn signal and veered into the right lane for the Newport Beach exit, he pushed the button on the side of his smartwatch.

Aiden McKenna, his longtime friend and owner of a massive bicoastal private security company had, shortly before Javi pretended to leave the ATF, provided him with a few pieces of tech. Equipment that would make available the surveillance Javi needed. Aiden hadn't asked questions. Not even the ones he should have. But that's what friends did.

Included in the tech package was the watch. It acted not only as a recording device, but it could also be also used to capture very low resolution images with an automatic upload to dedicated cloud storage that Javi kept in a secured lockdown facility.

Not that this particular conversation was going to provide much new information. It was simply Marcus's office assistant confirming changes to his schedule.

Still, it was better to record something that yielded nothing rather than miss something potentially important. Besides, recording it meant he could tune out the discussion and let his mind drift for the next few minutes.

The affluent Southern California community of Newport Beach was filled with homes ranging from nondescript bungalows to estates large enough to resemble small countries. Residents included a diverse group of people from blue collar workers to über-successful movie producers, fortunate heirs and fashionable corporate executives. It was the perfect place for someone like Marcus Antius to blend in.

Javi's brain jumped to an image of the slippery Reggie Bogart. He couldn't help but think—and hope—that thanks to the shady businessman, Caleb Flynn would walk through the front door tonight and sit down at the Antius dining room table. It would be stupid of the traitor, of course, and Flynn was far from stupid. But all Javi needed was one meeting, one confirmed sighting of the man, and what remained of the Valeri house of cards would come tumbling down.

Cut off the head of the snake and the body dies.

It was the mantra Javi had been chanting to himself for what seemed like an eternity. On days like this, he couldn't remember not chasing after Flynn or the remnants of the Valeri organization.

Funny. He'd talked that kid Kevin off the ledge of revenge while Javi had been stuck on his own for more years than he cared to admit. This investigation had cost him his job, his reputation, whatever contact he'd had with his negligible family and the love of one woman he couldn't allow himself to think about for too long.

Regret was a dangerous thing. It was easy to lose himself in the feeling. Flipping through the what-ifs of his life was never a good mindset: if he'd made different choices, if he'd not taken that undercover assignment in prison… But then he remembered the good things that had happened as a result. For Slade Palmer and his wife, Ashley; for Slade's cousin Georgiana. And, for a while, himself.

As usual, this train of thought circled back to the question that kept him up at night.

If he'd just been honest with Regan…

Regan.

He yanked the steering wheel a bit harder than necessary to dislodge the thought. Driving straight into the sun, he allowed the distraction of bright light and warmth to push the dangerous memories of her out of his head.

The only things regret would get him were depression and distraction, neither of which would help him accomplish his goal of tracking down Caleb Flynn.

He'd done what he'd done because it needed doing. Flynn was considered an embarrassment for the FBI, and the agency had gone above and beyond to sweep his betrayal under the rug. Other law enforcement agencies had given up on the Valeri syndicate for the most part. As far as the FBI, NSA and even Javi's own ATF was concerned, with the Valeri brothers dead, the organization once responsible for a huge portion of human trafficking on the West Coast was flailing. That was enough for them to step back and let the nefarious syndicate finish itself off.

It was not, however, enough for Javi.

If someone didn't take that final whack, there was the chance that the operation would quietly regroup and come back stronger. And that, for Javi, was unacceptable. So, when the offer to potentially destroy the criminal syndicate once and for all came later, from one man, he took it.

A deputy director who had been willing to fix it such that Javi would hang his professional reputation in order to get the job done. A deputy director who made no bones about his hopes that helping Javi would facilitate his own climb to the top of the agency ladder.

Javi stopped at a traffic light and took a deep breath. To see this through meant that he had to continue his ruse: a dishonored ATF agent looking to make a name for himself and amass a fortune big enough to retire on. He'd made it clear he'd cross lines other agents considered sacred. It had been daunting, setting himself up as a dirty agent after spending a lifetime of devoting himself to the rule of law.

But it had been far easier than it should have been.

One minute he'd been on the fast track to a leadership role, and the next, he'd been accused of altering evidence, taking payoffs and intimidating witnesses. His lack of pushback and protest hadn't gone unnoticed by those whose attention he was trying to get. The criminal element always had their ears open for corrupt agents and, as expected, they'd come calling.

In the end, the plan for him to infiltrate their ranks had gone seamlessly.

But he'd had to lie. To everyone. To Regan especially. It had crushed him, but it had been necessary. She had to believe he was capable of horrible misdeeds if his cover was going to hold.

He owed her for that. Not that she'd ever know her believing he'd betrayed his oath had been the biggest card he had to play when it came to locking in an undercover persona willing to cross the darkest of lines.

It would be worth it, he reminded himself, and switched off the classical music satellite station. Everything he'd walked away from, given up, turned his back on…it had to be worth it.

But there was a whisper of doubt, usually in Regan's voice. And with every day that passed, that doubt grew louder and more insistent.

"I hope Brigit makes up for lost time as far as relaxing," Javi said when Marcus hung up. He clicked the button on his watch to end the recording. "Where's she going on her vacation?" He wasn't a man who believed in coincidences, but that was probably just paranoia asking. Even a woman as dedicated to her responsibilities as Brigit Sweeney deserved time away.

"No idea." Marcus shuffled through papers before stuffing them into his briefcase. "Her sister is surprising her, apparently. I guess now I'll get to hear Celeste complain about having her new assistant split her duties. The young woman will be covering for Brigit, while trying to keep up with Celeste."

"New assistant?" Javi's ears pricked in delayed response to that bit of information. "What happened to Deborah?"

"She eloped last week. Don't worry. Brigit recommended a replacement. I know what you're thinking," Marcus added, while Javi hoped that wasn't true. "You're in charge of security. I should have run the idea past you, but I only just found out about this because Celeste forgot to tell me. At least Brigit mitigated the disruption by having the daughter of a friend come and take over. Young woman getting out of a bad marriage. Needs a job and a place to stay until she's on the other side of things. Brigit talked Celeste into giving her a try."

Javi locked his jaw. He might not have the law enforcement connections he once did, but he had enough backdoor access to be able to run background checks on every Antius employee currently working in the house. He liked knowing who he was interacting with and he hated surprises. Especially when he was undercover.

"Did you get a name?"

"Regina… Rita… MacKinny…something like that." Marcus waved off his answer as if it were an annoying mosquito buzzing too close. "Celeste insists she'll fit in just fine. I hope she's right. I can do without more drama."

Javi didn't respond. He wasn't expected to. Marcus didn't like being questioned about anything for too long. Javi had positioned himself as a sounding board, lending an ear to a man who often spoke without a filter or the acknowledgment that anyone else was in the room. It had paid off considerably and presented numerous tidbits of information that he had documented for future presentation to the appropriate authorities.

Tomorrow night's unexpected gathering, while an inconvenient development, could prove quite illuminating and fill in the larger blanks of his case.

The last few blocks to the Antius estate were lined with the familiar towering redwoods and various fruit trees swaying in the midsummer breeze. There were manicured lawns, meticulously maintained homes and mostly empty sidewalks, save for dog walkers out for their morning jaunt in the slightly less cooler climate than nearby Los Angeles.

Some might call it paradise, something to strive for.

It made Javi miss the apartment tenement he'd grown up in. Where the neighbors provided much affection and attention, just like his *abuela* and *tias*. But those days were a universe away, another lifetime away. A life he'd left behind.

He leaned down and hit the button on the gate remote before he made the turn.

"Unbelievable." Marcus gestured to the homeless man camped out a few yards away. "Send him on his way."

Javi slid the car into Park, climbed out and hustled around the SUV. "Hey." Javi nodded at the man. It was impossible to judge his age. The streets aged a person in their own regrettable way. His jeans were ripped and torn and about two sizes too big. He looked up at Javi from where he was sitting, his face obscured by a long, full beard and straggly hair. But it was the black-and-white terrier mix dog curled up at his side that had Javi bending down. He held out his hand for the dog to sniff, then gave him a reassuring pat when he wagged his tail. "What's his name?"

"Lucky."

Javi smirked. Of course it was. "I'm sorry, but you two can't stay here."

"It's nice here," the man said, his voice husky, like a smoker's. "I just wanted someplace nice to be."

"I get that." Javi continued to pet the dog, reached into his jacket pocket for his wallet. "There's a shelter about a mile in that direction." He pointed to the east. "They're good people. They'll take care of you. And your dog." He pulled out all his cash, a couple hundred bucks. "Take care of yourself." He knew some might blow the money on drugs or alcohol, but he never put strings on what he gave. "My boss will call the cops on you if you're still here in an hour," Javi added. "Don't risk it, man."

The stranger eyed the money with something akin to suspicion. But he snatched it anyway and began to gather up his things.

Javi stood and stepped back, waited until the guy was gone before he returned to the car.

The security fence slowly opened with nary a squeak. Javi drove through and down the curving road leading to the circular driveway.

Celeste Antius's gold-and-diamond wedding ring set glinted against the sun as she waved in greeting. Today's dress color was bright yellow and made her stand out like a human canary. Javi pulled the car to a stop and let Marcus out of the back. He heard the rumblings of greetings and introductions as he retrieved his and Marcus's bags from the SUV. He could smell the ocean, which was only half a mile away, wafting on the breeze. It was as close to home as he was going to get.

"I apologize for the abrupt change," Brigit was saying as Javi approached the group from behind. "But I wouldn't leave if I didn't think she wasn't a suitable addition to the staff. Not only as your assistant, Mrs. Antius, but filling in where needed for the rest of the household as necessary. You understand what this job will entail, don't you, Regan?"

Javi set the bags down with a thud.

Regan? No. It wasn't possible. He was hearing things. It had to be a coincidence. There was no way…

His legs went numb as Brigit and her "friend" turned and faced him. Politeness required that he offer a quick smile to Brigit, but his attention was immediately pulled to the familiar round, pretty face that had taken up far too much space in his memories. And his heart.

The surprise, or rather, shock, in her light green eyes erased any idea or hope she'd come looking for him. His mind instantly whipped back to the last time they'd seen one another, the day he'd officially left not only the ATF, but her.

Her gaze glinted for a fraction of a second, breaking the spell he'd been caught in.

"This is Javi Perez," Marcus introduced them before stepping closer to Celeste and slipping an arm around her waist. "He's my other right hand."

Celeste beamed at him, her sparkling teeth glinting as brightly as her rings. "Marcus so enjoys introducing him that way."

Javi blinked, as if attempting to reboot his brain. Regan's brown hair was a bit darker, quite a bit longer, her gaze a bit sharper, her curves…curvier. His hand flexed in response. It had been over two years since they'd seen one another. Two years since he'd smelled the rose-tinted fragrance of the lotion that danced off her skin. Two years since he'd touched her.

She offered a quick, nervous smile. "Regan McKendrick." She released her hold on the midsize roller bag and held out her hand. There was a flash of warning in her eyes as he accepted her greeting. "I'm filling in for Deborah while she's out. It's nice to meet you."

"Regan McKendrick." He couldn't stop from testing the name on his lips. Feeling her hand was like a bolt of lightning striking him dead center in his chest. The wedding band on her finger sent a cold chill racing down his spine. He couldn't help it even as that aforementioned regret sliced through him. "Pleasure." The smile he offered felt genuine for the first time in ages. "Welcome."

"Look at that," Marcus teased. "Even for a guy who never says much, he's almost speechless."

"Man's got good taste," Celeste gushed and beamed.

"Judging by that look on your face," Brigit said as she scrutinized Javi and Regan with that narrow-eyed assessment that always made him shiver, "I'm thinking I won't be missed that much."

"Don't be silly," Regan countered easily even as she shot him another glance. "I'm sure Mr. Perez is just being polite. Um. So." She turned her back on him. "Would it be possible to see my room? I'd like to get settled before diving in with the rest of the day's activities. I understand there's an important dinner coming up soon?"

She addressed the question to Marcus, who nodded. "Tomorrow night."

"Regan, I'll run through everything that's expected of you," Brigit said. "If that's all right with you, Mrs. Antius."

"Of course!" Celeste agreed eagerly. "Get yourself settled. Regan and I can put our heads together first thing in the morning. We're going to have so much fun!"

"Sounds great," Regan agreed. "Thank you for giving me the opportunity," she said to Marcus. "And the safe space."

She was good. Even Javi bought in to the damsel-in-distress ruse. Talk about playing a complete opposite. The woman could outshoot any ATF agent and held the record for training agility scores and nonviolent arrests.

"I'll take you upstairs," Brigit prompted before Celeste could say anything else. "I've chosen a lovely room for you with a view of the rose garden." She gestured toward the back of the house, where Regan's view would also include the separate guest quarters above the garage where Javi resided. "Come, please."

"I've got it, thanks," Regan said of her suitcase when Brigit reached for the handle. "You're on vacation, remember. Nice to meet you," she tossed over her shoulder at Javi.

"I like her already," Celeste gushed as she and Marcus both watched the pair of women walk into the house. "I think we're going to get along great."

"I'm counting on it. Javi?" Marcus was looking at him, a puzzled expression on his face. "You okay over there?"

Javi snapped his mouth shut. What in the world was Regan doing here? Obviously she was working. ATF agents didn't suddenly become housekeepers for suspected smugglers. "She reminds me of someone," he finally said and hoped he hadn't given anything away. "My apologies if I offended her. Or you."

"I don't believe any offense was taken." Celeste ran a hand down her smooth, shoulder-length blond hair. She was a woman who was always put together, a testament to her career as a personal stylist and fashion influencer.

To be honest, Javi thought her "carefree blonde" act was just that. It took pretty shrewd acumen to snag a husband like Marcus in less than six weeks, which was how long it took Celeste to get Marcus down the aisle. An elopement to Vegas.

"Oh, I'm picking up the possibility of romance in the air," Celeste singsonged playfully. "You all know how I love a happily-ever-after!"

"Let's not get ahead of ourselves," Marcus warned. "You can drop my bag off in my room, Javi." The couple disappeared into the house before Javi could respond or confirm.

Not that Javi was able to put a coherent thought together.

He picked up the dropped bags, torn between wondering who exactly was coming to dinner tomorrow night and what he could possibly say to Regan when he finally got her alone.

"I thought this room would work best for you." Brigit stood back as Regan went to the window and pulled aside the soft mauve curtain. The view of the estate was certainly stunning with a garden exploding with color and summer promise. Calm, peaceful beauty. If only Regan felt remotely peaceful. It was as if she was caught on an out-of-control carousel.

What is Javi doing here?

Had she somehow conjured him by thinking about him these past few days? The last thing she needed was a distraction and Javi Perez fit that description to a T. If only she could shake her head and erase his presence, along with that disarming smile he probably had no idea he'd momentarily flashed. A smile that almost had her somersaulting straight into the past and into his arms.

She hadn't realized until the moment she'd looked into his eyes just how much she'd missed him.

"This is typically used as a guest room," Brigit continued. "But I thought you'd appreciate the distance from the rest of the staff. Along with a private bathroom." She gestured out the open door. "The others reside downstairs in the rooms off the kitchen." Brigit paused. "I hope it's to your liking."

"It's lovely." Regan's response was automatic but that didn't make it less genuine. The room was large, airy and beautifully decorated in soft pastels of rose and sage green. White furniture accented with delicate traces of gold offered a timeless touch even as modern amenities like USB plugs and a cell phone stand on the bedside table were on display.

An old-fashioned writing desk sat beneath the other window, as if in homage to an era bygone when people took the time to handwrite correspondence, rather than impersonally type texts and emails on their phones.

Regan let the curtain drift back into place and faced the longtime housekeeper. "Thank you so much for your help, Brigit. I'm certain Dina would thank you in person if she could."

Brigit stepped farther inside the room and shut the door. For a flash of a moment, she looked uncertain. But the expression was gone almost as quickly as it appeared. "You know him." At Regan's silence, Brigit pressed, "Mr. Perez. Or, rather…" She inclined her head as if trying to see Regan from another angle. "He knows you."

Regan wasn't in a position to lie, not when Brigit was

risking so much by helping Dina. Still. Coming clean about her previous relationship with Javi could be problematic. If only because it was a topic she wasn't anxious to delve into.

"We worked together," she said. "A long time ago." Sometimes it felt like another lifetime. "I had no idea he was here." Her stomach pitched as anxiety tightened her chest. "Has he been here long?"

"Quite a while." Brigit's sensible black shoes made no sound as she walked across the thick cream carpet. She struck Regan as a no-nonsense type of person who gave off dueling auras of serious schoolmarm and attentive caretaker. She was slightly taller than Regan, stockier, and clearly wore her responsibilities as the head of the Antius house like a badge of honor.

The sharp I-see-everything expression in her dark gray eyes made Regan more than grateful the older woman was on her side. "Is this going to be a problem?" Brigit's voice was full of concern. "You and Mr. Perez knowing one another?"

"Not for me." Regan would do everything she could to keep that promise. That didn't mean her turning up wouldn't complicate things for Javi. Not that that was her business. She had a job to do and her ex being right in the middle of things was not going to deter her.

"Dina is doing well, then?" Brigit whispered, her smile hopeful.

"She's hanging in there," Regan confirmed quietly. "She misses her kids." Regan tilted her head. "I feel the need to ask, though. Why are you so willing to help her when you've worked for Mr. Antius for so long?"

Brigit's left brow arched toward her silver-streaked

hairline. "You've answered your own question." She shook her head, concern and something akin to regret crossing her Irish-rose complexion. "I've been very fortunate working for Mr. Antius. He's always been very generous and kind to me and appreciative of the work I do maintaining his home. But I've also had a front-row seat, not only to his business dealings, but to how he treated Dina." Her eyes narrowed. "She needed help, not combat. He blamed her for her issues rather than trying to be part of the solution. She loves her babies." Her observation carried a sharp edge. "They're why she went into treatment. As far as I'm concerned, he betrayed all of them by keeping them from her once she was better. Family should always come first. Especially before work." Brigit scoffed. "I've tried to do what I can to mitigate her absence, but children need their mother. It breaks my heart to say this, but they are not happy here."

Given Regan's conversations with Dina, none of this came as a surprise. "How do you view Marcus's relationship with Avril and Brandon?"

"He tolerates them." Brigit flicked her gaze to the window. "Sometimes it seems he forgets they exist and maybe that's for the best. They're wonderful children." Pride and affection shone on her face. "They're kind. Compassionate. Brandon has become quite the protector for Avril, but I can see how much he longs for his father's attention. I do what I can, but I can't replace their mother. No one can. I want to give Dina a fighting chance. That's all."

"And Celeste?" Regan asked about Marcus's current wife. "How does she manage with them?"

"She does as well as she can." Was that sympathy

or pity Regan saw in the woman's gaze? "She's very much focused on being Mrs. Antius and embracing all the perks that come with her marriage. That doesn't leave a lot of room or time to be maternal."

That sounded as if Celeste had made a choice.

Regan's own parents were incredibly driven when it came to their professions. Her mother, in particular. Elizabeth McKenna had made her way up the ranks, all the way to Boston police commissioner, the position she still occupied. Her father, Graham, a former police detective, had spent the past fifteen years as a criminal justice professor at a prestigious New England university. They were as solid, reliable and as loving as they came.

Work fulfilled them for sure. But when one of their children needed them—for anything—Elizabeth and Graham McKenna never hesitated to shift their focus to family. Regan was well aware she and her siblings had hit the jackpot in the parent department.

It didn't escape her notice, even for a second, that not everyone was so fortunate.

"Well, I appreciate you going above and beyond for Dina," Regan said to Brigit. "Hopefully, it won't take me long to… What's wrong?"

Brigit let out a long breath. "As I said, Mr. Antius has been very good to me. I don't like going behind his back." Uncertainty hovered. "I love those children. More than I should as they aren't mine."

"*Should* doesn't enter into it," Regan said. "Children need love. It doesn't matter where or who it comes from."

Brigit nodded and her unease visibly lessened. "I appreciate that. It doesn't make me feel any better about betraying Mr. Antius, but…" She took a deep breath.

"The children are…stifled here. And they miss their mother." Brigit blinked back tears. "Dina's in recovery now, isn't she?"

"She has almost a year sober. And her parents are close by for support." Regan squeezed Brigit's arm tighter. "It's a start."

"It is that." Brigit nodded again, more forcefully this time. "Being away from all this will allow me some space to think. About a lot of things."

"Why don't you give me a few minutes to unpack," Regan said. "Then you can go through my obligations as a staff member. And what I can expect, working for Celeste."

"The unexpected," Brigit said.

"Out of curiosity…" Regan caught Brigit when she opened the door. "Does Javi live in?" The instant she asked the question she wanted to take it back. Not only because of the knowing expression on Brigit's face, but because saying his name out loud had her stomach jumping for all the wrong reasons.

"Back there." Brigit gestured to the window and the two-story building Regan had spotted through the trees. "He lives in the apartment over the garage. He's on call 24-7 for the most part. Mr. Antius keeps long and unpredictable hours."

"Right." Regan flashed a quick smile. Good to know. "Thanks."

As soon as the door snapped shut behind the housekeeper, Regan retrieved Aiden's compact from her purse and did a quick check of the room. No electronic surveillance detected. That was some good news; she wasn't considered a big enough threat to spy on.

She returned to the window and peeked out. The garage looked more like a cottage situated amid a beautifully pruned grove of flowering trees and shrubs. It had a bit of charm to it and definitely provided privacy she had no doubt Javi found appealing.

The man had always liked secrets. Thrived on them in her experience. In the end, one of those secrets had nearly threatened her own career. Guilt by association was not something she'd ever anticipated surviving, but in the end, she had. She'd even thrived in spite of him.

Doubt that she'd kept buried for the past two years surged, now that she'd seen him again. Looked into his eyes again.

Doubt she'd never been able to fully shake.

She had questions. So many questions and it was obvious there was only one way to get the answers that would finally put the past to rest.

The only problem was, after all this time, after all that had happened between them and to them, could she believe anything he had to say?

Chapter 4

Javi took the stairs up to his apartment two at a time, key in hand. On the landing, the welcome mat was slightly askew, just the way he'd left it. He bent down and saw the paperclip he'd wedged into the bottom of the door-jamb was still in place.

Reassured no one had entered his rooms above the garage while he'd been away, he stepped inside. The door hadn't closed completely before he crossed the small seating area and dropped down in front of the windows overlooking the back of the property.

Withdrawing a switchblade from his pocket, he then slid the knife between a couple of scarred floorboards, twisted and popped one of them loose.

The receive-only cell phone that he'd been given shortly before he'd begun his job as Marcus's bodyguard sat exactly where he'd left it after his scheduled check-in with his ATF handler last month.

Picking the phone up, he unplugged it from the battery pack it was hooked up to and turned it on. Pulse throbbing heavy in his neck, he waited, barely breathing, for the screen to alert him to a message. An update. Something that would explain Regan's presence at the Antius estate.

Nothing.

The screen remained lit but blank. No messages. No alerts. No answers to be found.

"Great." He started to toss the phone back into the hole, then stopped. Considered.

As important as it was to protect the only person who knew the truth about why he was here, today's unexpected developments were a reminder that anything could happen at any time.

Javi pushed himself to his feet, retrieved his jacket and stashed the powered-down phone in the inside front pocket. *What next?* he asked himself. The house was partially visible through the window and he stared at it, trying to pull his thoughts together.

"Run through the facts," he answered. "Your handler hasn't reached out. That means he doesn't know she's here." That wasn't to say someone else in the ATF hadn't started looking into Antius. But he liked to think he'd have been notified if anything official was happening.

If that was the case and the ATF hadn't sanctioned her, that meant she was here on her own. But why?

She'd covered quickly, but it hadn't been so long since they'd seen one another that he'd forgotten about her tells. That brief pinching of her brows signaled she was processing news she hadn't anticipated. The pinching was slighter now; she'd learned how to cover better. But not enough for him not to see.

She hadn't known she'd find him here.

It should be good news, he thought. But the relief the realization should have brought never came. Instead, the pressure of uncertainty hit him like a sudden punch to the gut.

Lying full-time to Marcus Antius and everyone around him wasn't only part of his job, it was easy. Lying to Regan…

That was something else entirely.

In the galley-style kitchen he used primarily to store protein drinks and energy bars, he yanked open the fridge. His eye landed on the bottles of beer he kept handy.

"Not smart." He stepped back and closed the door. Normally, after all the recent travel, he'd give in to the urge, but with Regan around, he needed to stay sharp. Acting in front of Marcus, playing the role he'd been living for nearly two years where his boss, Celeste and the staff were concerned, had been tricky but not a huge challenge. With Regan around, that wouldn't be true anymore.

In typical Regan style, she'd just made his life—and job—a lot more complicated.

He headed into the bathroom, stripped down and stepped into the voice-activated shower. The second the water poured out of the massive waterfall showerhead and the pulsating body jets struck, the tension began to melt away.

He sighed, braced his hands against the marble tile and ducked his head. There weren't many luxuries that appealed to Javi. Growing up, he hadn't had any. But when all this was over, and he was on the other side of this assignment and he got to return to whatever life he still had, frivolities like showerheads that he had discovered an affinity for would exist in whatever bathroom he owned.

His body relaxed. He could feel the exhaustion begin to settle. He closed his eyes, tilted his head up into the spray. But Regan's guarded, suspicious face filled his thoughts. She was…inescapable.

During the time they'd been apart, he had made himself forget how much he had loved her.

When he stumbled, he braced a hand against the tile wall to keep his balance. He needed some downtime. He needed to get some sleep. Clear his head, let his system reboot. Maybe then he'd see his way through the maze of confusion that Regan McKenna's arrival had opened up.

"Water off." He snatched a towel from a nearby hook, dried himself and wrapped it around his waist. Barefoot, he padded to the front door, made sure it was locked and went to the bedroom. Out of habit, he checked his work phone and found a text from Marcus telling him there were no plans to leave the house tonight. Marcus and Celeste planned to have an early dinner by the pool, which meant Javi was in the clear for the rest of the evening.

"Perfect." He made note of the time before he tossed the phone aside and dropped face-first onto the king-size mattress. "Regan," he murmured into the soft comforter.

Only now, as his brain began to shut down, did he give in to the excitement and pleasure of seeing her again.

He'd missed her. So much so that he ached. Leaving her had felt as if he'd left half his heart behind. But now she was here.

For whatever reason, she was close by. So close.

For now, it was enough. He closed his eyes and let himself drift on the cloud of contentment that came with seeing her again. His lips curved into a slight smile as he imagined hearing her laugh again.

Seconds later, he was out.

* * *

Since "Regan McKendrick" didn't have more than a few cents or belongings to her name, everything Regan brought with her fit into one drawer and took up exactly three hangers.

Her first impression of the Antiuses had still been forming in her mind when she had suddenly found herself face-to-face with Javi. His appearance flustered her, and not in a good way, but in an "I can't believe I have to deal with him on top of Marcus Antius" way.

"Typical," she muttered. She closed the dresser drawer and stashed her suitcase in the spacious closet. Clearly the universe was pointing out it was time she dealt with her long-unresolved, purposely buried emotions about the man.

The universe's timing stank.

She changed out of her jeans and T-shirt and into one of the basic black dresses she'd been given to wear as a kind of uniform.

Times like this, she kicked herself for getting involved with a guy who was also her partner. Not just involved. She'd fallen in love with Javi. Not that the words had ever passed her lips. She'd almost said it, a couple of times. Especially after the cargo plane incident that had gone badly off the rails.

Their careers had shifted into a bit of a whirlwind after they had landed. The cargo they'd delivered ended up being a very specific blend of narcotics that aided the ATF and Mexican authorities in shutting down a significant portion of the drug supply into the States. The accolades and goodwill they'd earned professionally were cut short by the revelation of Javi's...misdeeds.

Regan pressed her lips into a thin, disapproving line. She and Javi never did make it to the beach before their lives—and careers—imploded.

Within weeks of the accusations of corruption and witness intimidation, she found herself assigned to a desk, while the investigation pushed Javi all the way out of the agency. It had felt as if she'd been caught in a riptide that she couldn't escape. And that had swallowed Javi, their relationship and any future they may have had, whole.

It was not something she had any interest in rehashing. Except...

Except for the nagging doubt that wouldn't keep quiet no matter how much she tried to stifle it.

As much as she needed to focus on Dina and the reason she was here, it was obvious that was only going to be possible if and when she finally put the past to rest. How she could do that was a question for the ages.

Regan left her bedroom and closed the door, headed down the hall to the steep, curved staircase.

The quiet elegance of the Antius home took her a bit by surprise. It wasn't as ostentatious as she assumed it would be. The simple whites, creams and golds definitely spoke of affluence, but she could see a bit of comfort throughout, as well. As she descended the stairs, she spotted a painting or two that would have set the Antius bank account back a bit.

In regard to the criminal activity Dina accused Marcus of being involved in, Regan didn't see a display of it in the furnishings or decor of his home.

Her thrift-store flats made no sound as she stepped onto the marble tile floor. Wanting to get her bearings, she wandered around the foyer. Beautiful arrangements of fresh flowers sat displayed on immaculate tabletops and the air carried a soft fragrance she couldn't place.

An open set of wooden doors showed off a substantial and brightly lit library with floor-to-ceiling bookcases. Another door led into a small sitting room with bright blue walls and soft white furnishings that felt more like Celeste than Marcus. Not that Regan had had a chance to form a complete opinion of her new bosses.

She poked her head inside the sitting room and made note of one garish desk situated in front of a giant bay window and another, quite a bit smaller, tucked into the far corner of the room. Stepping inside, Regan scanned the shelves lined with labeled boxes and framed photographs, most of which seemed focused on the couple's wedding.

She lifted a gold frame and looked into the recognizable eyes of Brandon and Avril Antius. There was a glimmer of joy on the children's faces and a closeness between them. Brandon's arm was locked protectively around his little sister's shoulders in what Regan now recognized as his go-to pose.

They were what was important, Regan reminded herself. They're who she needed to focus on. Not the past.

But what if...?

"There you are." Celeste Antius paused in the doorway before pivoting into the room. "Brigit said you would be making your way down pretty soon."

"Sorry." Regan flashed a forced, uneasy smile as she set the frame back down. "I didn't mean to intrude. I was just trying to map out this big house in my head." She gestured to the picture. "Brigit mentioned them. They're beautiful."

"Mmm." Celeste's skyscraper heels clicked on the polished hardwood floor. "I can't take credit. They're Marcus's children from his first marriage." Her own quick smile seemed tinged with regret. "I don't have a lot of say where they're concerned. They're at summer camp right now. Have to admit, I miss hearing them scampering about."

"So I don't need to worry about them?"

"You do not," Celeste assured her. "We might need you to fill in with the household chores from time to time, but for the most part, you'll be working for me. Since you're here, why don't I give you the lay of the land." She held out both arms and stepped back as if standing on a stage. "This is where it all happens."

Regan glanced around. "Where what all happens?" Some things she did not have to fake.

"This!" Celeste did a slight dip and picked a name plaque off her desk. "Willow and White."

Regan stepped closer and read Curator of Lifestyle Aesthetics beneath the name. Honestly clueless, she told Celeste, "I'm sorry. I don't know what that is."

"Oh." The sympathy in Celeste's voice and pity in her sparkling eyes grated. "Of course. I shouldn't assume everyone knows what a lifestyle curator does. I started kind of by accident. So many of Marcus's friends have elevated tastes, tastes I happen to share. Designer and luxury brands for everything from fashion to antiques, events to everyday decor. I'm a bit of a detective. People tell me what they're looking for and I find it or I come up with the ideas myself. I help create their own personal brands. I've got contacts all over the place and I've consulted on national brand launches and campaigns, as well as society events right here in Southern California."

"I see." Regan couldn't imagine this was even a thing let alone a real paying job, but to each their own.

"Well, if you don't, you soon will." Celeste laughed breezily and replaced the plaque, then scooted it a little to align it with the other items on the desk. "Brigit said you have computer skills? Anything with graphic design? Deborah is a genius with LogoLoom."

"Oh, some." What was LogoLoom? She could see she'd be spending a lot of tonight on her phone scrolling for how-to videos. "I can work a spreadsheet and I type eighty words a minute. Anything else I'm sure I can figure out. I'm a fast learner."

"Perfect." She all but flounced around Regan to the other, significantly smaller desk. "This is where you work. Do you have a laptop?"

"No. I'm sorry. My ex…" She trailed off, letting Celeste fill in whatever blanks she wanted.

Celeste waved off her concern. "Not to worry. I'll make a call and have one here for you tomorrow. I'll start making a list of clients who haven't been active in the last six months, so we can reach out to them. Oh, and I'll need you to drop that off tomorrow afternoon." She pointed to a large box beneath a table by the window. "They're linen samples for Sabina Trehune's wedding planner. I'll get you that information in the morning."

Regan nodded. "All right."

"Don't worry." Celeste walked over to her and wrapped both arms around one of Regan's. "You look like a deer caught in headlights. You're going to do great, Regan. I just know it." She gave a bit of a squeal when she squeezed Regan's arm and pulled her out of the office.

"Let's go introduce you to the rest of the staff. They're going to love you as much as I do!"

Javi had a lot of practice when it came to living by his internal clock. In his early years it had been vital to his survival to get out of the house before his father woke up from whatever bender he'd been on the night before. Later on, if Javi had wanted to get to school—and he'd always wanted to get to school—it was his mother he needed to avoid in case she couldn't cope with whatever the sunrise had brought with it and told him he had to stay home.

So, precisely four hours and three minutes after he'd dropped onto the king-size bed in the generous apartment on the Antius estate, his eyes popped open.

It took a second for his brain to catch up with reality, but his growling stomach soon clued him in to a way to gain a foothold with the Regan situation. He rolled out of bed and got dressed in somewhat professional garb. Just because Marcus had texted him that the couple were in for the evening didn't mean it would stay that way.

He strapped on his sidearm, placed his hand on the weapon resting at his hip. From the moment he'd become an ATF trainee, he knew he'd found his calling. Stepping into the law-and-order realm had felt as if he'd found the life he'd been born to live. He'd embraced it with every fiber of his being.

He'd given everything to the job, including a future with Regan. He thought he'd made peace with that decision.

Time would tell if that was still true.

Javi left his place and took the quiet walk slowly to the main house. He had to admit he found a certain peace living within the confines of the meticulously maintained and manicured gardens. The brilliant colors and cascading flora provided a respite outside the ugly, sometimes nefarious activities his boss participated in.

He entered the mansion through the mudroom, stomped his shoes on the mat before closing the door and heading into the kitchen.

"Javi!" Fred, wearing one of his colorful chef's jackets that made him look like a reject from a reality cooking competition show, waved him over. The cook was on the tall and slender with sunken features and hawklike eyes that never missed a trick. His acerbic sense of humor was always entertaining. "Brigit was sorry to miss you before she left. Shall we set a place for you for dinner?"

Fred indicated the large oblong table near the huge bay window on one side of the large room.

"Sure." Javi didn't often eat with the staff, but there were numerous mitigating factors this evening.

The main one was standing at the end of the kitchen counter, looking at him with an expression he couldn't quite read. That didn't unnerve him at all.

"Excellent," Fred said with enthusiasm. "I've just been getting acquainted with Regan. I understand you two met already." That twinkle in Fred's eye was all Javi needed to know the household gossip mill was already spinning. Courtesy of Celeste, no doubt.

"We did." He offered a short nod in her direction. "Settling in all right?"

"Yes. Both Celeste and Brigit have made certain I feel very much at home." Her smile was shy and timid, not at all in line with the Regan he was familiar with.

Regardless, that gaze of hers hadn't dimmed in its

intensity. The woman could still scorch him with the briefest of looks. Never mind what those hands of hers were capable of.

Javi ground his back teeth. Thoughts like that were not going to do either of them any good. Or get him any answers.

She'd changed into a plain black dress and practical flat shoes that did nothing to deter his bone-deep desire for her. Nothing ever had, not from the instant he'd met her. She'd tied her hair back in a simple knot, kept her face free of makeup, likely playing into the quiet and unassuming role she'd established during her initial meeting with the Antiuses.

"We were just going over the final notes for tomorrow evening's dinner," Regan explained to Javi. "Including yourself and Mr. and Mrs. Antius, there will be six of you."

Javi cleared his throat. "Sounds about right." Not that he'd had any idea how many people Reggie would be bringing with him. With only two additional guests, the odds that Caleb Flynn would be one of them weren't good. "If I remember correctly, Mr. Bogart is allergic to shellfish."

"Oh." Regan turned surprised eyes to Fred. "Will that be a problem, Chef Fred?"

Javi almost choked. True to form, Regan knew how to work people. "Chef Fred" would lap that title up like a cat with a saucer of fresh cream.

"Not to worry." The personal chef straightened with pride.

Despite the airs he attempted to present, forty-four-year-old Fred Armitage had graduated from an online culinary school and his experience in restaurants and eateries was limited to a celebrity's BBQ joint that hadn't lasted six months, and a food truck called Lettuce Turnip and Beet that served off-the-wall vegetarian and vegan fare. Ironically, the man cooked a great brisket and, given the aromas emanating from the oven, had made one of his famous roasted chickens for this evening's meal.

"For tomorrow I've already planned a chilled dill and cucumber soup for the appetizer course," Fred clarified. "And an herb-encrusted tenderloin of beef for the main. Vanilla *panna cotta* with roasted strawberries for dessert. Zero fish—shell or no shell—in sight."

"Oh, thank goodness." Regan pressed a hand against her chest and sighed in relief. "I'd hate to poison a dinner guest my first official day on the job." Regan turned as a young, uniformed blonde woman entered the kitchen. "You must be Natalia, the housekeeper. It's lovely to meet you." She extended her hand, which was accepted with obvious reluctance. "Brigit has spoken so highly about you. I'm looking forward to working with you."

"Ah, hello." Natalia stood a little shorter than Regan, had a slighter build and kept her wavy blond hair close to her face to hide a scar on her left cheek. Her accent had lessened only slightly during her time working here. "A pleasure to meet you, miss."

"Regan, please," Regan insisted.

"Miss Regan." There was a flash of something uncertain on Natalia's face before she offered a brief smile and touched a quick hand to her scarred cheek. "Of course."

Javi couldn't help but feel for the young woman. In the eight months since Natalia had started working at the Antius estate, Javi had only seen shadows in her eyes. She'd arrived from Eastern Europe shortly before her hiring and had been recommended for the household position through a mutual acquaintance of Celeste's. She was a little skittish, amiable and kept to herself for the most part, spending her days off working for a local church charity focused on helping refugees find housing and employment. She tended to give Javi a wide berth and most of the time had trouble meeting his gaze. It all spoke to something unpleasant, Javi assumed, but wasn't sure what.

For Natalia, trust was not a commodity she frequently exchanged. However, Javi could feel the tension around the young woman bend and release in Regan's presence.

It was Regan's nature to put everyone she encountered at ease. Javi had found that a common trait with all the McKennas, but to his mind, Regan had been given an extraspecial dose. One of the many things about her that he'd loved.

He recalled conversations with Aiden where her brother mentioned her being the family therapist, whether she wanted to be or not. She instinctively looked deeper, even, like in Javi's case, when they didn't want her to.

"Would you mind if I had a word, Regan?" Javi asked when she reached for the tablet computer on the kitchen counter. "In private? I'd like to discuss—"

"Regan, I wonder if you could—" Celeste Antius had bustled in, eyes a bit wide and frantic. "Oh, I'm sorry. I don't mean to interrupt."

"You're not," Regan said. Meanwhile, Fred turned away to the stove and Natalia scooted over to retrieve a stack of plates for the table. "What can I help you with, Mrs. Antius?"

"Javi, I believe Marcus is looking for you," Celeste

said before answering Regan's question. "Something about tomorrow night's guests."

Javi nodded. "I'll find him."

"Great. Regan, I heard once upon a time you worked in a bar."

"Oh." Regan blinked in surprise. "Well, yes. I served drinks at a country club back in—"

"Perfect! I'd like some help choosing the right wines for tomorrow."

"I, um…" Regan glanced at Fred, whose back suddenly went stiff.

"Come." Celeste held out her hand, waggling her fingers in a way that made her rings clink. "Please, Regan. Marcus doesn't want to be bothered. Normally, Brigit is a dear to take care of it, but alas, she's off on her well-deserved break." She sighed dramatically as if performing for the back row of a Broadway audience.

"Uh…" Regan looked to Fred, who was frowning at Celeste. "Perhaps Fred would be better suited—"

"Fred has his hands full with the food," Celeste insisted. "You don't mind, Fred, do you?"

"Oh no, ma'am." But it was clear, given the narrowing of Fred's eyes, that he did.

Regan didn't miss the look. "If you'll give me a moment to finish discussing the meal with Chef Fred," she told Celeste, "I'll be happy to meet you in the wine cellar, Mrs. Antius."

"Wonderful." Celeste backed out of the room with a wave and a twirl, which sent her floral dress fluttering around her knees.

Regan turned uneasy eyes on Fred. "Working in a bar as a cocktail waitress does not make me a wine expert," she said as Natalia moved around to the other side of the table. "What would you recommend for tomorrow, Fred? To complement your menu?"

Once again, Fred straightened as if her inquiry bolstered his ego. Which, of course, it probably did.

"The 2014 Chardonnay with the first course, and then a Bordeaux blend for the main."

Regan made a note on her tablet. "I'll be certain Mrs. Antius knows we have your approval." She flashed a grateful smile. "Thank you, Fred."

"Of course."

Javi was more than impressed with Regan's smooth handling of the whole situation. "Can what you wanted to discuss wait until after dinner?" she asked him.

"It'll just take a moment. Please." He gestured for her to walk ahead of him out of the kitchen.

Bad idea. When he followed, he caught a wisp of that familiar rose-scented lotion she wore. His head spun, catapulting him into the past and into her bed. Into memories of moonlight encounters and unending nights. Memories he shoved aside with more ferocity than he'd have liked. Before they reached the end of the hall, when he was certain they couldn't be overheard, he caught her elbow and tugged her aside.

"Don't." She wrenched her arm free, swinging on him with the ferocity of a cornered cat. She clutched her tablet against her chest like a shield. "No way, not now, Javi," she half whispered.

"We're all right for a moment." He swiveled left and right, making certain they weren't surprised. "What are you doing here, Regan?"

"Working." There was fire in her eyes. Fire that ignited the instant she'd looked at him. "What are *you* doing here?"

"The same," he snapped and wished he'd thought this through better. Anything he'd planned to say had flown out the proverbial window the second he touched her. "What's your case?" *What's with the ring?* he really wanted to ask.

"Seeing as you don't work for the ATF any longer," she said slowly, deliberately, as if choosing each word with precision, "I don't owe you any explanation. Unless you want to help me. But you wouldn't want to do that, would you, Javi?"

Dread settled from one end of him to the other. It shouldn't hurt as much as it did, that she'd believed the lies. It was, after all, what he'd wanted. "You're here for Antius, aren't you?"

She didn't even blink.

"You need to leave," Javi ordered. "He's dangerous, Regan."

"So am I," she shot back. "And I don't *need* to do anything." Instead of stepping away, she moved in, inched up her chin and locked her fiery gaze on his.

His fingers flexed; he wanted to sweep her up into his arms. But that would be madness. "Sorry. It took me by surprise… Seeing you," he added, as if she needed clarification.

"Ditto." There wasn't a hint of discomfort in her voice, but that wasn't surprising. Regan had never been easily intimidated. If anything, being faced with a challenge only intensified her determination to win. One of those McKenna genetic things. None of them liked to lose.

Probably had to do with having a police commissioner

mother, a US marshal for a brother, a sister in the FBI and a brother who ran one of the top private security companies in the country. He needed to come at this from a different direction.

"Antius shouldn't even be on your radar, Regan," he told her, voice low. "But if he doesn't worry you, his business partners should."

"And you'd know all about his business partners, wouldn't you?" She actually fluttered her lashes. "I don't need you lecturing me on what my job should or shouldn't be. I can take care of myself."

Of that he was well aware.

"Instead of protecting your boss, how about you give me a head start on tomorrow night?" she prodded with a sickly sweet smile. "Give me a name. Just one. Show me there's still a hint of an agent inside there somewhere."

He was all agent, but he'd managed to convince her otherwise, hadn't he? "And what do I get in return for a name?" he countered.

"Try me and find out."

He knew her better than that. But it was worth a shot, or at least a shot across the bow in whatever war she'd just declared on him. "Reggie Bogart," he said finally.

"Reggie Bogart." She frowned. "You're telling me that as if his name should mean something."

Javi searched her gaze and shook off the icy stare she was giving him. She was telling the truth. She hadn't heard the name before. But then Reggie Bogart had only been on Javi's radar for the past year. If the ATF didn't know about Bogart and his being the connection to Caleb Flynn and therefore the Valeri organization...

Neither did Regan.

He couldn't decide whether to be worried or relieved. He ducked his head but he could feel her breath against his skin. For a moment, one long, excruciating moment, he wanted to take her hand and run away from here. Run away from…everything.

Not that she'd have gone. He, *they*, had a job to do. "These are bad guys, Regan."

She smirked. "Takes one to know one."

For the second time, she hit the bull's-eye. At some point he'd become immune to her not-so-veiled accusations of corruption. After all, he had been the one to put them in place to begin with. "Bogart is no one you want to mess with. He's protected. If you aren't going to tell me why you're here—"

"It's none of your business," she said. "And don't even think about telling me to leave. You don't get to tell me what to do." She poked a finger into his chest. "Ever. You want me gone, then you give me some dirt on your boss."

"Dirt on…" He frowned, unable to put the pieces of whatever puzzle she was assembling together. "You want dirt on Marcus? Why? What kind of dirt?"

"I'll take anything I can use against him in court." There went those lashes again. "What do you say, Javi? Mix things up a bit. Do something honorable for a change. Help me make a bad guy pay instead of helping him get away with whatever you're helping him with."

She reminded him of a fire-breathing dragon with the way her eyes glinted. The heat in her words. The tension in her spine.

They stared at each other for a long, heart-stopping minute. It would be easy, so easy, to come clean. To admit the truth. To tell her what he was really—

"Javi?" Marcus's voice echoed from somewhere down the hall.

Javi didn't pull his gaze from Regan's, even as her brow arched high in challenge.

The truth wouldn't matter. She wouldn't believe that he was the man she'd fallen in love with, that he wasn't the criminal he'd convinced her he was. The words lodged heavy in his chest, unable to be pushed out by the pressure of all that was at stake.

"Your boss is calling you." Regan stepped back and away from him. "Guess that answers my question. You'd best get going." She spun away without another word, her shoes silent as they struck the marble tile.

Watching her rush off broke the spell.

Javi hadn't taken two steps before Marcus approached, irritation clear on his face.

"There you are," Marcus said. "I just got the names of our other guests tomorrow night. I need you to run a quick background check so we know who we're dealing with. I don't want any surprises."

"Of course."

With heavy steps, Javi followed. There was only one name he wanted to hear: Caleb Flynn. It could finally bring an end to these two years of lies and betrayal. The name that could, hopefully, erase the disgust barely covering the pain he'd seen in Regan's gaze.

Chapter 5

If Javi thought his conversation with Regan last evening was going to ease his mind or provide some answers, he was wrong. His head was filled with even more questions and none of them good.

Not that he had any time to address them.

The last twenty-four hours had him cooped up in his apartment doing a deep dive into Reggie Bogart's companions. A deep dive that had pulled him down into rabbit holes so dark and twisted he had trouble yanking himself free when it was time for dinner. A dinner he wasn't entirely sure he'd be able to stomach.

One thing was for certain: he did not like the idea of Regan—or any woman for that matter—being within ten feet of the guests coming to the estate this evening. He pulled on his suit jacket, double-checked his weapon and stepped out into the late-afternoon sun.

He allowed himself a brief bit of respite, closing his eyes and turning his face into the last bit of warmth at the end of the day.

Moments like this, after he'd spent hours with the horrific details about the absolute worst that human beings could do to one another, he wondered if what he—or any other law enforcement agent—did could ever make a difference.

The crisis of faith lasted a little longer than normal but giving up wasn't an option.

Especially now that he knew precisely who was coming to dinner.

He didn't take the shortest route into the house this time. He wasn't in any frame of mind to be around other people just yet. He needed the extra minutes to walk through the garden, around the side of the house, and embrace the last of the peace and quiet before Reggie Bogart and companions arrived.

He arrived at the front of the mansion with something akin to resentment flowing through his veins. Not just resentment, but anger and disgust at the information he'd been forced to absorb. Not that he was in any position to put his feelings on display. Especially since he worked for a man who expected Javi to embrace every awful element his life had to offer.

At the bottom of the curving path, the iron gate opened to allow a long, sleek limo to drive through.

"Here we go," he muttered as the front door of the mansion swung wide and Marcus emerged. Whatever fleeting hope Javi held that Marcus might cancel tonight's dinner and refuse to meet with Reggie and his associates evaporated the second Marcus offered him a nod of acknowledgment. Javi joined him, placing himself a few steps behind his boss, taking on his silent sentry post with practiced ease.

"Got your reports." Marcus smoothed a hand down the front of his gray V-necked sweater. "Interesting reading."

"*Interesting* isn't the word I'd use."

"Keep your head down and your mouth shut," Marcus said as the car stopped at the foot of the stairs. "I need tonight to go well and without incident. Understood?"

"Yes, sir." Javi crossed his hands in front of him, hit the record button on his watch and locked his jaw.

Marcus stepped forward as the chauffeur exited the limo and held open the back door. "Gentlemen." Marcus offered his hand in greeting the first of the three men. "Reggie. It's good to see you again. Glad we could make tonight happen."

"Marcus. May I introduce Niko Demchenko and Kasimir Vaya. They're most anxious to finalize the arrangements for this partnership." Reggie's beady-eyed gaze shifted briefly to Javi, who had long ago perfected the blank stare.

He stood by the door, ready for anything Marcus might need, per the man's order, as Marcus shook hands with the other men.

"A pleasure, Mr. Antius. Thank you for opening your home to us this evening." The younger of the two men, Kasimir Vaya, accepted the greeting, then turned to Javi. "And you are?"

Javi glanced at Marcus.

"This is Javi Perez," Marcus said with a warning glance. "He's the silent type."

"Sir." Javi offered a nod of acknowledgment.

"In my experience," Vaya said slowly, "those seen but not heard tend to be the most dangerous if not the most powerful people in the room."

Vaya represented the interests of Les Ecorches, or The Flayed—everything sounded better in French. He'd begun his rise through the ranks of the Paris-based organization a little over a decade ago. To gain entry, he'd run down a pair of would-be assassins trying to take out the then leader of the criminal group. Now, just shy of thirty, Vaya was second-in-command and oversaw their European black-market dealings as well as cybercrimes and political whisper campaigns designed to take down problematic do-gooders on both sides of the aisle.

Vaya's own reputation was problematic, especially to an undercover operative. He was considered quiet and polite, was a master chess player, and it was rumored he kept a black book detailing every betrayal made against him. *Ruthless* didn't come close to describing how he meted out punishment for perceived offenses.

As the four men made small talk, Javi focused his attention on the much taller, heavier man. Demchenko wore a suit that in Javi's ATF days would have cost him two years' salary. There wasn't an inch of weakness about him, from his sturdy stature to his steely gray eyes. Given the man's history as a mercenary in various world conflicts, it would make sense that he was connected to the Valeri syndicate. Playing sidekick to Reggie Bogart felt like a bit of a comedown in Javi's estimation.

Demchenko and Vaya together signaled one of two things to Javi. Either they were looking to take out the Valeri syndicate and had joined forces or, more likely given Reggie's presence, the new head of Valeri was looking to expand its criminal enterprises and needed help.

Neither option would be good news for anyone on the right side of the law.

Meanwhile, Reggie Bogart reminded Javi of a maniacal ferret, burrowing into situations just enough to benefit the only thing he cared about: his profit margin. His one and only arrest had come at the age of nineteen, almost thirty years ago. He'd been charged with operating a protection racket in his small New York neighborhood. With no one willing to testify against him, the arrest was almost immediately vacated. Reggie pivoted and shifted focus and soon clawed his way to the top of the list of trustworthy individuals that criminals relied on to facilitate their activities and dealings.

He was the ultimate middleman.

"Please." Marcus indicated they should follow.

Javi waited and brought up the rear of the disturbing criminal parade walking into the spacious dining room that overlooked the pool and garden currently bathed in the rays of the setting sun.

Celeste turned, a wide smile on her perfectly made-up face. She wore a knee-skimming dress of white and bright pink, the full skirt reminiscent of a certain movie goddess turned real-life princess back in the golden age of Hollywood.

"Good evening, gentlemen." She walked around the table, greeted each of the guests with a warm, welcoming tone that lowered the tension in the room. "I hope you don't mind if I join you for dinner."

"It is a pleasure, madam." Vaya took her hand and lifted it to his lips, brushed his mouth against the back of her knuckles. "We couldn't possibly refuse the offer of such a beautiful dining companion. Isn't that right, Reggie?"

"Of course."

Javi could only imagine Reggie's internal monologue.

The man wasn't fond of women in any capacity, but especially when it came to business. A mistake in Javi's eyes.

The exquisite aroma of roasted meat and freshly baked pastry wafted out of the kitchen. Reggie and Vaya chose high-back chairs across from Demchenko, with Celeste and Marcus at either end of the table.

Javi took up his usual post, standing within reaching distance of Marcus. He kept his focus though, on the room. No way was he going to take his eyes off this dangerous trio.

Before claiming his seat at the table, Marcus opened the pair of French doors wider, allowing the summer evening breeze indoors. Solar lights circling the grand pool and stationed around the well-tended yard blinked to life, casting a soft glow into the darker corners of the property.

Marcus said, "I find business discussions are best conducted after a good meal with friends, be they old or new."

"A most appreciated sentiment," Vaya agreed.

"And we appreciate you allowing us to host you this evening," Celeste said as Marcus sat. "Chef Fred has been hard at work creating a meal we hope you'll all enjoy. And don't worry, Mr. Bogart," she added with a slowly curving smile. "We were made aware of your food allergies and planned accordingly."

Reggie nodded in her direction.

So civilized. Javi took the final chair.

Hard to believe four of the five people sitting at this elegant table had reputations that would put the most violent criminals to shame. That said, their collective presence made complete sense when it came to the Valeri organization's motives. Better to work with your rivals than make enemies of them.

"Good evening, Regan." Marcus's greeting had Javi's head snapping to attention.

"No Brigit this evening?" Reggie looked distastefully at Regan in her plain black dress and makeup-free face. "I have to admit I rather miss the dragon-at-the-gate glare she's perfected over the years."

"Brigit's taking some much-earned time off," Marcus told him. "We're grateful to have Regan filling in for her until she returns."

"Happy to be here, Mr. Antius." She clutched her hands together and offered a shy smile. Casting her nervous gaze around the room, she hesitated briefly, attention on Javi. Or at least that's what he told himself. "We'll start the meal with a cold cucumber soup, fresh-baked brioche and a special wine selected by Mrs. Antius."

Out of the corner of his eye, Javi noticed Celeste straighten in surprise.

Regan lifted the bottle out of the marble wine chiller next to Marcus. She poured a small portion of wine into his glass. "This crisp Chardonnay should pair nicely with the first course. If you'd like to approve this bottle for the table?" Regan wiped the rim of the bottle with a cloth napkin as Marcus sipped from his glass. Brigit had obviously filled Regan in as to how Marcus Antius liked to be served. He had a routine and far be it from Regan to mess that up.

As expected, Javi's former partner paid attention to the details.

"Excellent selection, Celeste." Marcus nodded his approval. "Please, Regan." He gestured to the rest of the people at the table.

Javi watched as Regan made her way around, filling glasses.

"It's always a good sign when a beautiful woman is taking care of us," Demchenko said, just as Regan approached. He touched a finger to her wrist. She jumped, features sharpening before she quickly regrouped and continued pouring the wine, hands trembling.

Javi's entire body went cold.

He saw the warning in her eyes before she blinked it away.

Celeste gave a nervous little laugh and the others joined in, as if someone had told a good joke.

"If you'll excuse me, I'll have Natalia help me with the first course." Regan set the bottle on the table and backed away, heading for the door.

"Surrounded by beautiful women." Niko Demchenko raised his glass to Marcus, his eyes pinned to Regan's retreating figure. "You are a man of excellent taste."

Marcus returned the toast. Javi pulled at his collar and shifted in his seat as a smoldering fire of protectiveness for Regan burned in the bottom of his belly.

Yeah. Tonight is going to be a long one.

Regan was an expert in many things, but she excelled in identifying psychopaths. Not that the men in the dining room were making it particularly difficult. She could smell danger on them as soon as she saw them. Where Marcus Antius was on that chart hovered somewhere in the she-wasn't-entirely-sure area, but the others sitting in the dining room?

She paused in the hallway, just outside the kitchen, and gripped the edge of the doorframe until her fingers went numb. She'd heard names she didn't recognize—names she committed to memory. Names and faces that definitely struck high on the threat meter. Including Javi's.

Mostly. Or…not. Damn. How could she still be confused about him?

"Yuck." She shuddered, recalling the revulsion that hit when that hulk of a creep touched her. The questionable company Marcus surrounded himself with proved he'd gone over to the dark side.

Letting out a slow, controlled breath, Regan pushed on the swinging door, entered and found Natalia adjusting her white apron. She wore her black uniform dress and had tied her hair back, something required when they were serving food. It was very obvious she was not happy about it. The way the younger woman kept putting a hand to her scar made Regan's heart twist with sympathy.

"You doing okay?" Regan asked her and plastered on a happy-go-lucky expression. She knew Brigit had requested Natalia help serve dinner this evening, which Regan appreciated. But the poor girl looked like she was about to crumble. She watched Chef Fred sprinkle accenting sprigs of dill on the top of the cucumber-soup-filled bowls.

"Yes, ma'am. Regan," Natalia corrected herself in that apologetic tone of hers. Her hands were trembling. There was a small inked bird on the inside of her left wrist, its one wing hanging down as if it were broken.

Natalia caught Regan examining the tattoo and quickly

covered it with her other hand. Regan smiled and pretended not to have noticed.

"Don't leave before me. Let's go together, all right?" Regan picked up three of the bowls, balancing one on her forearm, and waited for Natalia to take the last two. "You serve the two gentlemen by the window." The farther away Regan stayed from Javi, the better. "I'll start with Mr. Antius's other guest."

Natalia nodded and, after an encouraging word from Chef Fred, she picked up two bowls and walked out of the kitchen.

"She'll be fine," Chef Fred assured Regan. "She's a good girl."

She was a terrified girl, but Regan nodded, letting him know she understood. Given Marcus Antius's business practices, there was no mistaking the edgy vibrations running through the entire house. It was clear this wasn't a simple dinner among friends. Or maybe that was just Regan picking up on Javi's constant guarded stare.

A stare that reminded her of his uncanny ability to make her feel as if she were the only woman in the world for him. She gave in to a momentary scowl.

The man should be listed as a lethal weapon as far as she was concerned.

She exited the kitchen and quickly caught up with Natalia.

"Serve from the right, remove from the left," Regan murmured, and Natalia nodded.

After doling out her soup bowls, Regan stepped back and looked to Natalia, who was standing beside the man known as Niko Demchenko.

The younger woman's hands trembled so much she

sloshed soup over the rim of the bowl when she set it down.

"M'yasnyk." Natalia's fractured whisper echoed around the room. She stood up straight, staring at the man in front of her, eyes wide with terror. And hate. *"M'yasnyk."* She sucked in a sharp breath as if the word hurt to say.

Demchenko lunged to his feet. Natalia leaped back, a cry of alarm squeaking in her throat. The color drained from her face.

"What incompetence is this?" Demchenko grabbed Natalia's wrist. The soup in the other bowl splattered across the table and landed on the hand-woven rug. "What did you say to me?" While still gripping Natalia's wrist, he jerked her closer to him. He said something else in a language Regan didn't understand.

But Natalia did.

Regan darted around the table as Javi catapulted out of his chair, caught the man's shoulder and spun him away. Regan saved a weak-kneed Natalia from landing on the floor and carefully drew the young woman into her arms.

Everyone was on their feet, voices raised in confused alarm.

Javi pushed the man face-first against the wall, twisted his arm high behind his back and leaned in. Demchenko went beet red as he pressed his lips together to stop from making a sound.

"In this house," Javi said quietly into his ear, yet loud enough for everyone to hear, "we don't put our hands on women without their permission."

Regan had a good idea what was going through Javi's

mind, seeing Natalia's reaction to the creep, and a twinge of sympathy slid through her.

"Do you understand me?" Javi demanded.

The man nodded, his face scraping against the blue damask wallpaper.

"Javi, let him go," Marcus ordered in a sharp tone that had Regan's inner agent seething.

Outwardly, she winced, but it wasn't her place to say anything.

"Javi," Marcus warned again.

Javi stepped back, held up both hands, but didn't take his eyes off Demchenko.

Regan cleared her throat. "If you'll give me a minute to clean up—"

Demchenko tugged his jacket straight, offered a short "Excuse me" and then walked out of the dining room. Moments later, the front door slammed.

Regan felt her lungs expand in relief. "I'll have fresh bowls for you quickly. Please." She turned pleading eyes on Marcus, hoping, praying he wasn't going to punish Natalia for any frustration or annoyance. It was obvious, had to be even to Marcus Antius, that something was very, very wrong. "I'll take care of her."

Marcus gave a sharp nod. At the other end of the table, Celeste remained in her chair, hand gripped around the knife at her setting. Her glassy gaze met Regan's and something clicked. An understanding between women when they knew something was bad.

Celeste's expression also left Regan wondering if events like this weren't uncommon in the Antius household.

"Come on, Natalia," Regan whispered and led the young woman to the door.

Muscle memory had her turning and glancing back to Javi, who was watching every move the two of them made. She gave a brief smile she hoped he'd take in the way it was meant. As a thank-you. Regardless of whatever else had happened, he'd given her a glimmer of the agent, of the man that, once upon a time, she'd known him to be.

"It's okay. You're all right." Once they were in the kitchen, Regan got Natalia to a chair at the table.

"What's going on?" Fred demanded as he came over, eyes filled with concern. "What's happened? Nat? Are you all right?"

Natalia's eyes filled with tears, but they weren't enough to erase the fear. She spoke, but not entirely in English. And the speed with which she did belied her terror.

"I need to clean up the dining room," Regan said, then stopped short when Celeste streaked into the kitchen.

"Natalia." Celeste bypassed Regan and Fred as if she didn't see them. All of her attention was on the junior housekeeper. She crouched beside her, clasped her hands around Natalia's shaking ones. "I'm so sorry." Sympathy shone in her eyes, but her jaw was locked so tight that Regan could see it pulse. "You okay now? He won't hurt you again. I promise."

Natalia nodded.

"Fred, why don't you fix some tea," Regan suggested. It was only then Celeste glanced up. "I can see her up to her room as soon as I've fixed things in the dining room."

"You go on." Celeste's voice left no room for argument. "I'll take care of her."

Natalia swiped at the spilled tears on her cheek,

seemed to breathe a bit easier. "Thank you. I'm sorry. I just…" She blinked, frowning. "His face." She whispered the words as if to herself. "I remember that face. It's him. *M'yasnyk*." She spat the word as if it were poison.

"Well, you won't have to see him again," Celeste confirmed. "Regan, really, go on. We need the rest of the dinner to go smoothly."

"Of course. Fred? I need more bowls of soup, please."

He bustled around without a response.

Regan grabbed towels and table cleaner and hurried back to the dining room. Marcus and the remaining guests had moved outside, the taller of the two speaking with him in a low register. The smaller, smarmy-looking guy seemed amused at the evening's events. She barely cast a glance in their direction before turning her attention to the spilled soup.

Regan gathered the discarded bowls and when she stood, Javi was right there, waiting for her. The heat radiating from his body nearly set her aflame.

"Is she all right?" His question was for her ears only. Regan nodded.

"She will be." Regan looked up at him. In that moment, the years, the doubts, the hurt evaporated instantly. Until she saw the telltale spark in his gaze. "You enjoyed that, didn't you? Putting him into the wall."

His brow arched, but he didn't deny it. "It needed doing."

She supposed he was right. Men like the one who had touched her, touched Natalia, they didn't see anything beyond their own ego and desire. And the fear Natalia had been displaying hadn't even registered with him.

Regan wanted to say more, but how could she without showing there was more to her and Javi's relationship than two strangers who had just met? But she knew… she *knew* what buttons of Javi's had been pushed. Because she knew him.

Or at least she had. Once upon a time.

She stepped back, picked up the dishes and sodden towels. "I'll be back with the rest of the appetizer course."

"Thank you, Regan," Marcus said, entering the room. "Please." He motioned to the men. "Let's sit back down."

A cell phone beeped at the table. Reggie reached for his phone, glanced at the screen. "We'll bring Niko up to speed once we're back at the hotel." He tucked the phone into his inside jacket pocket as if nothing had happened. "In the meantime…" He shifted his gaze to Regan as she walked past. "I look forward to what the main course brings in terms of entertainment."

Chapter 6

Regan didn't make it back to her room until well after midnight.

Unexpected worry accompanied her up the stairs. She gripped the banister so hard her fingers went numb. What was going on inside this house?

Celeste had returned to the table after escorting Natalia to her quarters on the other side of the house, but she'd displayed no concern other than to make certain their remaining guests had a pleasant rest of their evening.

For Regan, there had not been an opportunity to enquire as to Natalia's state of mind and all she got out of Fred was tight-lipped nods when she suggested Natalia might be suffering from PTSD.

Pressing for details when Regan was so new would only raise red flags. While every instinct inside her wanted to help the younger woman, who was clearly traumatized, it would be another case of Regan pushing her luck.

Being nosy was never a good idea on undercover assignments—even off-the-books ones.

Dina. Regan had to focus on Dina, the kids, and now that she'd gotten a glimpse of the situation the young ones were living in, getting them to a permanent home filled with love rather than tension and fear.

Relief surged when Regan closed her bedroom door. She turned and sank back against it, closing her eyes for a slow count of thirty. It was a routine habit she practiced during her undercover assignments. It was something she'd learned from Javi—a mini-reboot of sorts to process an overload of information so she could apply it and move forward.

Being undercover was a nonstop adrenaline rush, not to mention an energy suck, even in a situation like this when the danger wasn't nearly as threatening as it had been in her last case.

Here, if she thought herself in trouble or her cover was blown, she could walk out the door and not look back.

But months ago? When she'd been living out in the middle of nowhere in a swamp surrounded by survivalists and gunrunners? There had been nowhere to hide or run to if things went sideways.

She squeezed her eyes shut again. Nausea churned in her belly, but she swallowed hard, shook her head as if refusing the threat of vomiting. Like Natalia, she had her own trigger when it came to the past.

Javi's face floated into her thoughts.

Embrace the feelings, she told herself and gave in to the emotions swirling like a tornado on a crash course toward Dorothy's house. What Regan wouldn't give for a magical yellow brick road to be waiting on the other side.

She pushed through the memories of the friends and colleagues she'd lost. She needed to stay on target, if only because the here and now was far more under her control than the past.

She opened her eyes, took a deep breath and retrieved the phone Slade had set up for her.

Waiting for an answer, she suddenly remembered what time it was. Regan cringed when he answered. "Sorry," she said on a rush. "You're probably catching up on sleep since you're away from the baby."

"No worries." But there was exhaustion in his voice. "What's going on? You okay?"

"I'm good." She kept her voice low, uncertain which, if any, rooms nearby were occupied. "It's been a weird day."

"Weird how?"

"I don't even know where to start." It felt good, having someone to talk to. Someone she didn't have to confront, like she would have to if she had called her brother. Slade considered Javi a friend. He'd even named his kid after her former partner. How did she even broach that part of her current situation?

"Are you okay?"

It was, Regan knew, what her brother would want to know before anything else.

"I'm fine." She swallowed hard and tried in vain to find the right words. "Javi's here."

"Here." Slade seemed to be testing out the word. "*Here*, as in…"

"He works for Antius. He's his body man."

The silence pressed on for a long moment.

"I don't suppose you have the how or why nailed down," Slade said in a measured tone. "What could he be thinking—"

"I know." She ducked her head, pinched the bridge of her nose. Her mind was spinning. "I'm right there with you but as many questions as I have, he isn't what's important right now." Or at least she couldn't let him be. "I've got some names I need information on."

"Sure. Okay, we'll come back to Javi. Give me a sec."

While he did what he needed to, she hugged an arm around her waist, trying to temper her churning stomach. She flexed her free hand in frustration.

What had Javi gotten himself involved in?

"Okay," Slade finally said. "Go."

"First name is Reggie Bogart." She offered a quick physical description. "Struck me as a kind of middleman. Not muscle, that's for sure. Not particularly scary or intimidating. More…skeezy."

"Copy that. Bogart." She could all but hear him frown. "That name rings a bell or three. Running him now." She heard the clicking of keys. "I've got full access to Aiden's system here so this shouldn't take long… Right. Here he is. Reggie Bogart. Oh, yeah, I remember this guy. Your instinct is spot-on. He's a connected little rat," Slade murmured. "I'll dig deeper but the short story is he's an intermediary—makes his money bringing rival criminal organizations to the table for partnerships or truces. Ruthless reputation and is noted in this particular file as a greedy cockroach."

"Don't insult the roaches," Regan suggested. So far, her instincts were proving accurate. "He brought two men with him to meet with Marcus—Niko Demchenko and the other's last name is Vaya. I didn't get a first name."

While Slade typed, Regan walked over to the small desk by the window and opened the laptop Celeste had delivered this afternoon. She hadn't had the chance to do more than skim over the programs Celeste needed her to learn, but the basics were familiar.

The machine immediately connected to the household WiFi. She clicked online and pulled up a search engine. "There's a word I heard at dinner. Not sure how to spell it." She was talking more to herself than to Slade. "It sounded Eastern European." She remembered the background info Aiden's people had run. "Where was Natalia from again?"

"Pulling up her file now," Slade said. "Says here she arrived from Ukraine a little less than a year ago."

A new pit opened up in her stomach. "She called Demchenko something. It triggered him." Big time. "It sounded like *miasma*." She typed in a bunch of possible words and spellings. "But there was a *k* sound in there somewhere."

"*M'yasnyk*?" Slade asked in a tone that didn't sound particularly positive.

"Yes!" She typed it in phonetically and hit Translate.

"That was definitely it and it says here it means… butcher." Regan swallowed hard. Suddenly the terror she'd seen in Natalia's eyes made absolute sense. "She called Demchenko a butcher."

"That should make his name pop," Slade muttered. "Give me a few hours to do a deep dive. I'll have something on him and this Vaya then."

"Great. Thanks. I'll call you tomorrow," Regan told him. "Maybe by then I'll have answers about Javi."

"Be careful," Slade warned. "We both know Javi doesn't like being cornered."

Regan agreed. "I remember. Thanks, Slade."

"Sure thing. Get some sleep."

She hung up, feeling slightly better or at the very least, less alone. Not that anything took the edge off of the Javi issue.

But she knew something that could.

She kicked off her shoes and practically sprinted to the bathroom, stripping off her clothes as she went. Time to wash off the day.

After her shower, she swiped a towel across the steamy mirror of the impressive bathroom. She forced herself to breathe deep, to let it out. And inhale again. The tension trickled away but still hovered like a swarm of irritated wasps.

Hair knotted on top of her head, towel wrapped above her breasts, Regan stared into her foggy reflection as if looking at a stranger. Tomorrow, she told herself, as she returned to the bedroom. Tomorrow would be better. Tomorrow she'd get more answers.

Two hours later, lying in bed, blinking into the darkness, her frustration mounted. She needed to sleep. Recharging was the only way to make certain she was ready to tackle the morning and build on the information she was collecting for Dina. Her friend was right. There was something criminal going on in this house. She just had to collect more pieces to the puzzle before she could put it all together.

Regan covered her face with her hands, tried to relax.

She could literally feel the time ticking away to the staccato beating of her heart.

"Gah!" Regan flopped onto her side, punched her pillow. Stared out the curtained window. She closed her eyes. Tried to box breathe. *Four counts in, hold for four, four counts out, and...*

It was no use.

She threw back the luxury sheets and goose-down duvet, got out of bed and, after slipping her bare feet into a pair of foldable ballet flats, grabbed a long sweater to put over her thin tank and sleep shorts and quietly opened her door.

Regan poked her head out. Looked up the hall and down.

Empty. And creepily quiet.

Why did she feel inclined to sneak? It wasn't as if she was on lockdown or something. It was a new place, a big place. Wandering around at night could easily be explained away. For all anyone knew, she could be a nighttime snack thief.

Her footsteps sounded like firecrackers going off in the silent house. She shuddered. She'd always hated mansions like this. Maybe she'd ridden on one too many amusement park rides as a kid—as far as she was concerned, there were too many corners and tucked-away places to hide.

She walked down the stairs, toes scrunching in her shoes. When she hit the landing, she wrapped her arms around herself and followed the rays of moonlight streaming through the large bank of windows.

The dining room was absent of any evidence of the dinner that had taken place just hours before. The heavy furniture sat stoically in the room, adding to that gloomy tension she couldn't shake.

The kitchen was, not surprisingly, spotless to the point of obsessive on Chef Fred's part. Not even a fingerprint on the stainless steel refrigerator door.

Between the silence, the huge rooms and the shadows

shifting against the moonlight, she felt as if she were trapped in an Agatha Christie mystery, where everyone was suspect.

Well. She smirked. That wasn't too far off the mark.

Unlocking the back door, Regan stepped outside. The cool night air swooped in and filled her lungs with promise. Ah. She closed her eyes and lifted her chin to the sky, shivering slightly at the California chill. There.

She heard the gentle lapping of the ocean in the near distance and the sound immediately offered the peace she'd been thirsting for.

Regan felt the tension melt out of her bones as she walked down the marble steps.

The narrow path at the side of the stairs gave way to lush grass and meandering, manicured shrubs and flowering plants that had her bending down and plucking off her shoes.

The instant her feet sank into the damp grass, the last of the anxiety eased. She continued walking, curious as to the limitations and boundaries of the property. When she'd arrived, she had seen an indication of neighbors along her route, but they were far enough away that the Antius estate felt rather isolated.

Near as she could tell, the garden stretched on forever. Or, at least, far enough for her to get lost in. Not entirely unappealing.

Crickets chirped in the distance, playing their nighttime melodies. She heard rustling in the bushes and bid a silent greeting to whatever nocturnal creatures had joined her on her middle-of-the-night sojourn.

She stopped short as the two-story cottage with garage

attached rose out of the ground behind a thick grove of trees. Regan lifted her gaze to the darkened windows.

Javi's windows.

As quiet and still as the house she'd left behind.

Temptation surged, almost as powerful as the regret.

Every question she'd had, every ounce of hurt she'd felt when he'd turned his back on her flooded into her heart, removed all thought and reason. She put her shoes back on, wedged herself through the shrubbery, rustling the branches as she approached the side staircase.

The doors of the multicar garage were down. A floodlight flashed on as she passed. Regan immediately hurried forward, flattened her back against the side wall until the glow blinked back off.

Her pulse kicked into overdrive. Common sense told her to leave but she let the impulse, to discover what she could, drive her onward and up the stairs.

The wood groaned quietly. She climbed faster, fingers barely brushing the smooth painted handrail.

Just before she reached the top of the stairs, she froze.

What was she thinking?

Her foot hovered inches off the ground, as if she were incapable of taking that last step. Whatever answers she hoped to get from Javi wouldn't be forthcoming. Besides, could she even trust anything he said? She might want to.

But could she?

He'd made it clear two years ago that she didn't factor into his decisions or actions. Otherwise, he wouldn't have done what he'd done. She'd been a convenient distraction, a cover of sorts, as he'd manipulated the privileges his position in the bureau had provided. He'd used her and then discarded her when she was no longer of benefit and was happy to fill her in on the gratuitous details.

Was it possible— Were the desperate shadows of her heart right and that all of it had been a lie? Even if that was the case, what was she thinking, running straight to him the second he reappeared in her life?

It was as if she wanted her heart broken all over again. Not to mention…

What could he possibly say to her now that would change any of what had happened?

She pivoted, took one step down and…

The door opened.

She spun back around, nearly lost her balance on the step.

Her heart nearly forgot to beat.

Moonlight streamed down, catching against the black of his hair, the gleam of interest in his dark eyes. The bare skin of his toned torso narrowed to hips wearing low-riding pajama bottoms the color of the evening tide.

His arms flexed as he held open the door and for an instant, she remembered what it felt like to be held in those arms. Worshipped in those arms. How she'd clung to him to the point the entire world could have melted away and she wouldn't have cared.

She could see the question in his eyes, the challenge. The understanding.

She despised him for it. Even as she…

He came forward as she lowered her foot. Her toes scrunched again as her fight instinct battled her desire to flee. She waited for one of his clever comments, an observation that would set her teeth on edge.

Instead, he simply stood there with the open door in his hand.

She glared at him even as she felt herself softening beneath his heated gaze.

"I didn't see a light on," she finally said. "I figured you were asleep."

"I was." He inclined his head. "Now I'm not."

Still, she hesitated, turning her loathing on herself. "I don't know why I'm—"

Javi only opened the door wider.

She couldn't very well walk away now, could she? And he knew it.

Keeping her gaze on his, stomach clenched, she took the last few steps up and into his house.

Javi closed the door behind him, reached down and snapped on the lamp next to the sofa. The dim glow took the edge off the night and put a spotlight on the woman who still had a claim on his heart.

"Coffee?" It was the only thing he could think to distract himself from the sight of her. He'd learned early on not to give anyone any power over him, but with Regan McKenna, all bets had been off from day one, hour one. Minute one.

"No. Thanks." She hugged her arms around her torso, turned as he moved around her and headed for the kitchen.

No point in even pretending he was going to sleep again tonight. It had been difficult enough dropping into oblivion knowing she was in the main house only thirty yards away. Now that she was in his personal space?

He flipped on the coffee maker. "Still working on those stealthy skills, I see."

She blinked before understanding glinted in her bold green eyes. The same color, the same fierceness all the McKennas shared. "You heard me."

"People probably heard you half a mile away." It was a lie, but a necessary one to maintain an emotional distance. Yes, he'd heard her moving around, but his hypersensitivity to his surroundings alerted him more than anything that someone was outside the cottage. "Couldn't sleep, I take it? Needed one of your midnight walks to ease the nerves?"

Irritation flashed. He knew she would not appreciate the idea that he remembered everything about her. She'd appreciate even less the fact that those memories were sometimes the only thing that kept him sane in his upside-down, dangerous world.

"It's a beautiful garden" was all she said.

She hadn't moved from the center of the living room. Not that it was very big. The space only consisted of a small sofa, flat-screen television he rarely had time to watch and a coffee table covered with books he'd borrowed from the Antius's library.

"I didn't plan to ever see you again." She frowned and tightened her arms to the point it looked as if she were shrinking. "I don't know what I'm supposed to say to you." She looked to him for answers he didn't have. "What have you gotten yourself mixed up in, Javi?"

He smirked, more because he knew it would irritate her than convey an actual emotion. The further he kept her away, the better. "A nice profit margin." Even as he said it, his stomach rolled. "What's the ATF's interest in Antius?"

"None of your business." She turned away as she spoke, shifted her attention to the collection of books on the coffee table. Regan leaned down, pulled one from the stack. "I remember trying to get you to read this." She flipped the dog-centric borderline-horror novel, with elements of adventure and romance, around to show off its cover. "It's one of my favorites."

"Is it?" He knew very well that it was. She'd had multiple copies of the book, one of which ended up in his bag when he'd packed up and left. It had become one of his comfort reads. He focused on the brewing coffee rather than the truth, which had no place in his life now. "I don't think I've gotten to reading it yet." He winced. He just couldn't help twisting the knife deeper, could he?

She tossed the book back down, followed him into the cozy kitchen. "The men Reggie Bogart brought with him tonight. Who are they to Antius?"

"Are you interested in bachelor number one or bachelor number two?" He looked over his shoulder, specifically down at her hand displaying the simple gold band and negligible diamond. "Or maybe you aren't interested in either."

She blinked, frowning. She followed his gaze. Surprise jumped into those amazing eyes of hers. "Oh. That." She waggled her hand in a way that felt like a red flag in front of a bull. "It's fake. Part of the cover Aiden built for me."

"You're working for Aiden?" He frowned. "You left the ATF?"

"No." She looked baffled at the very idea. "Of course

not. I've been on leave and he's backstopping me on this…job."

"Why are you on leave?" Back in the day, the very idea of Regan taking leave would have been seen as some kind of a joke.

"Because the world keeps turning and—oh, yeah—sometimes it sucks." She seemed to surprise herself with that response. "Slade Palmer's my handler. You remember Slade, don't you? According to him you got him out of a tough spot a couple of years ago. Was that when this obsession with the Valeri syndicate started? With that whole prison break situation?"

Prison break situation. That was one way to put it. His hand shook when he poured his coffee. It was because of his work on that case that he'd been approached for the deep cover operation run by his superior at the ATF. "How is Slade? Is he still with the FBI?"

"No. He's working for Aiden now at Minotaur. But he's good. Married," she said as she moved away from him again. "She's a doctor. I met her once. She's nice."

"Ashley." Javi recalled her instantly and thought of the curvaceous blond doctor who had survived a kidnapping and multiple threats against her life at the hands of Edik Valeri's brother and henchmen. At the time, Javi had been taken aback by the instant attraction between Slade and Ashley, but it had worked in their favor. Slade staking a romantic claim on the good doctor had probably saved her life. "Glad it worked out for them."

"They have a baby now." She was looking at him when he faced her. "A little boy. He's a year old," Regan went on. "His name is Micah." She tilted her head. "Micah Javier."

Some gut punches were impossible to ignore. Everyone's life had moved on while he'd been frozen in time. But the idea…the very idea Slade had named his son after Javi…

He swallowed hard, took a sip of scalding coffee and embraced the pain. "I haven't seen him in years."

"So he said." Her smile was quick and without humor. "You aren't going to tell me anything about those men at dinner, are you?"

"Why do you want to know?" Until she was honest with him, he couldn't risk blowing his cover just to appease her. It didn't matter what her case might be. "I thought this wasn't official."

"Do you really need a reason, or should I just name my price? What pay app do you use? Or…" She snapped her fingers and he almost jumped. "That's right. You prefer cash for your payoffs, don't you? I forgot that detail."

"Cash is easier to move around," he admitted with practiced ease. "If Antius is who you're after, you won't get to him through them. They aren't working together."

"Yet." She smirked at his arched brow. "You were going to say they don't have an arrangement with him *yet*. That's what dinner was all about, wasn't it? Coming to some kind of agreement to use DriftCore Global for whatever activities they're involved in?"

She saw everything so clearly. Too clearly perhaps. One of the many reasons he'd fallen in love with her. And the main reason he had needed to distance himself from her. "Okay, how's this?" he tried instead. "A quid pro quo. I give you their names, you tell me why the ATF is running an off-the-books investigation into Antius." It was, he thought, the only explanation that made sense.

She snorted, rolled her eyes. "Seriously?"

He shrugged. "Humor me." The more he knew about her current investigation, the better he could protect his own case. That was, after all, his one and only focus these days. "Deal?"

She shrugged. "Sure."

He hesitated on his next sip of coffee. That had been way too easy. But…at this point, what did he have to lose? "The larger man who went scurrying off with his tail between his legs is Niko Demchenko. He's a mercenary. An expensive one. Works a lot in Eastern Europe. Doesn't know the meaning of subtlety let alone empathy or compassion." He was a blunt tool for a violent world.

"What does the Valeri syndicate want with this Demchenko?"

He'd wondered when she'd drop that question on him. "I said I'd give you his name, not his résumé."

"Do *you* work for the Valeri syndicate?"

It took all his control not to react. "I do not." But that didn't mean he hadn't spent the last two years setting himself up as an approachable asset. Once Marcus was in, Javi would be in by association and that would get him closer to Flynn. That's what this entire thing was about, after all. Getting in so he could take down Caleb Flynn once and for all. "I know you don't understand why—"

"I know why," Regan cut him off. "Or, I know what you told me the night you left. Money." Was it his imagination or was she scoffing at him? "You were tired of watching criminals make gobs of it while members of law enforcement scraped by on peanuts. You did it because you could, and despite spending most of your life trying to distance yourself from your father, you ended up just like him. Maybe even a little worse."

He couldn't exactly argue with her when he'd been the one to open this door to the past.

But she wasn't done, reciting almost word for word the script he'd rehearsed for when he'd had to leave. "You also said you did it because it was easy and because you didn't care who got hurt. You accepted cash in exchange for compromising physical evidence in a case. You lied under oath and intimidated not one, but two witnesses the prosecution had in protective custody. And because of you, because you did those things, a three-year FBI investigation was destroyed and two killers went free." Each word seemed to build her spine into steel as she straightened. "So, spare me whatever excuses you've come up with to justify why you betrayed every oath you ever took. I wouldn't believe you, anyway."

But there was a wobble in her voice. A slight one. One that made him wonder if somewhere deep down she still believed in who he'd been.

He stared into the depths of his coffee, wishing not for the first time that he and his handlers hadn't done such a phenomenal job of setting up his cover. He'd told his handlers she'd be impossible to convince and so she'd become their litmus test. A personal challenge, so to speak. They'd manufactured evidence Regan McKenna would believe despite how much she'd loved him.

And she had loved him. That's what had hurt so much.

Using and exploiting that love had been the final key to locking in his cover story. If Regan McKenna thought him guilty…

He had to be dirty.

That belief had been like a key to the golden gate.

"The other man is Kasimir Vaya." There was no point in arguing with her. Or defending himself. Nothing could restore what he'd already sacrificed. "He's second-in-command of Les Ecorches. And don't let the charm fool you."

"I'm immune to charm," Regan said. "Now."

He took it on the chin. "Niko is a blunt tool with half a brain. Vaya got the other half along with plenty of smarts of his own. Of the two, Vaya is the one with the power. Power that Antius needs on his side if he's going to finalize his deal with whoever is running the Valeri organization. He's a sadist and probably a psychopath."

"Albeit a handsome one," Regan observed. "Okay. Demchenko and Vaya. Got it." She nodded. "Thanks."

"Your turn."

She blinked in that overly innocent, "I have no idea what you mean" way that set his teeth on edge. "My turn for what?"

He set his mug down with an irritated clack. "What is the ATF's interest in Antius?"

"They don't have any." She dropped her arms. Her entire posture shifted to one of confidence. A sure sign she was telling the truth. "I'm not working an ATF case. I told you I'm on leave. My being here is personal."

"Personal?" That didn't make any sense. "How do you have any personal connection to Marcus Antius?"

"I don't." She was enjoying herself, if that small smile curving her lush lips was any indication. "And don't go accusing me of going back on our deal," she warned when he started to speak again. "You're the one who offered the terms. You're the one who assumed I was here on behalf of the ATF, even after I told you I was on leave. I just didn't correct you. So, thanks for the information. FYI, I already had their names. But I appreciate the added details." She gestured to the door. "I'll be going now."

"Now hang on—" He stepped in front of her, but this time she was ready for him. She dodged to her left, faking him out before she shoved him away.

"Don't." The word whipped out of her mouth like a lash. "You hold no high ground, Javi. Not in any way, shape or form. And you certainly lost any right to touch me when you threw me away along with your career. Do not do it again."

She flung open the door and walked out.

How did it hurt more the second time?

She'd have been better off drowning in the nearby ocean than attempting to have a cordial conversation with Javi Perez.

The night felt warmer now. Or maybe that was just her temper simmering below boil. Behind her, the door slammed open a second time. She ducked her head, walked faster, keeping the pool in sight as her destination. Her ears roared with white noise produced by a brain determined to keep her safe. Tears burned behind her eyes. As if she'd let herself shed another tear for him. Whatever he was involved with, it had nothing to do with her.

She'd bring him down along with the rest of them.

Wouldn't that be a boon to her record.

"Regan!" Her name split the air. She would not turn around. She would not…

He caught up with her, touched her shoulder and she jumped.

"I said do not—"

He spun her around, pulled her against him and dropped his mouth onto hers.

She moaned, every cell and synapse in her brain firing at full strength. Her lips trembled beneath his as he kissed her. She would not let herself surrender. She would not remember that this was where she felt the most safe. The most loved. She could not allow herself to think about all that might have been had Javi truly loved her.

"Kiss me back," Javi murmured against her lips.

"What?" She pulled her head back, but when she did she saw he wasn't looking at her, but over her head. To the pool. Where she heard splashing.

Her entire body tensed. Panic she couldn't stop surged to the surface even as her hands moved up his arms to his bare chest. His bare, taut skin felt perfect beneath her fingertips. Fingertips that trailed gently higher until they caressed his shoulders.

"I'm sorry," Javi whispered as he brushed his mouth against hers.

In that moment, just for that moment, she let everything else go. She slid her hands behind his neck, threaded her fingers through his hair as she pulled his head down. "Don't be," she said, and rose up to meet him this time.

She was torn between trying to stay alert and sinking completely into his embrace. So many things had changed since they'd last been together, but one thing remained the same. Javi knew how to make love to a woman.

When she was in his arms, she had no doubt he was fully focused on her. He pulled her higher against him. His fingers slipped beneath the hem of her sleep tank even as he hardened against the heat of her.

She gasped into his mouth and his tongue swept over hers, engaging her in a familiar, enticing dance of intimacy she'd forced herself to forget. She kissed him back, not because he'd told her to, but because she wanted to. Needed to.

If only to say goodbye one last time.

Someone cleared their throat. A female someone who added just enough attitude to establish her rank in the house.

Javi lifted his head, looked over Regan's before she stepped to his side, her arm still wrapped securely around his bare waist.

"Oh, no." She made a show of pulling away from him, of trying to escape as Celeste climbed out of the swimming pool and retrieved a robe draped over one of the lounge chairs. "Mrs. Antius, please—"

"It's Celeste, remember." The bright blue bikini she wore defied gravity and, if Regan wasn't mistaken, would short-circuit many a male's nervous system. She slid her arms into the robe, drew it across her bare shoulders and tied it quickly. "I had a feeling about you two." The smile on her face as she stepped into her high-heeled sandals was both knowing and secretive, as if she'd just hit the jackpot on household gossip. "Sparks from the second you two met on the driveway." She walked over, waving away Regan's sputtering, false concerns. "Don't worry, Regan. If anyone understands the pull of an attractive, unattached man, I do."

She stopped in front of them, the glow of the light from the pool highlighting her wet blond hair. "This evening has been chock-full of surprises, hasn't it? Sorry I had to interrupt. Wasn't entirely sure if I could extricate myself from the situation without notice."

Right, Regan thought as she caught a glimmer of glee in the other woman's eyes. Celeste Antius struck her as the kind of woman who could do anything she set her mind to. Including quietly vanishing out of her pool during a middle-of-the-night swim.

"It's not what you think," Regan tried again. She squeezed Javi's waist, urging him to say something, anything, as a misdirect.

"Yet," Javi said, throwing her own word back into the fray. "She's a beautiful woman who deserves a fresh start. And some fun." He looked over at her, a sly smile curving his swollen, delicious lips.

Regan bit the inside of her cheek. "I don't think—"

"Don't think on it too much," Celeste suggested and reached out her hand, which Regan felt obligated to take. "Grab happiness where you can. With whomever you can. You never know when it's going to be taken away from you." She squeezed Regan's fingers, shot her another quick smile before she left them and *click-clacked* beyond the pool and inside the house.

"I have to say…" Feeling a bit dazed and confused, Regan couldn't find the energy or inclination to remove herself completely from Javi's hold. "I didn't think this day could hold any more surprises. Celeste Antius is a romantic? Who would have thought?"

"Not me, that's for sure," Javi agreed. "You need to be ready for tomorrow."

"What about tomorrow?" Regan's brain was still filled with the scent, the taste, the feel of Javi's kiss. She couldn't begin to fathom just how much she'd missed him. Why she still cared.

"Celeste might be a romantic." His voice lowered into that seductive, determined tone that sent shivers down her spine. "But she thrives on gossip and secrets. She'll either hold this over our heads or serve us up to the help. Either way, she's going to tell someone we're involved and that someone is going to be Marcus. Which means…"

"Oh, no." Regan's head finally cleared. She pushed away from him, held up both hands even as she whispered, "We are not continuing this charade."

"Don't see that we have a choice." He reached for her, a smile on his face this time, but she dodged his hands. "We'd best figure out how we're going to fake this to keep everyone entertained. Otherwise, they're going to get suspicious and start asking a lot of nosy questions."

"Please." She shrugged. "What questions? I've only been here a couple of days. No one is invested in anything connected to me."

"They will be once they get an earful about tonight," Javi countered. "So, how about you tell me what you're really doing here?"

She shook her head. "It's none of your business."

"It might not have been before, but it is now," he told her. "You and I are involved, at least as far as anyone else is concerned. That means I need to know everything about why you're here."

"Not going to happen," she insisted as she straightened her top and sweater. "I mean it, Javi. I'm not here to play games, especially not with you. I'm here for something important."

"Uh-huh. Convince me."

"Why? Because you used to be my partner?" The sad thing was it never crossed her mind to be honest with him. She simply looked at him, replaying that last day they'd had together in her mind to the point she knew it reflected in her eyes. "I can't trust you, Javi. Not anymore. And never again. So no, I won't tell you. I meant what I said. It's important. I have a job to do and people's futures depend on me doing it. You are the last person I can rely on to help me see it through." She clutched at her sweater and backed away. "Good night."

She turned and walked all the way into the house, up the stairs and into her room. She went to the window, pulled back the curtain and saw him standing where she'd left him. Alone. In the moonlight. Looking up at her window before he turned and disappeared into the night.

She tossed off her sweater, her shoes and climbed into bed.

Touching a finger to her well-kissed lips, she squeezed her eyes shut and willed her brain to shut off. To forget. Everything. But especially him. *Sleep*, she told herself. *Just go to sleep.*

But she never did.

Instead, she spent the rest of the night staring at the dusty pink walls until the sun came up.

Chapter 7

"Heard you took a little walk in the garden last night."

Javi reached into the center console for his travel mug of coffee, sipped slowly. "Moonlight was nice" was all he said and ignored the disbelieving chuckle that Marcus offered in response.

Parked overlooking the teeming site of the Los Angeles port, the midmorning sun burned off some of the city smog that blanketed the collection of ships lining the maze of docks. A short distance away another black SUV sat parked against the side of the building, awaiting the same signal Marcus was anxious to receive.

The lung-scorching stench of diesel permeated the air, thick and oppressive against the growing summer heat. The lack of a breeze today added to the stifling atmosphere that felt out of place in the open air of one of the biggest waterways in the country.

Shipping containers of all sizes, all colors, were loaded on and off various vessels. Behind them, the warehouse DriftCore Global used as their primary intake arena awaited the cargo from its latest arrival from Tunisia, the *Ink Tide*.

"You moved fast with Regan," Marcus tried again,

proving his affection for beating a dead horse. "I figured you'd give it at least a week or two before you made a move."

"She's a beautiful woman." Javi hoped that didn't sound too rehearsed. "Didn't want to miss my chance." All the sleepless hours he'd spent last night and that was the best he could come up with. He rubbed a hand across the back of his stiff neck. As amusing and arousing as his time with Regan had been last night, in the light of day, he began to realize their "involvement" could turn into more of a problem than a benefit.

Marcus's cell rang and after a quick conversation he hung up. "Deal's done." He gathered up the papers he'd been sorting through and shoved them into his soft monogrammed briefcase. "Let's go."

"Don't forget your phone." Javi gestured to the cell on the back seat.

"Demchenko's paranoid," Marcus said with a distasteful grimace. "He doesn't want cell phones around during business deals. Best leave yours behind, as well."

"Right." He made a show of tossing the phone Marcus provided onto the passenger seat, but kept his burner stashed in the inside front pocket of his jacket. As soon as he opened Marcus's door, the other SUV's doors opened and Niko Demchenko dropped out of the back, along with Reggie Bogart, the team builder himself.

Marcus shook Reggie's hand, then Demchenko's, without giving Javi a passing glance. No doubt this was an effort to appease Demchenko's bruised ego following his and Javi's interaction last night.

"Gentlemen." Marcus took the lead while Javi stood back like a silent sentry. "The *Ink Tide* arrived fourteen hours ago and has now been cleared through customs per our arrangement. The cargo you asked us to ship in as a test run is ready for pickup. If you'd like to follow me. Javi?" He held out a hand when Javi moved in ahead of him. "You don't need to join us on the ship," Marcus said. "Niko and Captain Drajic are old friends. No need for added protection."

Javi frowned. This wasn't normally the way they did things. "I'm not familiar with Captain Drajic or his procedures to feel comfortable with that suggestion."

"I appreciate the concern," Marcus assured him, but there was a "don't argue" edge to his voice that seemed forced. "I'll be fine. Wait back at the car."

"Yes, sir." Javi didn't budge from his spot even as resentment rose. He barely moved as the three men walked together toward the gangplank that offered access to the huge vessel measuring more than eight hundred feet in length.

Paranoia struck and he turned back to the vehicle. Usually without fail, Marcus demanded Javi's presence at his side. Why the sudden change in routine?

Maybe he was overreacting. Or maybe Demchenko's bruised ego had him demanding limits on Javi's presence. Javi couldn't be sure of either, which left him questioning everything.

No sooner had he slid behind the wheel again than he caught sight of Marcus's briefcase on the floor behind him.

His heart skipped a beat. Maybe this wasn't such a bad turn of events. He wouldn't have a better opportunity to examine the shipping documents Marcus had brought with him.

Javi got out and opened the back door. He made quick work of the combination lock as his boss used his birthday in reverse for nearly everything.

Javi made a mental note of the order of the papers he pulled free as he flipped through them. Just as he thought. The ship's manifest Javi had accessed on Marcus's home laptop, the one on record with import officials, was completely different than the one printed out here.

Peak capacity for the *Ink Tide* was over five thousand containers, but it had come in less than half full. Javi glanced up, checking to make sure the nasty trio hadn't unexpectedly headed back.

Marcus had worked especially hard on creating a coding system for items transported on his ships. But he'd also had to write everything down and, over the past few months, Javi had been able to catch, memorize and document that code.

The organic turmeric powder called Golden Dust was heroin. Siren's Milk, described as a skin rejuvenation tonic in custom-made amber glass bottles was actually ketamine. There were similar notations for amounts of fentanyl-laced counterfeit pills, meth and cocaine bricks.

But it was the weapons that had really earned Marcus high marks on creativity.

Javi sneaked a look at the ship again, then focused on the rest of the forms, which he quickly scanned through. Street irrigation piping listed as Black Rainsticks were AK-47 rifles. Bulletproof tactical gear was renamed safety equipment, while C-4 explosives went under the guise of beekeeping starter kits with mesh screens and wax blocks.

"If only he used his powers for good." He stacked the papers in order, and quickly aimed his watch face at them, pushing the side button to snap low-resolution images of the documents. It wasn't ideal; they wouldn't be backed up until he was in his apartment, but it would have to do. He righted the papers, slid them back into the briefcase, then stopped.

A new invoice, a different one with a ship's name was still inside. He snatched the paper free.

"The *Deadlight Express*." He'd heard that name before, but not where Antius was concerned. Back when he'd been undercover with Slade Palmer at Folsom Prison in the early days of Javi's investigation into the Valeri syndicate. The *Deadlight* was a Valeri ship. And yet here was an invoice for an incoming shipment being run by Marcus.

"What the—" His pulse kicked into high gear as his mind raced to catch up. Was it possible…? Was this the evidence he needed to connect Marcus to the new and reborn Valeri organization?

The manifest for *Deadlight*'s cargo listed mannequins for luxury boutiques, and sculpture pieces, along with glass display cases. But it was the notation for temperature-controlled shipping containers that rang alarm bells in his head.

Glass display cases didn't require climate control, and neither did plastic mannequins.

But people did.

He reached into his inside jacket pocket, pulled out the phone that until yesterday he'd kept under the floorboards of his apartment. It might be receive only, but the device could serve as a backup for storing critical information, especially if the images he'd captured with his watch were somehow compromised.

"This qualifies as an emergency," he muttered and powered on the receive-only phone.

On the back seat, Marcus's phone blinked on for an instant, but the screen went blank again.

"Glitchy," Javi said and quickly began taking photos of each manifest page for the incoming *Deadlight Express*. He stopped at one point. The hair on the back of his neck prickled, as if he were being watched.

He glanced up. He was alone. No one was around.

Demchenko's paranoia must be contagious.

He still had two pages to go when he caught sight of Marcus, Reggie and Demchenko emerging from the ship onto the gangplank.

Determined to finish, Javi took the last shots, stashed his phone in his pocket and forced himself to calmly stack the papers in the correct order.

He slipped the case into its old position, put his phone away and ducked down before pretending to exit the car normally. Demchenko, Marcus and Reggie approached Javi with Demchenko carrying a metal case a little larger than a normal briefcase.

Javi headed straight for them, but his mind was still on those papers and on that incoming ship that he figured would be carrying trafficked human beings. A ship scheduled to dock at 10:00 p.m. in Los Angeles in less than four days.

Four. Days.

Was it possible…? Could he actually be done with this case, with his undercover work in less than a week?

Instead of Reggie and Demchenko moving on to their

own car, they followed Marcus to the SUV. When Demchenko handed off the case to Marcus, Javi had to stop himself from looking at the exchange with anything other than calm acceptance.

"I'll be in touch," Demchenko said coolly.

"Excellent." Marcus gestured for Javi to pop the trunk before handing him the case.

Javi assessed what he could as he placed the case inside. It was lighter than he expected, given the titanium edges. Whatever was inside was well protected.

"We'll get this taken care of for you," Marcus assured them.

It didn't escape Javi's notice that neither Reggie nor Demchenko looked in his direction before they walked away. Only when Marcus was in the car and Javi had slid behind the wheel did Javi finally ask, "What's going on?"

"Your disciplinary antics at dinner left a bitter taste in Niko's mouth." The disapproval in Marcus's tone was evident. "He doesn't trust my judgment as much as he once did. We can head home."

Javi flinched. He started the car, pulled out and turned to head back to North Beach. "I apologize for putting you in a difficult position."

"But you aren't sorry for planting his face in the wall, are you?" Marcus countered with a wry smile. "I'd be surprised if you were. But that doesn't change the fact I need Demchenko to trust me. At least as far as he's capable. I don't care if he trusts you, because I do. But we need to make him believe he can. That's going to take some work, especially on your end."

Javi braced himself. "What is it you need me to do?"

"Deliver that case in the back to one of his clients by 6:00 p.m. tomorrow night."

"All right." Didn't seem so difficult and, bonus, it was another entry on Marcus's list of criminal activity. "Where's the drop-off?"

"Las Vegas. I'd let you use the plane, but Reggie and I will be leaving in the morning to meet with another potential investor. And before you ask, Reggie has two of his men accompanying us. We'll be perfectly fine."

"You're grounding me." And shutting him out. Definitely not a good result.

"I'm appeasing one of my partners because of your lapse in judgment. Seeing as Celeste and I have a late dinner party to attend this evening, you can leave in the morning."

Marcus had it all planned out, didn't he? It seemed Javi hadn't only lost Demchenko's trust, but some of Marcus's, as well. He was going to have to work on getting that back, given how things finally, hopefully, were coming to a head.

"Until you make good on this delivery, it's best I put some distance between us." Marcus picked up his phone and dialed. "If the delivery goes smoothly, I anticipate things will return to normal once you get back. I'll text you the details on where to make the drop as soon as Niko sends them to me."

After hours sitting at her new laptop in Celeste's office, Regan's eyes were beginning to cross. It hadn't taken her long to get the hang of the design program Celeste had insisted she use to create endless marketing memes for various collections and products. She'd caught on quickly to editing the various "review" videos Celeste had stored in the cloud and knocked those off her to-do list.

In between projects, she'd ridden in on the WiFi in an attempt to get a handle on the computers hooked up to the private home network. She'd found the system analysis that told her at least six unique IP addresses had logged in over the past month. She compared them to the ones currently connected so as to eliminate as many as possible and identify Marcus's personal laptop. She'd spotted the laptop on his desk earlier this morning when she was doing her scheduled walk-through as Brigit had instructed. She needed to get into his office if she was going to find evidence of shady or illegal financial dealings to bolster Dina's custody case.

It was Chef Fred's day off and Natalia moved around the place like a ghost. Celeste had met friends for lunch at her country club and with Javi and Marcus also out, there was no time like the present.

She grabbed her cell and headed out of Celeste's office. The second she reached Marcus's office door, however, her screen lit up. Incoming call. She tried the knob, found it unlocked and quickly scooted inside before she answered.

"Slade. Hey." She kept her voice down and her eyes moving around the spacious, tastefully decorated room. "I was planning on calling you this evening."

"Didn't think this information could wait. Can you talk?"

"Sure." She went straight to the large mahogany desk and the laptop on top of it. She cracked it open, slowly sat down in the chair. "I was just going to see about pulling information off of Marcus's laptop."

The computer woke up and blinked on. She stared at the familiar owl icon looking back at her. "Wow. He's got Sentinex installed. I thought only federal agencies use that security system."

"Federal agencies and well-connected individuals," Slade said.

"Is there a work-around?" The second she tried to gain access the program would save her attempt and show it as the last log-in. Most people probably wouldn't pay attention, but she'd bet Marcus would. Besides, she'd only get three attempts at a password before it locked down.

"No work-around that I know of."

"Great." So those bank statements and records weren't going to be easy to get ahold of. "I'll need his log-in information." She closed the computer before it timed out of its sixty-second window and started pulling open drawers. Maybe he had a password book around here somewhere. "What information did you find on Demchenko and this Vaya guy?"

"Kasimir Vaya," Slade said. "Guy's connected to just about every criminal organization out there. Same goes for Demchenko, but he's more hired muscle and mercenary whereas Vaya is leadership. Add in Reggie Bogart and I'm guessing there's an alliance being formed."

"Dinner definitely had a 'meeting of the master villains' feel to it." She didn't find anything in the desk and moved on to one of the multiple bookcases. "Did you find out what Natalia meant when she called Demchenko a butcher?" She searched for out-of-place books, notebooks or other items that stood out on the shelves.

"I did." It was clear from his tone he wasn't anxious to share details. "The man's wanted for war crimes in multiple countries. Atrocities I don't even want to go into details about, but murder is probably the least disturbing. I've got reports on him going back more than three decades."

"And now he's in the US. Awesome." A wave of revulsion washed over her and she swallowed the rising bile in her throat. "Judging by Natalia's reaction to him, I'm going to assume she experienced some of those atrocities firsthand."

"It's a good bet," Slade confirmed. "She fits into his timeline of travel. But that's not what caught my attention, sadly. Demchenko disappeared for a while only to resurface about four years ago, working for the Valeri syndicate. He was one of their enforcers and who they brought in to oversee human trafficking transport from overseas."

Regan abandoned her search and slowly stepped back. "The Valeri syndicate. That's the organization you and Javi brought down, isn't it?"

"We tried to. Took a good whack at it, but we didn't get everyone involved. Javi took that personally."

"Yes, he did." Some things were impossible to forget. But she almost had because of everything else that had happened with her former partner. Her mind raced as she tried to pluck seemingly obscure pieces of the puzzle and fit them together. "Is there any connection between Caleb Flynn and Demchenko?" she asked Slade. "Or Reggie Bogart or Vaya?"

"Nothing on Vaya that I've found, but hang on." He

went quiet for a moment. Her phone dinged. "I just sent you something."

Regan pulled the phone away from her ear and tapped open the attachment. Flipped through to the second picture. And the third.

"I had to call in a favor with my DOJ friend to get ahold of those. That first image was taken in Russia a little more than six years ago. That's Demchenko and Flynn together when Flynn was still working as an FBI agent. The others are of the two of them with Reggie back in New York last summer a week after Edik Valeri was killed in prison. Flynn is the rumored heir apparent to the Valeri syndicate."

"Caleb Flynn." The plant in the federal agency who had nearly cost Javi and Slade their lives. She glanced around, her eyes landing on the closed door.

Was it possible…?

"I can bet what you're thinking," Slade said. "I'm thinking the same thing."

"Yeah?" Her voice cracked as her breath froze in her lungs. "What's that?" She didn't want to go there, but at the same time it was the only place she wanted to go. Because it was the only thing that made sense. "When did Marcus Antius show up on the DOJ's radar?"

"It wasn't the DOJ who caught wind of Antius," Slade said. "It was the—"

"ATF," Regan cut him off. "Javi's undercover." The second she said it she knew she was right. "All the accusations, him leaving the agency, lying to…" She sucked in a shallow breath. Lying to *her*. "Everything that happened with him was to get him in deep enough to infiltrate and find Caleb Flynn."

"It makes more sense than believing Javi Perez suddenly turned traitor," Slade agreed. "Regan, I think you should take yourself out of this. Let Javi—"

"No." She shook her head as if Slade was standing in front of her. "No. If we're right, Javi's still my partner. He needs backup. He needs us."

"You've been with him a few days now," Slade reasoned. "Why hasn't he come clean?"

She laughed. One sharp sound that felt like a slice across her heart. "Because he's Javi and he always thinks he has to go it alone." She shook her head, cleared the fog. "You need to talk to Aiden. Tell him everything you've told me. And then find out from your contact at the DOJ exactly what they're waiting for where Javi is concerned."

"I'm not sure they know. My contact—"

"Knows more than they've told you. They put you on the path to finding those pictures, didn't they?" She had to remind herself to lower her voice. "They know more. Find out what it is."

"Aiden won't like you staying under when he hears about all this."

"I'm not walking away from this now." Not only because Javi was risking everything to bring down Caleb Flynn but because he knew enough about Marcus Antius to be of benefit to Dina getting her kids back. And that was her way in. "I'll stay in touch, Slade. I promise."

"You'd better. Daily check-ins from here on, Regan. Otherwise, Aiden will come blasting through those gates to get you."

"Remind him he's not the only one who can do some blasting," Regan said. "But I get your meaning. Stay close to the phone. We might need you."

"Understood. Stay safe."

Regan hung up. She dropped her arm to her side. A cool, detached acceptance washed over her.

Finally, the last few years made complete sense.

He'd broken her heart for a case. For a cover story. For…

Revenge. Although he'd probably call it justice. Either way, she wasn't going to let him finish the fight alone.

She returned her attention to the shelves, only to jump at a loud crash upstairs.

Freezing for a split second, she then rushed to the door, poked her head out and quickly stepped into the foyer.

Soft crying echoed from upstairs, followed by a pair of soft, muted voices.

Regan tracked the sounds and found Natalia in one of the guest rooms on the second floor. She had a sheet clutched in one hand and was staring down at a shattered vase on the hardwood floor.

Celeste was stooped over, gathering broken ceramic shards into her hands. When she glanced up at Regan there was a flash of irritation and anger in her eyes.

"Is everything okay?" Regan reached out a hand to Natalia. "Are you all right? If you want to talk about what happened at dinner last night—"

"No. Thank you. I'm fine," the young woman whispered as she turned uncertain eyes to Celeste. "It was an accident."

Regan agreed. "Accidents happen. There's nothing to apologize for. Truly."

Natalia swiped her fingers under her eyes and turned her back on Regan, continuing to sob quietly.

"I didn't mean to disturb you," Regan told Celeste, realizing she must have interrupted something.

"Turnabout is fair play," Celeste said, but the teasing in her voice didn't match the taut expression on her face. "Is there something you needed, Regan?"

"No." This guest room was decorated in beautiful shades of robin's-egg blue with white-and-gold-accents. "I just heard the vase break and wanted to see if there's anything I can do."

"There's nothing you can do," Natalia said softly, and when she turned back around she displayed a tight smile. "I'm still a bit nervous. I didn't mean to cause a scene or make any problems."

"You have nothing to apologize for, Natalia," Celeste responded sharply. "There's no reason to keep doing so. Regan, a word, please?"

"Of course." Why did she have the feeling she was about to be called into the high school principal's office?

Celeste guided her into the hall. "Interrogating the staff isn't an appropriate use of your time."

The sentiment, not to mention the word choice, struck Regan as odd, given the messenger. She saw only shadows of the flirty, boisterous woman she'd been hired to assist.

"I apologize," Regan said contritely. "I was just concerned is all. Last night felt—"

"Familiar." Celeste lowered her voice. "Yes, I'm sure it did, given the state of your marriage. And while I'm very sorry about what happened with your husband, let's not project things onto someone else."

Regan bowed her head, not out of shame, but because it was expected, given the role she was required to play.

"You're right. It's not something I like to talk about. I shouldn't expect anyone else to want to."

"Precisely my point," Celeste agreed. "She's had a rough go of things and she's doing her best to adjust and move past them. Last night was simply a setback."

"She called Mr. Demchenko *m'yasnyk*," Regan said, curious as to whether Celeste had understood what that meant. "Do you have any idea—"

"No." Celeste's eyes sharpened before they cleared with what looked to Regan like forced calm. "I'm afraid I have no idea what it means. Please don't ask Natalia or push her into discussing that which she'd rather forget. I want her to feel safe in this house."

"Yes, certainly." Regan nodded. "I won't bring it up again."

"Thank you." Celeste took a slow breath. "We all have our secrets, Regan. We each need to respect that. Don't you think?"

There was a warning in her words. One that Regan took to heart as Celeste returned to the bedroom and closed the door with a quiet click.

Chapter 8

"Javi."

Javi peered around the open refrigerator door where he'd been looking for some of Chef Fred's leftovers before driving Celeste and Marcus to their dinner party. Regan stood there, arms crossed over her chest, that familiar yet concerning determination shining in her eyes.

"We need to talk."

"Okay."

"Not here." She jerked her head toward the double French doors and walked out of the kitchen and into the backyard.

Seemed as if today simply wasn't going to break his way.

He grabbed a bottle of water and followed her outside.

"What's going on?" He joined her at the far end of the pool where she stood beneath the overhanging branches of a fully blooming crepe myrtle and its cascading blossoms. "What's wrong?"

Either she was ready to blow her own cover or she was tired of pretense. Gone was the subdued, go-along persona she'd adopted upon her arrival at the estate and in her place, in all her glory, stood the Regan McKenna he knew and loved.

"Caleb Flynn." She shot the name out like two bullets, each word in quick succession that struck him dead center of his heart.

He cracked open his water as panic attempted to grab hold. "I don't know what—"

"Caleb." She took a step closer and narrowed her eyes. "Flynn." Another step. She was so close now he could feel the heat of her radiating, setting his body on high alert. It took every bit of control he possessed not to reach out and smooth those lines of tension from her face. "You're working undercover, aren't you?" she accused. "The last few years, you leaving the ATF, breaking things off with me." There were no tears in her eyes, only steely resolve that told him he had no hope of winning any ensuing argument. "That was all a setup so you could get to Flynn through Antius. You're still on the job."

He might have swallowed hard had he had any moisture in his mouth. But that didn't stop him from at least attempting to keep up the ruse. "Regan, I—"

"No more lies."

He hated the concern in her voice, the pain he saw in her eyes. Pain he'd last seen when he'd walked out of her apartment, out of her life in order to keep the promise he'd made to himself.

"Please, Javi," she whispered and inched her chin up to stare directly into his eyes. "You've made a fool of me long enough. Stop with the lies and come clean."

"You aren't a fool." He couldn't help himself now. He lifted a hand to her cheek, steeled himself against the wave of desire that struck when she turned her face into his touch.

"Aren't I?" She grabbed hold of his hand, gripped his fingers so tight he almost flinched. "You convinced me. I let myself believe. All this time I thought—"

He was too tired to keep pretending. "You thought exactly what I needed you to think and believe." Her believing the lies had, in the end, protected him.

"You didn't do any of it. You didn't intimidate those witnesses. You didn't take the payoff. You didn't tamper with evidence." She paused, took a deep breath. "You didn't betray your oath to the agency."

"No." What was the point in denying it when they both knew she could win any fight with him? "No, I didn't." A surprising sense of relief surged through him when he finally admitted the truth. "Antius wasn't going to hire me if he didn't think I'd cross lines. I needed to be disgraced. To hit bottom professionally. It was the only way I could get in and track Flynn."

"You didn't trust me with the truth or with your plan." She frowned, as if still unable to process. "You didn't even try. You didn't even give me the choice."

"No. I didn't." Because he hadn't been given that option. It was a clean break or no break. No in-between.

"I was your partner," she whispered. "I was more than that. We were more than that to one another. I loved you, Javi."

He didn't think it would still hurt, hearing the past tense of her feelings, but it was the bed he'd made years ago. He'd been lying alone in it ever since.

"I had the chance to do what no one else was willing to do," he said, attempting to explain the unexplainable.

"Pulling you in with me would have destroyed more than both our careers. It could very well have hurt your family. I wasn't worth that risk, Regan."

"Then you're a fool." The grief vanished behind a flash of anger. "We could have worked together. We could have found another way."

"There was no other way." He glanced around, feeling more exposed than he had in years. "Look, this is too involved a conversation to have at the—"

"Javi!"

They both turned to Marcus calling from the house, signaling for him. Javi swore under his breath. "We can't do this now. I need to work. We can talk once I'm back from Vegas."

"Vegas?" She balked. "When are you going to Vegas?"

"In the morning. A special errand for Demchenko." It was a crumb of faith he could offer to her. Too little too late, no doubt, but it was something.

Because he needed to, he dropped his head and kissed her, quick and hard.

"Be careful," she whispered against his lips.

"Always am." His smile was quick and cursory before he turned and walked away.

Regan spent most of the rest of her evening pacing her bedroom. Natalia had taken the dinner Regan prepared back to her room, no doubt avoiding any additional chit-chat Regan might have attempted.

The young woman reminded Regan of a stray cat she'd once encountered: skittish, uncertain and clearly afraid of saying or doing the wrong thing. There wasn't much

Regan could do except offer a shoulder or an ear for whenever Natalia might need it.

Her own lack of appetite annoyed her, but she'd put that aside to focus on her reason for being here. Heading back down to Marcus's office to finish giving his shelves the once-over, she tried to review what she knew so far. She was careful to tackle various rooms in the rest of the house, avoiding the kitchen area and suites where Natalia and Chef Fred resided.

Normally the promise of pasta loaded with cheese and black pepper brought a smile to her face. Instead, the very idea had her stomach churning. She touched a hand to her chest, felt the wild, unsteady rhythm that came with a broken heart.

She'd expected a fight where Javi was concerned, but he'd acted as if destroying what they'd shared had been nothing more than an inconvenience and a necessary action.

Maybe it was. She chewed on her thumbnail, something she only did when she was anxious and stressed. But, admittedly, she was capable of her own inconvenient and necessary actions.

She needed him. Needed the information he could give her to use against Marcus in Dina's custody battle. She could forget tackling the illegalities of obtaining banking records and private communications if she had Marcus's second-in-command in front of the judge. But that would only work if Javi's reputation was restored.

Regan stopped short, blinked in surprise at her own train of thought. Was that possible? Restoring everything he'd destroyed on his way out?

Would that include…

Tears filled her eyes before she blinked them away. Useless to cry, but the emotion welled up at the idea of getting him back, not only as her partner but as…more.

She'd spent hours and hours convincing herself she was over him, that she'd been duped into believing he was something other than what he'd pretended to be. Except he was exactly the man she'd always believed. His actions might not have been honorable or on the up-and-up where she was concerned, but when it came to doing what he'd given his word he would do? He hadn't faltered. He'd doubled down.

How could she not love a man like that?

And as soon as this case—both their cases—were over, she was going to do her best to convince him they deserved a second chance.

Early the next morning, Javi stashed his overnight duffel into the back of the SUV. Tempted as he was to examine the contents of the security case, he hadn't had the chance since Marcus had kept it with him after they returned to the mansion.

Even now, he was waiting for Marcus to bring it down. The handoff wasn't until six this evening and the drive to Vegas was less than five hours. He'd have plenty of time to examine the case and document its contents.

He touched a hand to the phone inside his jacket. He hadn't received any new messages since he'd last checked. His next scheduled check-in wasn't for another three days. Hopefully by then Javi would be able to say they were close to completing the case.

"Good morning, Javi." Marcus emerged from the open front door of the house, looking far from bright eyed. Ever since the meeting at the dock, his boss had worn a perpetual frown. Even Celeste's ever-chipper mood hadn't broken through the doom-and-gloom attitude on full display. Hopefully, once Javi got back from Vegas and Marcus returned from Seattle, everyone would have righted themselves.

He was near, so near to seeing this deal happen between Marcus and the Valeri syndicate, which meant Caleb Flynn was in the offing.

Just a little more time, perhaps a few days, and he could finally put this case and the Valeris behind him. Once and for all.

"Morning, sir." Javi stepped back to allow Marcus to put the case into the back beside Javi's bag. "Would you like me to drive you to the airstrip on my way out?"

"Not necessary," Marcus assured him. "Reggie is sending a car for me in about an hour. You can flip off your bodyguard switch for the next forty-eight hours or so." He shot Javi a quick smile. "Text me when the delivery's done. I'll notify Demchenko."

"Yes, sir." Javi started to close the door only to stop short at the sight of Celeste racing for them, a not-so-happy-looking Regan trailing behind her.

Celeste's needle-thin heels clacked on the cobblestone driveway and she waved Javi down. "Wait! Javi, please, wait a minute!"

"Celeste?" The confusion in Marcus's voice mirrored what Javi was feeling. "What's going on?"

"I got a call from Amara Bridal Couture about an hour ago." She almost sounded out of breath. "The custom dress one of my clients ordered is in early." She reached behind her for Regan's arm and tugged her forward. "I told them I'd send Regan to pick it up in person."

"I thought Amara had couriers for those kinds of things," Marcus said.

"Their courier can't deliver until next week, they don't trust commercial senders, and seeing as Javi is headed there anyway…" Celeste offered one of her playful shrugs before turning that beaming, self-satisfied smile on Javi. "I've got meetings the next few days anyway. The two lovebirds should go and…have some fun. You know. After he makes his delivery."

Marcus's brow furrowed. "I don't recall mentioning—"

But Celeste waved away his concern. "I'll call ahead and get you our usual suite at the Elysian. It's our favorite place to stay." She looked back at Regan. "Very romantic. You'll love it."

Regan's gaze skittered to Javi's. "I'm not sure…" she said at the same time Javi said, "I don't think—"

"Marcus won't mind you taking some downtime," Celeste cut them both off. "You've earned it, Javi. And as for Regan, well, she's working out like a dream. Tell them it's okay, Marcus." She stepped closer to her husband and touched his arm. "Please."

Marcus shook his head. "I know better than to get in the way of your matchmaking efforts." He looked back to Javi. "Just make sure the delivery is made on time."

Celeste actually squealed. "Thank you!" She kissed his cheek and spun on Regan. "You need to pack."

"Uh." Regan looked to Javi again. "Fifteen minutes?"

Celeste grabbed her hand and pulled Regan back toward the house. "We'll be down in ten!"

Terrific, Javi thought as he avoided his boss's gaze. *Just…terrific.*

* * *

"Just so you know," Regan murmured to Javi as she climbed into the passenger seat of the SUV. "This wasn't my idea."

"Believe me, I know." Javi didn't come close to meeting her gaze before he closed the door.

Regan wasn't complaining too much. Celeste's obvious matchmaking might make things a tad uncomfortable, but at least they had an excuse to be alone together, and alone time with Javi had been at the top of her list ever since he'd left her out by the pool.

"Celeste is a die-hard romantic," Javi said as he buckled his belt. "She wants everyone to be as blissfully happy as she is, so tag, I guess, we're it." He started the car and they exited the gate, but suddenly he stopped. She noticed a car now at the front gate. "Hold up."

"What's wrong?"

"I need to check out that plate," he said before he pulled around and drove past the vehicle. "Reggie sent that car for Marcus for their trip to Seattle."

She dipped down to dig into her bag for the compact Aiden had given her. She flipped it open and quickly took a snapshot of the car under the guise of checking her nonexistent makeup. While she was at it, she hit the blinking yellow electronic scanner light on the bottom right of the mirror. It strobed once, then settled back into its normal rhythm without making any sound. "What's Marcus going to Seattle for? Don't worry," she said when he shot her a look that told her to be careful with what she said. "The car isn't bugged."

Javi frowned. "How do you—"

She waggled the compact in the air. "One of Aiden's

new toys. Document scanner, camera and surveillance detector. Pretty cool, huh?"

"So you were telling me the truth before." Javi sounded surprised. "You're not here as an ATF agent." He glanced over, changed lanes in order to head onto I-5 North. "If that's the case, then why are you here?"

"A friend asked for my help." She debated just how far to take the truth. "Dina Antius."

"The kids' mother." His knuckles went white gripping the steering wheel. "This is about the custody case."

"It's about a loving mother who's been unfairly cut off from her children and she wants them back." It took an effort to keep her temper in check. She was well aware of Javi's family history, especially what happened with his mother. "She's turned things around, Javi. She's in a good place now."

"Yeah, now." He pressed his foot down on the accelerator as they headed up the freeway ramp. "We both know that can change with the wind."

"I'd rather see them with a woman trying to make her life better than with a father who's a criminal."

He shook his head. "Unbelievable."

"She's got a good support system in place, Javi. She's been sober for a year, her parents are in town. She's working a steady job and…" She trailed off. "You're about to put their father in prison. Do you really think they'd be better off in child protective services than with their mother?"

"Maybe."

"You weren't." It wasn't an argument she wanted to have, or an observation she wanted to offer, but they had to get through this conversation to move forward.

His jaw tensed and for a moment she considered easing back, but they were beyond tip-toeing around one another. "I'm not only doing this for Dina. I'm thinking of Brandon and Avril, too. And I wouldn't be pushing for something that I thought would hurt them." But her heart ached for the neglected little boy he'd been. Until someone had stepped in and stepped up for him. "You could help me, you know. And help Dina. The way your *tias* and *abuela* helped you. You know where Marcus's proverbial bodies are buried. If you agreed to testify on Dina's behalf—"

"I'm not in any position to do anything but what I've been doing for the past two years." Javi cut her off. "The only thing that I'm focused on is getting to Caleb Flynn and that means using Marcus as much as I can. Everything else is a distraction."

"Does that include me?"

"You are most definitely a distraction." But he sagged a bit in his seat, the tension he held in his arms easing as his fingers relaxed. He checked the rearview mirror before switching lanes.

"I don't have to be," she told him. "You aren't alone in this anymore, Javi. Or you don't have to be. I'm right here. I can help you finish this once and for all." She was practically shouting but she couldn't hide her emotions anymore.

"Okay, okay. I'm right next to you, you know? No need to yell, Rey." It was the first time since they'd met again that he grinned the way she remembered. "So, are you going to tell me why you've been on leave?" He turned to look over his shoulder, then up at the mirror again.

"Why what?" And just like that, her optimistic mood evaporated.

"And you've learned how to deflect," he countered as his grip on the wheel tightened once more.

"I've got three siblings," Regan reminded him. "I've always known how to deflect."

"Rey—"

"Not now," she said and looked out the window as they left Newport Beach behind. She squeezed her eyes shut against the memory of bullets flying and children screaming. "Just…not now, Javi."

She reached over and snapped on the radio, turned the volume up and let the pulse-throbbing beat of classic rock fill the car.

He switched it off.

"What the—"

"I need the music off to concentrate," Javi said.

"Concentrate on what?"

"The road," he said calmly. "And the car following us."

Thirty minutes later, I-5 opened up into the vast nothingness of the desert. The heat was bearing down through the windshield, despite the AC. Javi's hands ached from holding on to the wheel so hard.

"No one for them to hide behind now," he muttered and glanced over at Regan. She had her eyes pinned on her side mirror. "But also less risk of collateral damage."

"No plates," Regan said. "Can't tell what make and model the car is. Don't bother slowing down," she said when he took his foot off the gas. "They removed whatever emblem there was. You think they're after what's in that case?"

"Odds are," Javi agreed. "We've got three and a half hours to Vegas." He checked the GPS. "Another seventy minutes to the next rest stop and gas station. I'm thinking we get it over with sooner than later, yeah?"

"Just like old times." She pulled on her seat belt and sat up straighter. "Let's do it."

He slowed down, nearly pulling his foot completely off the gas. They dropped back almost immediately, like coming out of warp speed. The car behind them swerved, caught off guard by their sudden deceleration.

"That got their attention." He hit the gas again and rocketed forward. This time the other car followed and stayed right on their bumper.

"Determined, aren't they?" Regan twisted around to look behind them. "Tinted windows. No idea how many are inside. They're going to hit!" She threw herself back in her seat and braced herself.

The car plowed into them, bouncing their SUV forward but not enough that Javi lost control. A car driving in the other direction blasted its horn as it sped past.

"We could just give it to them," Regan yelled. "Want me to throw it out the back?"

"No." Something told Javi that might be exactly what they wanted.

"So you want to play bumper cars for the next three hours?"

He shook his head. He didn't plan to do that, either. He looked into the rearview mirror just as the car hit again. This time he felt it in his teeth. "Hold on!" He hit the brakes, yanked the steering wheel to the left and spun.

"Steer into it!" Regan yelled just as the other car clipped their back end.

Two wheels came up off the asphalt before Javi righted them. The smell of burning rubber filled the car as he took off again, sliding and slipping through the shoulder dirt and back onto the road.

"Let's see how they like it." Javi punched down on the gas and caught up, never taking his foot off until they knocked hard. The crunch of metal on metal erupted around them. He backed off.

Regan leaned forward, looked over the hood. "Aim for the left!" She pointed to the damaged rear bumper. "They'll have to skid off to keep going."

He did as she said, moving over into the lane of oncoming traffic to get a better angle.

"Javi!" Regan screamed as he jerked the wheel back and avoided the 18-wheeler coming right at them.

"Sorry." He winced. "Should have noticed that."

"You think?" Regan shot him a look. She rose up in her seat. "You're clear for a few minutes. Go again. Clip him on the left."

He zoomed ahead, made contact, then pulled even with the car and swerved into them. The other car went flying off the highway, dirt swirling all around them.

Javi and Regan sped beyond the other vehicle before pulling to the side and stopping.

"You armed?" Javi yelled as he pulled his sidearm out of the center console.

"Housekeepers don't carry guns," Regan countered.

"Glove box." He pointed before he climbed out of the car.

By the time he'd circled around the back of their SUV,

Regan was armed and almost at his side. Weapons raised and trained, they advanced, Regan taking left, Javi staying right. Two men dropped out of the open doors, scrambling for their footing even as they pulled their own guns free.

"Don't!" Javi yelled as he and Regan closed in. He didn't recognize their faces, but their features were similar enough that Javi had to wonder exactly what their purpose had been.

Regan circled around as one man dropped his gun. He had a good three inches on her, but she walked behind him, slammed a hand on his shoulder and shoved him to his knees. She bent down, pulled a large knife out of the holder on his hip.

Javi turned his attention to the weapon aimed at his own head. "Not again," he muttered. "Who sent you?" he demanded of the second man.

"He works for Demchenko," Regan called out, pointing to the guy on his knees. "The ring." She gestured to the man's hand. "Niko was wearing one like it at dinner the other night."

The armed man had wild-looking eyes as he glanced between Javi and Regan.

"You've got one shot," Javi told him. "One shot to take me down." He wasn't normally one to call someone's bluff, but there really wasn't another option.

"Shoot him and the next bullet is for you!" Regan released the safety on her weapon and re-aimed. "Think it through."

Javi could see the man's eyes spinning as he did just that. He dropped the gun but remained on his feet. Javi shook his head in disgust, but as he bent down to pick up the weapon, the man kicked out his foot, caught Javi in the jaw and sent him flying back.

He pivoted the second he hit the ground, gun still in hand as the other man reached for his weapon.

Regan fired. The bullet hit the dirt next to the gun and sent debris flying into the man's face. Javi was back on his feet and returned the favor, sending his man sprawling face down on the side of the road.

A trio of cars sped past, horns blaring, lights flashing.

"Someone's going to call the cops!" Regan yelled as she holstered her weapon and grabbed her guy's arm, hauled him to his feet.

Javi knew what she was saying. If the authorities arrived, he'd either get arrested for assault or he'd have to blow his cover and tell the truth.

He bent down, grabbed the discarded weapon, shoved it into the back of his waistband before he rolled the guy over. He was still conscious, enough to grin at Javi.

"Was it the case?" Javi demanded. "Or was it me?"

The man simply stared. The answer didn't matter. They were one and the same.

Javi crouched and pulled the ring off the man's finger. "You can tell Demchenko he can get this back from me, or you can disappear. You and your friend."

Fear filled the man's eyes. "He'll kill us."

"He'll kill you no matter what." Javi leaned in. "He doesn't abide failure. Go." He nodded to the car. "Now. Before I change my mind."

Regan shoved the other man forward. They both went toward the car. Immediately, the engine started and they sped away. Cutting across traffic, the car headed in the opposite direction.

Regan sauntered up to him, knife in one hand, the gun from the glove box in the other. She kicked out a hip and rested a hand on his arm. "Just like old times. We didn't miss a step, did we?"

He touched a hand to his jaw. "Maybe a little one." Man, he was already beginning to ache. He held the ring up into the light. "A trophy."

"A small one." Regan arched a dismissive brow. "I'm thinking you weren't supposed to make that delivery."

"I'm thinking you're right."

They turned and walked back to their SUV. He opened the back and pulled the case forward.

"Do you even know what's in this thing?"

"I do not." He snapped the locks and pulled the top up. Foam insulation lined the interior of the box. Underneath were a couple dozen thin, square plastic boxes. He lifted one up to inspect it.

Regan grabbed another box and opened it. "Microchips." She took one out, held it up to the light. "I can send pictures of these to Slade and Aiden. See what they can find out about them. Could work against Demchenko. Maybe even Flynn." She looked at him. "If you're okay with their help?"

"I'm okay with their help." He slipped a hand around her shoulders and pulled her in close, pressed his lips to the top of her head. "And yours."

Chapter 9

"You sure this is the place?" Regan leaned forward and peered through the windshield. The strip mall boasted a handful of storefronts, two of which were boarded up. That left a Chinese restaurant, an old video restoration business and a dry cleaner. She checked her watch. "It's only three. You're early."

"Considering they're probably not expecting to see me at all, I think I'm right on time. No." He held out a hand when she started to unbuckle her seat belt. "I'm going in alone. They're connected to Demchenko. I don't want you anywhere on his radar. They see you, he'll know."

Regan wanted to argue. She didn't want him going in there without backup, but she also knew he was right. Demchenko getting wind of something awry at the Antius household could ruin everything. Some battles weren't worth starting. "You've got ten minutes." She still took her belt off, then slid across the center console to take his seat once he got out of the car. "Then I come in."

"Understood." He closed the door, headed to the back to get the case, then made his way across the lot to the dry cleaner's. The neon Open sign flashed on and off.

She could practically hear the fizz of power surging through the tubes.

She buckled back up, had her hands waiting on the wheel in case she needed to come to his rescue.

Unexpected laughter bubbled up in her chest. She caught it behind a quick hand to her mouth. Her life had fully flipped upside down in the space of days and yet…

And yet she wouldn't have wanted it any other way. But while she could understand—and forgive—the past few years, she wasn't capable of forgetting. But that would come. In time.

Under the passenger seat, her cell phone buzzed. She scootched over, dug it out, flipped it around and tapped open the speaker. "Slade."

"You've got me and Aiden." Slade's voice echoed in the car. "We're curious about these microchips you found."

"You recognize them?" She set the phone on the dashboard and kept her gaze on the dry cleaner's ahead. "What are they for?"

"They match the description of upgraded programming chips used for casinos. Chips that went missing in Switzerland just weeks ago."

"Casinos," Regan muttered. "That makes sense considering where they wanted them delivered. Slade, is there any mention of casinos where Demchenko is concerned?"

"Nothing official that I can find," Slade told her. "But it would make for a good laundering operation. Any idea who they're being delivered to?"

"Not yet." She winced. She caught hold of the locket she'd been wearing. "Aiden, don't get mad."

"Nothing good has ever followed that sentence," her brother muttered. "What did you do?"

"The tracking chip you put in my locket? You said you could remote activate it, right?"

"I did. I can."

"I cut a small hole in one of the pieces of foam and wedged it in there. Maybe keep an eye on it and see where the chips end up?" Assuming they stayed in the briefcase. But she wasn't going to mention that.

"When I said test my equipment out this wasn't what I had in mind," Aiden said. "I'll get it handled. Good thinking, by the way."

"Trying to stay ahead of things. Demchenko sent two guys after Javi. Either to kill him or make sure he didn't make the delivery on time, in which case…"

"He would have been taken out either way," Slade said. "Making an enemy out of Demchenko isn't a smart move."

Regan sighed. "What's done is done. Aiden? Did Slade fill you in?"

"On the fact that Javi's misdeeds with the ATF were to build up his rep for an undercover op? Yes. I've been filled in." He paused. "You're on board with that story?"

"It's not a story," Regan said calmly as she caught sight of Javi exiting the shop. "I believe him, Aiden. I need you to, as well."

There was a long pause. "I believe in you, Regan. For now, that's enough. But there will be discussions about this later."

"With both of us," Slade chimed in.

"I'll warn him," she assured them. "We're taking tonight in town, will head back tomorrow. It would be helpful if you could put a pause on turning over the tracing of the chips to anyone official. Javi thinks things are coming to a head with Antius and Flynn. It would be a shame to blow up his investigation just before he gets a result."

"I'll slow walk anything we get," Aiden assured her. "I want you checking in every twenty-four hours now that you're tracer-free."

"Understood." She started the engine as Javi approached. "Gotta go. I've got a wedding dress to pick up."

"Excuse me?" her brother exclaimed before she disconnected with a grin. *Let him sit with that for a while.*

"Everything okay?" she asked when Javi pulled open the door and climbed in.

"If Demchenko doesn't already know his men missed, he will shortly." He looked down at the phone. "You talk to your brother?"

She nodded. "He and Slade are in standby mode. I told them I'd get in touch once we're back in Newport Beach." She reached out and caught his chin in her hand, turned his face toward hers. "He really clocked you, didn't he?"

"Nothing a few hundred ice packs won't help." But his smile was tired. "Hotel?"

"One more stop first. But don't worry. You can sit the wedding-dress portion of the day out."

"I don't know," Javi said slowly and in a tone that set her pulse to thumping. "It is Vegas after all."

So many thoughts raced through her head, but she clung to the ones steeped in reason. She refused to even think about weddings or marriage until both of them were clear of the past. And that, she reminded herself, could be a long, long way off.

"Look up the hotel's room service menu, would you?"

She handed him her phone to keep him distracted. "I'm starving."

"Shocker." He offered a weak laugh. "Adrenaline crashes always make you hungry."

"That and other things."

The Elysian rose up from the Strip like an oasis of melded glass and steel. Bursting with glistening panels of green, blue and gold and reaching more than fifty stories high, only the Palazzo and Fontainebleau stretched taller. The circular drive that welcomed guests boasted thick tropical foliage and an attentive bell staff that immediately hurried forward to take the SUV to valet parking.

With their bags in safe hands, they went straight to registration. The air was filled with the scent of jasmine and the sounds of trickling water from the numerous indoor waterfalls spread out across the lobby.

"No shortage of oxygen in this place." Javi kept his hand on the base of her spine.

"Welcome to Elysian." A dark-haired, middle-aged woman with tortoiseshell glasses offered a welcoming smile. "Do you have a reservation?"

"I believe so," Regan said. "Our boss arranged a room for tonight. Celeste and Marcus Antius?"

"Oh, of course! You're Regan and Javi." Her smile widened and she held up a hand to gesture someone over. "We have the Antius's suite all ready for you. Armand will take you up and make certain you have everything you need."

"My pleasure." The short, stocky, dark-haired man offered a heel-snapping bow. "If you'll follow me."

"I could get used to this," she murmured as they followed Armand past the bell desk, where he picked up their bags.

"Don't," Javi said quietly in her ear. "Neither one of us can afford this in our real lives."

"Please. Sir. Ma'am." Armand stepped back to allow them into a private elevator that zipped them up to the forty-second floor. Their room was at the far end of the hall. Once they stepped inside, they were offered a spectacular view overlooking the Strip.

"Like being in a fishbowl," Javi muttered as he walked past the kitchenette and into the bedroom.

"Thank you so much, Armand." Regan reached into her purse only to have him refuse.

"Gratuities have already been taken care of, ma'am," Armand told her. "Would you like a tour?"

"Ah, no, thanks. I think we'd both like to be surprised." Like they hadn't had enough surprises for one day.

"Good evening, then."

She walked him out, gave the hallway a quick check, then closed the door and snapped the lock in place. Regan grabbed the extensive room service menu off the coffee table and was flipping through it as she strolled into the bedroom. "How hungry are you?"

She stopped short just inside the room.

"Huh." Her plans for the evening went up in smoke at the sight of Javi lying on the king-size bed, sound asleep.

Regret didn't linger long and was replaced by concern for that still-forming bruise on the side of his jaw. After plugging in her phone to charge, she found ice in the refrigerator along with a liner for the ice bucket in the tidy kitchen. Making use of the liner, she filled it, wrapped it in a towel and carefully crawled up the mattress. She pressed the ice gently against Javi's face. He shifted slightly, turned toward her, but didn't wake up.

Her stomach growled as a reminder that the burger they'd stopped for a few hours ago hadn't done its job. She started to turn away, but Javi's hand reached out, gently touched her arm.

Emotion swamped her as she looked at him. She slipped a hand into his hair, brushed a strand off his forehead. Only days ago, she'd believed she'd never see him again. Never hear his voice or feel his touch. Remember what it was like to be loved by him. And now here she was. Exactly where she'd longed to be.

Room service could wait. Reality could wait.

She lifted his arm and lay down beside him, scooting close. She placed her head on his chest. His heartbeat throbbed in perfect rhythm to her own as she closed her eyes.

"Regan."

"Hmm?" Regan snuggled into the warmth of Javi's body. "Five more minutes." She shivered as his lips brushed against the side of her neck.

"You sure about that?" His voice rumbled in her ear and broke the fog of sleep. His hand ran up her arm and back down, catching her fingers between his. "I assume you crawling in next to me is a sign I'm forgiven."

She blinked her eyes open and found him leaning over her, those glistening dark eyes of his filled with restrained passion, happiness and the barest hint of uncertainty. She lifted a hand to his face, to the bruise on his jaw. "Hi."

"Hi." That smile of his could temper a raging storm. "It's late."

"Is it?" She didn't want to take her eyes off of him to check. "Are you hungry? I left the room service menu—"

He silenced her with a kiss. A kiss so perfect, so tender, so promising that the last three years melted away into nothing.

A passion she'd tried to forget, to keep quiet for so long, surged as his tongue swept into her mouth to dance with hers. She moaned, arched her back and rose slightly up off the mattress to press herself against him.

Kissing him stole her breath and rescued her heart. She found herself grabbing at his shirt, unwilling to relinquish his mouth when he started to pull away.

She clung to him, determined never to let him go again.

There wasn't a thought in her head other than want. Need. Desire. The feel of his lips against hers drove her wild and she opened her mouth against his. She drew him in, accepted what he offered and took what she wanted. She'd missed this. She nearly sobbed with the need for him. She'd missed this so much.

"Regan." Her name was a panted whisper that had her opening her eyes. "There you are."

Tears burned the back of her throat. "Here I am." And there he was. Exactly where he was meant to be. "Now," she whispered insistently. "Now and forever."

She didn't wait for an answer. She kissed him again, deeper this time. Putting every ounce of built-up passion into tasting him. Filling her senses to the point she couldn't breathe. Arms tightened, tongues dueled.

They sat up as one, shifting and moving and twisting

out of their clothes as they teased one another with more kisses. They were on their knees facing each other, barely a breath of space between them. The instant her fingers touched his bare flesh she nearly went up in flames.

She wanted him. Near her. Around her. Inside of her.

His hands moved like lightning over her body, leaving a scorching trail of desire. He swiftly drew her shirt over her head and with nimble fingers unhooked her bra. He cupped her full, straining breasts. His palms were rough against her nipples, which instantly hardened beneath his touch.

"You're sure about this?" he asked. He stared into her eyes. "I can't let you go again."

She touched a hand to his face. "Then don't," she whispered.

He slid his hands down and lifted her fully against him. She wrapped her legs around him, felt his arousal pressing hard against her core, almost sending her over the edge.

She threw back her head, tightened her hold on him and tilted forward. When she could, she put her mouth against the side of his neck and kissed him.

He turned in a way that told her he expected her to release him, but she threw her weight to the side and sent them tumbling onto the bed together. Arms and legs tangled as they got their bearings. She grabbed his shirt and hauled it up, dramatically flinging it away. His fingers unbuttoned her jeans, drew the zipper down slowly before he slid the denim and her panties off and flung them to the floor. He looked at her then, his expression full of fervor and want.

She hissed out a breath, anticipating him surging to

her, but instead, his fingertips teased the soft curls between her legs.

Regan whimpered. The pressure built from within, pushing hard, unrelenting. She glanced up, found his face mere inches from hers. She spread her legs, caught his hand with one of hers and brought it where she needed and wanted him.

"Yes… Yes… Right there," she murmured, her breathing steady, but she knew she was starting to lose control as he stroked and teased her wet heat. She arched her back, her groan echoing through the suite. He kissed her and kissed her, never stopping. The rhythm of his touch had her panting and pressing up into his hand. When she finally tumbled into what felt like absolute bliss, she cried out, but the sound was quickly captured by his mouth. His tongue resumed dancing around hers.

She didn't take a minute to enjoy the relaxing sensations streaming through her. When he stopped and gazed at her, she took the opportunity to reach, boldly, for him.

"More." She breathed him in and rose up to remove his pants with a ferocity that had her feminine power soaring into the stratosphere.

"Tell me there are condoms."

He smiled a smile she felt in her core, and switched his gaze to the nightstand. "There was a box in the bathroom."

"I love this hotel," she said and laughed at the same time. "Suit up already." Regan put a hand to his chest, more than prepared for what would happen next. Javi ripped open the condom wrapper and sheathed himself.

She settled back on the bed, and he came to her. Right away, she wrapped herself around him. Her legs about his hips, her arms at his neck, she opened herself to him willingly, wantonly.

"I never thought…" he murmured against the side of her throat.

She squeezed her eyes shut against the tears that formed. Tears that spoke of her love for him that had never left her, despite the countless times she'd willed it to. It was almost too much to bear. She needed…

She needed control.

In one fluid, controlled movement, she spun and rose over him, reached down to grasp his hard length and slowly took him deep within her.

He groaned. Or maybe it was her. She couldn't be certain. All she knew was that in this moment, having him beneath her, like this, was the most perfect thing she could have ever wished for.

He stretched her as she moved up and down, pressing her hips forward and increasing her tempo. His breathing came in short, controlled pants. His hands grasped her shoulders, moved down her arms until he captured her hands. Their fingers mingled, joined, threaded as she rocked, deliberately hard over him. Every moment of their joining was a memory she would never forget.

The tension in his body shifted as his pace grew frantic. He thrust up and into her, throwing her off rhythm, and she felt the orgasm building inside of her once more. Powerful, perfect, a promised wave of passion she only wished she could ride forever.

Her hands tightened against his and she drew his arms up, then wide. She arched her back, thrusting her breasts forward as he filled her and only then, when she looked down into his ecstasy-filled face, did she allow herself to let loose.

And follow him over the edge.

"I need to talk to your brother." Javi turned his head and pressed his lips against Regan's temple.

"For the record, that's not the thing a girl likes to hear right after sex." She snuggled against his side, her head nestled in the crook of his shoulder. Her leg rested between his and nearly had his eyes rolling back in his head for the second time that night. Her hand became restless and moved across his belly, short nails teasing against his skin.

"Is this some new kind of torture they're teaching at the ATF these days?" If so, he was all in favor of it. He caught her roaming hand before it moved into the danger zone. "Regan." He turned his head, pressed a kiss to her forehead and tried not to read too much into this. "What are we doing?"

"Starting over." She sighed. "Don't overthink it or you'll ruin it." But when she started to move away, he held on. He'd let go of her once. He wasn't inclined to do it again. Not so soon, anyway.

"I ruin everything."

"Yes, you do." She shifted, rested her chin on the back of her hand, which she pulled free from his and looked up at him. "You're such a silly fool, do you know that?"

"So you said before." Not that she was wrong. "It doesn't come as a complete surprise. But if you'd like to be more specific—"

"Caleb Flynn." When she looked at him, there was

fresh pain in her eyes. Pain he hadn't seen before. A resignation of sorts. Or acceptance. "You lied to me."

That mental precipice he'd been standing on began to crumble. "And sex was my punishment?"

Her smile was tight. "Trust is a scarce commodity in our line of work. More so with the personal. As fun as this is and as happy as I am to have you back in my life, there's a lot still standing in the way. This won't be an easy fix, Javi. It's going to take a lot of work to get back what we lost." She paused. "On both our parts."

"I've never been afraid of hard work." Especially with a promising payoff. He tilted her chin up, swooped in to kiss her. He could feel the tension in her body. How she stiffened at his joke, as if she worried he wasn't taking this conversation as seriously as she was. He needed to offer an olive branch. "Deputy Director Seth Dunning."

Her brows pinched. "What does our boss's boss—"

"Dunning came to me after Mexico, while I was still recovering in the hospital. It was his idea to put me in deep cover with Antius to get to Flynn. He pulled all the strings."

"You're serious." It was clear she didn't want to believe him, though. "That's just…cold." She shook her head. "He was the loudest voice against you. He's the one who pushed for your outright dismissal."

"We needed it to look legit," Javi explained. "He's the only one I've been in contact with. The only person who knows the truth about what I've been doing. You're the second." He didn't have to add that telling her now showed just how much faith—and trust—he had in her. "Add in Slade and Aiden and we're up to four." He flinched. "That's a lot of people really fast." He'd stayed in control for so long, he didn't know how to let go. But this was a start.

"What is it you need to talk to Aiden about?"

"Hmm?" Distracted, he ran his hand up and down her bare arm.

"You said you wanted to talk to him." She shifted away slightly. "About what exactly?"

"I came across a manifest in Marcus's paperwork the other day for a ship called *Deadlight Express*. It's supposed to dock in LA in a couple of days. I think it's going to be carrying human cargo."

"Human cargo." Regan froze. "You mean trafficking victims? I assumed it was drugs or weapons he was helping smuggle in, but people? That's a whole different level of evil." The agent inside of her woke up. "Are you sure?"

He nodded. "I deciphered Marcus's coding for his shipping notations. It would fit the pattern. But I want Aiden's eyes on it. He has contacts I don't who could confirm it."

"I want to see them. The documents," she added at his slow blink. "You made copies of them, didn't you?"

"I took pictures with a receive-only phone. No SIM card so there's no way to send them to anyone. If we can get them to Aiden, he'll be able to forward them to where they have to go." Plus, federal authorities would be more inclined to believe Aiden McKenna than they would him these days. "But it has to happen fast. From what I read, the ship will be in the LA harbor the night after next."

"You didn't have to tell me all this."

He touched her again, dragged the back of his finger down her arm. "I know."

"You could have found another way—"

"I trust you." It was, he realized, what she'd been waiting to hear. Still, he held his breath.

She stared at him for a long moment. For the first time, he couldn't decipher the expression on her face. Either she'd gotten really good at wearing a mask, or he was out of practice.

"Are you in there?" he asked.

"I can set up a meeting with Slade once we're back at the mansion tomorrow and he can get the documents to Aiden."

"It's that simple?"

Her brow arched. "Amazing what happens when you let someone help you." She sighed and flopped back down, rolled onto her back. "Aiden gave me a few things to use. Like that tracker I put in the briefcase full of microchips." She looked down at the locket dangling between her breasts.

He picked it up, snapped it open, looked at the picture inside. A little white dog with a ring around one eye. He remembered her mentioning him before. Croissant? Cupcake? No. That wasn't the name. "Donut."

Her eyes misted. "He had the cutest little bark. Let me see if I can…" She let out a sharp, almost pathetic whine of a sound that had him laughing.

"Dogs are the best."

Her lower lip wobbled and she caught his hand. "How did I ever believe you'd turned traitor?"

It had definitely taken a lot of work on his part. "You believed what I needed you to. Thanks for your help with Aiden."

"Ah." She held up a finger. "I have a favor to ask in

return." She waited until he met her gaze. "I want your help where Dina's custody case is concerned."

Now it was his turn to move away, but as he'd done earlier, she held on and kept him in place. "That's a complicated situation, Regan. I don't want—"

"You either trust me or you don't." The statement now wedged between them like an inconvenient boulder. "Do you really think I'd put those kids into a scenario where I thought they'd be in danger? Javi." She caught his chin in her hand so he couldn't look away. The bruise on his jaw throbbed as a painful reminder to their earlier takedown. "They're already in danger. Look who their father lets into the house. But whether the kids are there or not, they're his weakness. Demchenko and Vaya wouldn't hesitate to use either or both of them to further their agendas. Those children need to be with their mother."

Javi had trouble thinking of a response that didn't make him sound like a total jerk. "Marcus's business arrangements aside, that doesn't mean Dina—"

"She's not your mom," Regan reminded him for a second time. "She's made the changes. Changes your mother wasn't able to, Javi." She touched his face. "Don't let your past get in the way of their future."

He shook his head and shot her a glance. "You're just pulling out all the big guns, aren't you?" With her psychological leanings, he should have remembered she wielded certain weapons with stealth. "What exactly—"

"A statement of support, detailing Marcus's activities," she said, as if expecting the question. "Once your case is closed, of course. Simply tell the judge Marcus's parenting abilities and skills are questionable at the least.

Dina's lawyer will take care of the rest. Tick tock, Javi," she added. "When does that ship arrive?"

"Didn't think you'd resort to blackmail."

"It's deal-making, not blackmail. And I believe I've earned some latitude. And keep in mind, even with Aiden's connections, it'll take time to get a federal warrant for the *Deadlight Express*."

He didn't have to verbally agree. She already knew she had him backed into a corner. He'd do what she wanted, but he'd also stay close when the dust settled, just to make certain Avril and Brandon were safe and happy.

"I guess we're unofficially partners again," he said. "I've missed working undercover with you."

Her face darkened. "Don't get used to it. My undercover days are over."

"Why? What happened?"

She looked away but then focused again on him. "Nothing." She kissed him, but there were ghosts in her eyes he'd never seen before. "Suffice it to say that after my domestic-assistant duties are complete, I won't be rushing into any other assignments like this anytime soon. If ever."

"No?" There was a definite story there. "Why? What happened?"

She winced. "I don't want—"

"I think we can agree the mood has been broken. Talk to me, Regan." An ironic request, he knew, but one that was necessary. "Does this have to do with why you took leave from the ATF?"

When she extricated herself from his embrace, this time he let her go. He knew what it was like to carry ghosts and couldn't begrudge her obvious desire to put some distance between them.

She curled her legs in, wrapped her arms around her knees and stared straight ahead. The way her spine curved and she all but huddled in on herself had him scooting back against the headboard. Whatever had happened, she didn't want to look at him when she told him. He could understand that. Probably better than most.

"We received reliable information that a major ghost gun operation was being run out of Southern Florida. I went in undercover as a potential buyer to suss out the informant and get additional information. It took a while." She turned her head and looked at him out of the corner of her eye. "You know how that goes. But I finally narrowed the list down to three people. One was a young mother of two who had gotten caught up in this group because of her boyfriend. She was so scared, Javi. I mean down-to-her-bones terrified, especially for her kids, but I assured her everything was going to be okay. That we could protect her. So…

"She agreed to testify to what she'd seen in exchange for witness protection and a fresh start. The ATF came in on my signal, before the final details were in place. The firefight…" She squeezed her eyes shut and a solitary tear escaped. "She was there when her boyfriend set off a bomb. She was injured protecting her kids from the blast." She swiped at her damp cheek. "She died in my arms with her children watching." Regan sobbed. "I didn't do enough. I failed her."

It was impossible, Javi knew, to convince her otherwise. She was wrong about not having done enough, but what he believed didn't matter in this moment. All he could do was listen and support her. He touched her shoulder and felt some relief when she reached up and grabbed hold of his hand.

"What happened to the kids?" he asked.

"Foster care." Her voice broke. "I managed to pull some strings, and they were placed with a good family who had other kids from similar experiences. Last I heard they were doing okay, but…" She paused again. "They've lost their mom. Nothing is ever going to be the same for them."

"So when Dina Antius came to you asking for help…"

"I couldn't say no. I'm really predictable, right?" She actually laughed. "It was like being given a second chance to get it right. To make sure two other kids got a life with their mom that my witness didn't get. I had trouble coming back after the fallout from that case. It felt…hard. Difficult. So I requested additional leave and well, you know the rest." Her sad smile broke his heart. "Here I am."

"Yeah." He squeezed her hand and tugged gently. "Here you are." Giving him the second chance he never believed they'd get. "I'm only going to say this once," he said quietly. "And I know you aren't going to believe me, but what happened wasn't your fault, Regan. Given that world, her surroundings, chances are the same thing would have happened if you hadn't been there. Maybe because you were, those kids are alive today. They're safe now because of you." Deep down she knew that, but she had to come to terms with it on her own.

"I want to believe that." She leaned back, curled into him once more and wrapped her arms around him. He could feel her shaking, shivering against the grief and guilt she'd no doubt carry for the rest of her life. "You're the first person I've been able to talk to about this. Wren tried to pull it out of me, but…" She shrugged. "My sister is easier to fight than you." He could feel the dampness of her tears on his chest. "With you…"

He leaned down, pressed his lips to the top of her head. "I'm glad I could give you something you needed."

Now she smiled and when she tilted her head back and looked up at him, the shadows had lessened. "You're always what I need. Always."

He turned his mouth to her palm and kissed her hand, wishing, hoping this was true.

"So." She cleared her throat as if ridding herself of the melancholy. "How about we take another trip around the bases."

"Baseball analogies and sex?" Javi wrapped his arms around her and squeezed. "I have missed you so much, Regan."

"Yeah?" She grinned and pulled his mouth down for a kiss. "Prove it."

Chapter 10

Regan's eyes snapped open.

She sat up, peering into the semidarkness of the hotel room. Beyond the nearly shut double doors of the bedroom, the twinkle and glow of the midnight Strip streamed into the suite. She rested a hand on Javi's arm, straining to hear.

She was inclined to dismiss whatever had woken her up, but she'd learned a long time ago to trust her instincts first and verify later.

Something shifted in the sitting room.

She nudged Javi before leaning over and retrieving the sidearm Javi had loaned her earlier.

He bolted up, hand already reaching for his own weapon. "What?" His voice was barely a whisper.

She touched a hand to her ear, then pointed at the open door. The silver dome gleamed on top of the cart that had delivered their room service order a few hours ago.

He nodded, slid out of bed and grabbed his pants from where they'd landed on the floor. She felt around for her own clothes, set the gun down long enough to pull them on before joining him.

They stood there, on either side of the doorway, weapons raised. Trigger fingers at the ready. She reached out, pulled the door open a little bit more to get a better view of the main room. Two shadowy figures moved about the space, clearly looking for something as they dug into the seat cushions of the sofa before one quietly switched to the dining area, while the other vanished into the kitchen.

She held up two fingers to Javi, pointed in one direction, then the other before exploding her fingers out, indicating she'd hit the lights.

He nodded before pointing left. She'd go right. Their usual routine. Funny how it came back to her like second nature.

Javi wrapped his hand around the door, nodded three times as a countdown and pulled it open.

Regan moved out first, heading directly across Javi's path as he crossed behind her. She kept her weapon aimed and trained, scooting past the breakfast bar to reach the light switch.

The second she switched it on, the intruder spun and launched himself at her. Regan kept her weapon high as he tackled her. She heard a distinctively male grunt, smelled the stench of cigarettes and beer before the back of her head bounced off the floor. Even as stars exploded in her eyes, she kicked out, spinning slightly, and caught her attacker against the back of his knees. He went sprawling face-first. Another groan as he tried to drag himself back to the door.

Behind her, Javi landed punches that sent that intruder rolling over the dining room table. Regan blinked against the harsh light, walked over and planted her foot firmly on the back of the man who was coughing and spitting up blood. She pressed the barrel of her gun to his back.

He froze.

"Javi?" she called just as he landed a punch into the guy's jaw. He went down hard but was back up on his knees in an instant.

"Got him!" He loomed over the attacker, gun in hand. "You good?"

"Yeah." But her head hurt something fierce. She engaged the safety on her weapon, eased back and grabbed the man's shoulder. She rolled him over. He spit blood, coughing and wheezing as he looked up at her.

"You broke my nose!" He swiped off the hood and exposed stark white dyed hair.

Regan was disgusted. "It's a kid." Seventeen at most. And scrawny as anything.

"So's this one." Javi shoved the other's hood off, revealing a nearly shaved skull. "What the…? He was at the dry cleaner's." He kicked at one of the dining chairs, motioned for him to sit.

"They were looking for something," Regan said as she grabbed hold of the shirt of the guy she'd tackled and hauled him to his feet. "First one to talk gets to walk." Taking either of the intruders into custody wasn't realistic. Not without burning both her and Javi as law enforcement.

The boys looked at one another. She saw desperation in their gazes, and more than a little fear. They shook their heads, pinched their lips tight.

"Aw, man." Regan sighed and went into the bedroom, pulled open the drawer next to Javi's side of the bed, snatched what was inside before returning to the living room. "Is this what you wanted?" She held up the ring Javi had taken off of Demchenko's goon.

Their eyes went wide before their faces drained of color.

"I'm beginning to question Demchenko's recruitment policy," Javi muttered. "This is the second duo of dummies he's sent after us." He retrieved the kid's discarded gun, shoved it into the back of his waistband.

"They aren't so dumb," Regan commented. "They had a key card to get in."

"Which means they had help here at the hotel." Javi seemed to be studying the two of them. "Who's the connected one? Let me guess. Sister? Girlfriend?"

Her kid's gaze dropped immediately to the floor. "Girlfriend."

"No. No, we don't know her," Javi's guy insisted with a hint of panic on his face. "We were just told to meet her in the lobby and she'd give us the key card."

"Please. We need that ring. They won't let them go if we don't get it."

"Shut up, Ivan," Javi's guy muttered.

"Won't let who go?" Regan asked, gentling her tone.

"Ivan…" the other boy warned before Ivan spat out a litany of Russian that had Javi's eyes narrowing. They argued back and forth, the words flying faster than Regan could hope to interpret. But she understood fear and being trapped in any language.

"Stop!" Javi ordered. "That's enough. They're brothers." That earned him a pair of surprised gasps.

"Since when do you speak Russian?" Regan was dumbfounded.

"It's been a long couple of years," Javi said. "Their family's coming to the States. Parents and two younger sisters. They were sent ahead to work for the people arranging their transportation." He met Regan's eyes. "They're supposed to arrive in a couple of days. By ship."

The *Deadlight Express.*

Javi shot off a round of questions. The kids were too shaken not to answer, but they did so in their own language. When Javi held up his hand to silence them, he gave her an all-too-familiar look.

He wanted to let them go.

"You sure?"

"I'm sure." There wasn't a moment's hesitation in his response.

She grabbed the kid's gun, ejected the chambered round as Javi did the same with the brother's weapon. "Here." She handed Ivan the ring and his gun. "Tell them you found it on the counter. That you were in and out without incident. As far as you know we never woke up. Wait!" she said when the teens moved to the door. "Just…hang on."

She grabbed the hotel notepad by the phone on the desk by the window, scribbled down a couple of names and phone numbers. She ripped off the paper and handed it to them. "When your family gets here and you're all safe, you call this number from a secure phone." She indicated the top one. "They'll help you. All of you."

"Go. Now," Javi said before either of them could process what was happening. "If you're gone much longer, they'll think something went wrong and come looking for you."

They looked shell-shocked yet relieved as they closed the door behind them.

Javi leaned back against the dining room table. "Not the way I like to wake up." He scrubbed a hand down his face before facing her. "Whose number did you give them?"

"A friend." She shot him a smile.

"You McKennas have a lot of those, don't you?"

"We do." She shook out her arms to get rid of the tingles. "What did you ask them before?"

"Details about their parents' arrival. They gave me the same information I read on that shipping manifest of Marcus's."

Well. That took care of that, didn't it?

In the distance, she could see the sun beginning to peek up over the horizon, setting the Strip on fire. Before she forgot, she opened the hall closet and pulled out the garment bag containing an obscenely expensive one-of-a-kind wedding dress. She draped the bag over the fancy sofa so she'd be sure to remember to bring it with her when they left. "As much as I'd like to enjoy a couple more hours of connubial bliss, I think we should get out of town. Maybe call down for room service to go?"

"Good idea." Javi walked over, touched a hand to the back of her head. "Hurt much?"

"Only a little." The second he was out of eyesight she was going to take some painkillers. "Go grab a shower. I'll get the food. Go," she urged when he was about to suggest something they didn't have time for, despite how much she wanted to. "We need to get back and put an end to all this once and for all. We can talk downtime later."

"Not going to argue with that. Which reminds me, I still owe you a trip to the beach, don't I?"

"Yes," Regan said as she began to straighten up the mess the scuffle had made. "And I still have every intention of collecting."

"Thank goodness you're back!"

Regan didn't have both feet in the foyer before she spotted Celeste racing down the stairs. She reminded Regan a bit of an animated princess with her perfectly arranged hair, bright white pleated tennis skirt and a flowery peach-pink tank. All that was missing was a flock of tiny birdies twirling around her head.

"Here's the dress." Regan held up the garment bag and resisted the temptation to look back at Javi as he entered the house. There was no stopping the heat that rose into her cheeks, however. "The manager of the shop made sure to remind me that whatever changes might need making, he'll arrange for a top seamstress to take care of it."

"Wonderful!" Celeste clapped her hands together and waved Regan into her office. "I can't wait to see it. Have you seen it? What did you think?"

"Oh, uh…" It probably wasn't very typical of her not to have taken a peek. "I'm afraid I didn't get around to looking." She ducked her head but not before catching a knowing expression on Celeste's face. "I was a bit distracted."

"I'll bet," Celeste chuckled, following her. "I've got a door hook around here somewhere." She rummaged in a drawer until she found one. "Let's hang it here." She opened a closet door and gestured for Regan to hang up the bag. "I've been dying to see how it turned out." She unzipped the bag, stood back and gushed over the dress.

Regan tuned out the commentary. She imagined this was what astronauts felt like returning from space. Regan felt the need to decompress and be reprogrammed into what was expected of her. Especially since she was far more in her element with car chases, flying bullets and teenage burglars.

"Celeste?" Marcus poked his head in and offered a quick, cursory nod to Regan. "I'm heading out."

"Okay," Celeste murmured absently, then snapped to attention. "Don't forget about tonight." When Marcus didn't respond, she added, "The Pacific Reverie Gala." Celeste's tone said she was used to Marcus forgetting their engagements. "The Worthingtons are sending their limousine for us at seven thirty. And don't tell me you didn't know about it." She pouted. "I called your office assistant yesterday to confirm it was on your schedule. That reminds me, Regan, I'd appreciate it if you could pick up Mr. Antius's Armani tuxedo from the dry cleaner's today? And I've laid out a selection of dresses on my bed. If you could steam or press them and leave them on the back of our bedroom door? I'll choose which one I'll wear once I get home from the club."

"Of course."

"And I've made note of other items for you to address just there. On your desk."

Regan retrieved the two full pages of notes and let out a held breath. She could knock most of these tasks, including the social media graphics, out with ease.

"Not a problem," she assured her boss. "If there's nothing else? I'd like to unpack and get settled in."

"Go, go," Celeste said and shooed her out. "You're

a lifesaver, Regan. I appreciate you!" she called out as Regan retreated down the hall and into the kitchen.

Picking up dry cleaning wasn't at the top of her want-to-do list, but it would give her the excuse she needed to meet with Slade and pass off Javi's receive-only phone. Which reminded her…

"Please tell me that's fresh coffee," she pleaded with Chef Fred the second she stepped into the kitchen. "I'm running low on caffeine."

"Third pot of the morning," Fred confirmed with a grand wave to the machine. "Help yourself."

"Good morning, Natalia." She offered a quick wave and earned a timid smile in response as the housekeeper continued folding laundry.

"Excuse me," she murmured to Javi and he shifted slightly away. She kept her voice purposely low. "I need your phone."

"Right." Javi grabbed an apple out of the countertop basket. "Got any big plans for today?"

Other than handing off potentially case-closing photographs? "Oh, tons." Regan smirked. "After I pick up Marcus's dry cleaning, I get to steam press a bunch of dresses I couldn't afford in any lifetime. And this afternoon I get to inventory our office supplies, help Natalia with the first-floor cleaning and upload a bunch of social media posts I'm betting no one will see."

"Never really thought about you as domestic before." He grinned. "It's kind of a turn-on."

"Hearing you say that is not," she deadpanned, then straightened when Natalia joined them.

Javi's cell phone pinged. He checked for messages. "I'll get that thing we talked about before I head out.

Have a good day." He smiled in that way he had that often short-circuited her senses. "See you later?"

"Uh-huh." She did her best to sound casual, but after Javi left, she found Natalia watching her. "Something wrong?"

"No." Natalia glanced away, twisting her hands together. "I'm sorry. I wasn't being nosy or spying. It's just…" She looked to the doors Javi left through. "He's different with you."

"Is he? Different how?" If that wasn't a leading description, she didn't know what was.

"Less…intimidating," Natalia said finally. "You make him smile."

As nice as that was to hear, Regan didn't particularly like the idea of being a distraction. Javi needed to focus on his work and closing this case. It was the only way they were ever going to be in a position to see what might come next for them.

"He's kind," Regan said. "I haven't had kind in a long time."

Natalia rubbed a thumb against the inked marking on her wrist. "Kind is always good."

"That's an interesting tattoo." Regan walked over, and Natalia clutched her clasped hands to her chest. Regan tapped her own left shoulder. "I have an owl. My—" she almost said *sister* "—my best friend and I got matching ones when we graduated." She didn't add that it symbolized their graduations from law enforcement programs. Regan from the ATF training school and Wren from the FBI Academy. "They can be very special."

"Mine is not special." Natalia tilted her chin up, tears flooding her eyes before she blinked them away. She extended her arm to show off the broken-winged bird. "It was not my choice."

Regan looked down at the rather crude image. The lines were uneven, the color thicker in some places than others. A rush job. Probably, Regan realized, one of many that had been given at the time. She swallowed hard, understanding far more than she wanted to. She gently took Natalia's arm in her hand and covered the image with her other. "I'm sorry."

It was routine, she knew, for human traffickers to "brand" their "property." It wasn't only to keep track of them and remind them that they were no longer living their own lives, but it also acted as a sign to anyone outside their inner circle that they were already claimed by someone.

Considering Natalia's reaction to Niko Demchenko the other night, it was a given he was somehow involved in what had happened to her. Or Demchenko was just known in those circles. Regan wanted to ask, to dig deeper, but Celeste was right. It wasn't a kindness to make Natalia relive something that clearly still caused her trauma.

"I'm saving my money," Natalia said, and bravely held Regan's gaze. "I want to have it removed. But it is very expensive."

Regan nodded. She knew of an organization dedicated to removing such brands and markers for survivors. If an opening to share such information presented itself… "I'm sure you'll get there. Natalia?" she called when the younger woman moved away. "If you ever want to talk about anything—"

"Mrs. Celeste says I should not burden anyone else.

She listens. She cares." Her smile was small but carried no hint of resentment that Regan could see. "It is enough."

Regan nodded. It wasn't her place to push. Not yet at least.

Had Javi put two and two together where Natalia's tattoo was concerned? Or had he even noticed it? Sometimes in deep cover, you missed the simple, everyday things. Marcus Antius was, if not already involved, about to step fully into the trafficking business himself.

And Regan found herself as committed as Javi was to making sure he was held accountable for that.

Chapter 11

"He does not trust you."

Hearing Kasimir Vaya state the obvious when it came to Niko Demchenko did little to stop the chill racing down Javi's spine.

The offices of DriftCore Global took up most of the tenth floor of the West Tower of a high-rise that offered spectacular views not only of downtown Newport Beach, but also the mountain ranges in the distance. Located close to the major freeways, Marcus had created a comfortable atmosphere here for his twenty-five employees, half of whom worked overnight shifts to facilitate communication with Marcus's worldwide clientele.

Marcus Antius might sleep, but his business never did.

From the second they'd walked off the elevator this morning, Javi felt the penetrating, assessing eyes of Niko Demchenko. Even now, across the conference room, Niko waited for his scheduled meeting with Marcus with a visible sense of impatience.

"Funny," Javi said to Vaya without a hint of humor. "And here I was wondering if he planned to ask me out on a date."

Vaya chuckled. "What is the phrase you Americans

use? Poking the bear? You must enjoy putting yourself into dangerous situations."

Enjoy? Not remotely. But he responded with a shrug and said, "It's a living."

Demchenko was no doubt processing the events of the past couple of days. His cool facade didn't come close to hiding the disgust he felt at seeing for himself that Javi had returned from Vegas relatively unharmed. Men like him, and even less in-your-face men like Vaya, did not react well to being taken down or out or being one-upped. Especially in a room full of witnesses. A miscalculation on Javi's part? Maybe.

It wasn't just pride or ego that Javi had attacked the other night at dinner. It was the idea that Demchenko's authority had been questioned. Javi had weakened him in the eyes of everyone in attendance. Demchenko wouldn't forget it.

In the meantime, Javi needed to find a way to use the other man's anger to his advantage. He saw Marcus approaching the conference room and quickly pushed the record button on his watch.

One side of the heavy double glass door opened. Marcus strode in. "I apologize for keeping you waiting," he said as Vaya left Javi to join Marcus and Demchenko at the table. "I've spoken with Reggie. Our mutual friend's arrival will coincide with that of the *Deadlight*."

Mutual friend? Javi didn't want to get his hopes up yet again, but the only person he could think of that could unite all these factions swas Caleb Flynn. Anticipation surged.

"And the cargo?" Vaya asked.

"The distribution company will be waiting at the dock.

The harbormaster has received his payment. He'll make certain the only workers around are those we've secured. Javi."

He'd mastered the art of feigning ignorance. "Yes, sir."

"Your previous experience with law enforcement," Marcus said. "I think it will come in handy for the arrival. You'll come with us to make certain the off-loading and transfers are made without any issue, or outside involvement. You know what to look for surveillance-wise."

"Yes." Javi nodded. "Of course." There wasn't any other answer to give.

"Excellent. Then it is all arranged." Marcus folded his hands on the conference table. "Now, I'd like to get into the details of our future. We've already agreed that this shipment will lock into place DriftCore's position as the primary shipping company for both of your businesses, along with those of the Valeri organization. I would very much like to lock in a contract for subsequent arrivals along with expected time frames. I think we can all agree we need to keep things moving as expeditiously as possible in order to maximize our profit margin."

Javi locked his jaw as the negotiations began. He could only hope, when all was said and done and all the evidence he'd gathered over the past two years was evaluated, that he could finally, once and for all, walk away from this life.

And maybe, if he was very lucky, step into a new one with Regan.

"Javi didn't come with you?" Slade stepped back to let Regan into the Los Angeles apartment. The forty-minute drive had acted as a reset. With the music blasting, she was almost, *almost* able to set aside the new kind of nerves that had set in. Nerves that hovered whenever she sensed big change ahead.

Not just with her assignment and Javi's case. But with...

Not now. Letting herself head down that road was only going to distract her.

"He's working," she told her handler. "Although, if you ask me, most of his job is just standing around looking intimidating." Regan dumped her purse on the table beside the array of computer technology. "Personally, I think he's a little afraid of you at this point."

"He should be," Slade said. "Ashley says I'm being too hard on him. But I don't like being lied to."

Regan could see his side of things. "He didn't lie to your wife, he lied to us, didn't he?"

The guarded look in Slade's eyes eased. "Nice to know I'm not alone."

"You are not." She was definitely still working on that forgetting thing. "But you're also who he needs right now." She dug out Javi's cell phone. "His superior at the ATF gave this to him when he went under. It's receive only, so he couldn't send the pictures he took himself. They're images of a shipping manifest he found in Marcus Antius's briefcase the other day."

Slade took the phone, sorted through a bunch of cords before connecting it to his laptop. He sat down. "Let's see what he got."

Regan moved behind him to read over his shoulder.

"*Deadlight Express.* Well, there's a blast from the past," Slade said.

"Yeah?"

"This is the vessel long suspected of being the Valeris' main smuggling vehicle. Always clean as a whistle when it got boarded. Hasn't been back this way for a few years."

A thought flickered in Regan's mind. "Like maybe before Caleb Flynn was exposed as a plant at the FBI?"

"Timing seems right," Slade muttered. "Looks like it's bringing in a bunch of mannequins and display cases."

"Yeah, Javi's convinced that's code. Hang on." She pulled out her own cell and tapped open the notes app. "He wrote down what he thinks it all means."

Slade skimmed it, continued clicking through the pages. "I mean, it makes sense. On the surface at least." He shrugged. "We've only got his word that this is what the ship is actually carrying. There's nothing indicating anything criminal and before you say it, no, we can't take previous supposition into account. As far as I know, they gave up on the *Express* along with Flynn. That means starting over and getting new information to use."

Regan's stomach dropped. Her expectations had been skyscraper high. "You don't think the manifest is enough to take to the justice department or ATF?"

Slade shook his head. "I can't imagine any judge signing off on a search or seizure warrant of a foreign ship based on a disgraced ATF agent's belief."

One way Javi's reputation worked against him. "Whatever you and Aiden can do to make these pay off we'll take."

"We?" Slade teased. "I take that to mean you two have come to an…understanding?"

"We're running out of options. Let's look at everything, okay? Oh, can you do me another favor?"

"Sure."

She grabbed a piece of paper and sketched out the bird tattoo she'd seen on Natalia's wrist. "Can you do an image search on this?" Her artistic skills left a lot to be desired. "If I can get a picture to you I will, but—" she stepped back "—it's pretty close."

When she was done, he turned the paper around. "Any context you want to give me as a place to start?"

"Human trafficking. I assume out of Eastern Europe. And use Demchenko as a reference point." Natalia had said it had been done against her will, and her reaction to Niko at the table had been intense.

"You've got it."

"Thanks, by the way."

"Just doing my job."

"No." She pulled open the door, turned back around. "I mean about Javi. You were right about him, Slade. You never did lose faith in him." She only wished she could say the same.

"Be careful, Regan," Slade warned. "He isn't the only one in danger anymore. Those guys in Vegas could have a lot to say."

"That's why I have you and my brother for backup." She flashed a smile before walking out.

Whatever hope she'd come in with had pretty much been deflated. She and Javi had been so sure the manifest was the answer to everything. Now it might prove more troublesome than beneficial. They needed solid evidence to build a case on, not pipe dreams and assumptions.

She returned to the parking lot, found her keys and climbed into the beige sedan that smelled of old french fries and wet dog. It fit her fictional background and this neighborhood with its run-down stores and beleaguered, sagging restaurants. She made the half-hour drive south to the dry cleaner's to pick up Marcus's tuxedo.

As she came out of the shop, suit in hand, she spotted a familiar white convertible turn the corner and zoom down the street, whizzing right past her. Blond hair fluttering in the wind as it sped by.

"Celeste?" But…the country club where Celeste took tennis lessons was a good half hour in the other direction. Regan checked her watch. Almost one. Celeste should have just been finishing her first hour of practice by now, before lunch.

What was Celeste doing in this area?

Regan unlocked the car, tossed the suit into the back seat and climbed in. She pulled out of the lot and turned left, keeping Celeste's car in sight.

She drove in silence, keeping half a block between them. Wherever her boss was headed, she was in a rush and didn't possess a penchant for hitting her turn signals.

Celeste stopped alongside a neighborhood park where a smattering of food trucks had gathered. Regan drove past her, looking back as Celeste parked and climbed out of her car. Horns blared as Regan shot into the other lane, made a quick loop around the block. She parked on a street a short distance away, grabbed her bag and headed back toward the park.

The air immediately filled with the intoxicating aroma of grilled meat, wood smoke and hot butter. All things that made Regan's stomach rumble loudly. Ignoring the pull of the neon-painted taco truck called Guac-n-Roll, Regan walked the perimeter of the park, looking for Celeste's bright blond hair and even brighter pink tank.

Kids raced around the swings and slides. Not too far

away was a group of picnic tables that, for the most part, were full with a happy summer crowd. Lines at the trucks were long, giving Regan cover as she searched the crowd.

"Sorry," she murmured when she bumped into a pair of teenage girls trying to decide what to order at Rolling Scones.

Regan felt antsy. She was really getting hungry. She shielded her eyes against the sun, finally catching sight of Celeste standing at a café-style table on the edge of the playground. The tall, hefty man she was speaking with was around thirty with dark hair, dark eyes and burn scars on the left side of his face that Regan could see from where she was.

The table was more secluded, which, given the intensity of the conversation, was probably why Celeste and the guy had chosen it. There was no way to hear what they were saying without exposing her presence—at least, not without a plausible excuse. And her lip-reading ability sucked.

She could use her phone's camera to zoom in, maybe get a picture…

Of course! She dug around in her bag for the compact Aiden had given her. She snapped it open, pretended to look in the mirror as she zoomed in. The small picture was not too bad and she snapped an image of the two of them. Then shifted slightly to get the man's face. *Click*.

She was about to close the compact to transmit the images, but instead moved around to the other side of a group of kids on their bikes. From here she could get a shot of Celeste, which she did. She closed the compact, pulled out her phone and called the number Aiden had provided for Minotaur.

"Minotaur Security." The deep female voice echoed across the line. "How may I direct your call?"

"Hi, this is Regan McKenna. My brother—"

"Please hold a moment, Agent McKenna. I'll put you right through."

"Oh." She blinked. "Cool." She stepped back into the shadow of yet another truck, this one called Bread Zepplin, which offered an astonishing array of uniquely crafted sandwiches on fresh-baked bread. "Chef Fred would never." She grinned. *Or would he? Hmm...*

"Regan? What's wrong?" Aiden's voice came over the line like a whip being thrashed.

"Nothing." She was watching Celeste's conversation intensify. The emphatic clenching of her fists, the tightness in her face. Who on earth was this guy she was talking to? "I just sent in some images from the compact thing you gave me. I wanted to make sure they were received."

She heard her brother breathe a sigh of relief.

"Something's off with this guy, Aiden. I need to know who he is." She couldn't help but think Celeste was in trouble here.

"Hang on." She heard typing in the background. It echoed in an odd way.

"Where are you?" Regan winced at the noise.

"Surveillance duty" was all he said. "Okay, photos received. Huh. Good resolution. Works better than I'd hoped."

"Yay," Regan muttered. She watched a customer walk away from the sandwich truck with some kind of monstrosity in a cardboard takeaway boat. "Do you recognize him?"

"Nope. I'm running him through one of our ID programs right now. Might take a couple of..." Beeping erupted on the other end of the line. "Never mind. Well. That's interesting."

"What is?"

"He's not popping. Anywhere." Aiden typed some more. "Okay, we'll take this to another level and..." A few seconds later he stated, "Who *is* this guy?"

"That's my question," Regan said. "You're not finding anything?"

"No," Aiden replied. "And that's a problem for me. This program gives me access to nearly every photographic database around the world. Granted, that's a lot of pictures to process in..."

"Oh, come on..." Regan rolled her eyes. "Cut to it, already."

"There could be a block on his ID. Someone doesn't want him identified, so they've made sure he can't be. They can go in, remove his picture or, when his image is put into the system, it's prevented from giving an authentic answer. Something like that costs serious money and takes a lot of influence. Not the good kind."

Great. More questions. And more bad guys. "Not what I was hoping for."

"You want me to run Celeste Antius through the system? Maybe something will catch with him that way."

"May as well." Regan stood up straight as Celeste stepped abruptly from the table. "I need to go. Talk later."

"Okay, but—"

Regan hung up and jumped into line for the sandwich truck, turned her back and hugged her arms around her chest as she examined the chalkboard menu.

"Regan? Is that you?"

Regan spun around, eyes wide with fake surprise. "Celeste! Hi! I thought you were at the club this afternoon."

Celeste frowned and stepped closer. "What are you doing here?"

"I was out running those errands and saw the trucks." She waved behind her. "Couldn't help myself. Everything sounds delicious."

"It doesn't, doesn't it?" But Celeste didn't seem particularly convinced as she eyed the menu. "My tennis coach called in sick, and I heard some women at the club talking about this place. What are you going to get?"

"Um." Regan hadn't gotten that far. "For myself? That Bahn Mi Cubano sounds good." Any kind of Cuban sandwich always appealed to her.

"I think that's an excellent choice." She checked her watch. "I just finished eating, otherwise I'd stay and chat. I'll see you back at the house." She hurried off, her pleated skirt swinging as she walked.

Regan took a step out of the line and peered back to the table where Celeste and her companion had been talking—but he, like Celeste, had vanished.

Chapter 12

In the main house, Javi pulled open the refrigerator door and stared at the chaotic contents. His stomach had been rumbling for hours. The protein bar that he'd had for lunch hadn't made a dent in his hunger.

Marcus had been on a tear all day, micromanaging his upcoming business deal with almost maniacal attention. His boss's shift in moods could be easily explained by Javi's assumption that Caleb Flynn was about to make an appearance, but Javi needed to pull back on his expectations. Until he actually heard the man's name, he had to keep control and figure Flynn was lurking around the next corner.

Before heading home from the office downtown, they'd gone to the warehouse for a few hours where Javi could have cut the tension with a butter knife. That could have been because Demchenko and Vaya hadn't gone off on their merry way after the meeting. Instead, they'd assigned themselves to be Marcus's shadows, which meant Javi didn't get any kind of break, either mentally or physically. He'd been running on adrenaline since leaving Vegas that morning.

Now that Javi had escorted Celeste and Marcus to the

limo that had been sent to pick them up for the gala, he planned to embrace his downtime with Regan.

If only to hear about her meeting with Slade.

He picked up a brown paper package with the words "Bread Zepplin" stamped on it along with the notation "Holy Mole" in Regan's writing. He'd just pulled it out and closed the fridge when Regan walked into the kitchen.

She'd changed for the evening into wide-legged yoga pants and T-shirt and covered her bare arms with that long beige sweater she'd worn in the garden the first night.

Her face was locked down in a rather stern, if not concerned expression, but it was good to see her. Almost normal, even.

"Hey." He hefted what he assumed was a sandwich and grabbed a plate out of the cabinet. "Thanks for this."

"Sure." Her smile seemed distracted. "I remembered you talking about your *abuela*'s chicken-mole a while back. Thought that might bring back some good memories for you."

Or make new ones.

"What's wrong?" He gestured to how she was massaging her right wrist. "You hurt?"

"Huh?" She glanced down, frowned, pulled her hand away. "No. Not really. Just took some unexpected effort to help Celeste tie up the corset on the back of her dress."

He carried his sandwich over to the table, sat down and unwrapped it while she wandered over to the window overlooking the backyard. The sun had given up its spot in the sky as the night crept in. Javi peeked under the top of the sandwich roll to take inventory of the rich, sauce-covered chicken, cheese, toasted pepitas and plantains. She really did know him well.

"How did things go with Slade and Aiden?" He went in for a bite, then sat back and tried to relax his body. The spices and familiar flavors zinged through his system. "We a go for the docks tomorrow night?"

"Huh?"

That was the second time in as many minutes she'd *huh*-ed him.

"Regan?" He stared at her back until she turned around. When she did, that concern had taken over her expression. "Something's wrong."

She grimaced. "You should enjoy that sandwich. This can wait." A minute passed before she got a glass of water and downed it in one gulp.

While he ate, she sat across from him, fingers tapping on the table. He was pretty sure she wasn't even aware she was doing it. "Okay." He took his last bite, crumpled up the paper and sat back. "Let's have it."

She pressed her lips for a moment, wincing. "I think we have a problem."

"I got that." He nodded even as the sandwich sat heavy in his stomach. "Let me guess. The manifest didn't match up."

"The manifest? Oh, no. I took the phone to Slade." Her tapping sped up. "We looked over the manifest together. I think it's fine. Exactly what we thought. He doesn't think it's enough for a federal warrant, but Aiden's going to push."

Javi paused and let the words sink in. "I see." It was difficult not to feel disappointed.

"You must have other evidence to use against him," Regan pleaded. "Is there something, anything else that would lend credence to your interpretation of the manifest's listings?"

"My interpretation." Interesting phrasing. That ping of dread he'd been fighting off all day landed with a thud in the center of his chest. "Slade doesn't buy my explanation for the coding."

"He does," Regan insisted. "And so do I. But your explanation, that interpretation, might not carry much weight given your history. And circumstances."

His circumstances. There it was. He'd always known the lengths he'd gone to in order to establish his cover would work against him one day. Naively, he didn't think it would happen before he got himself out from under the case.

"It isn't a done deal," Regan went on. "But we all agree we're going to need more to take this to the next level."

"I have other evidence." He inclined his head, second-guessing himself. "I'm not sure how well it bolsters my *interpretation* of the situation." The idea he'd gone to this much effort only to have it be called into question because of his manufactured history seemed comically ironic.

"Shortly after I started working for Marcus I installed spyware in his computer that sends copies of everything he does to an off-site laptop. That computer also has backup copies of my own reports and recordings of any conversations I was close enough to get." He touched an absent finger to his watch.

"But that's great!" Regan immediately brightened. "That's evidence in real time. Perfect. So all we need is to get that information turned over along with an official statement and… What?" She sagged back in her chair. "What's wrong with that idea?"

"I can't get to it," he admitted. "Not for at least forty-eight hours."

"You can't…" She blinked. "Where did you stash it? Japan?"

He wished he saw the humor. "It's in a secure locker at a company called DataSentra. It's a high-security private data vault that requires forty-eight hours' notice to gain access."

Disbelief and frustration flashed in her eyes. "If you needed to secure the laptop, why didn't you ask Aiden? Oh." She snapped her fingers. "That's right. You didn't ask for anyone's help."

He wasn't going to apologize for the decisions he'd made. What was done was done. "I needed to stay as far away from my old life as I could. That included separating myself from the McKennas. I couldn't take the chance that if something went wrong, they'd connect us." And turn Aiden and possibly Regan into targets.

She looked a bit taken aback, as if she hadn't considered just how far he'd thought this through.

When she finally spoke again, it was to ask, "You can't just walk in and get the laptop?"

"Not without that two days' notice, a retinal scan and voice-recognized passcode." Overkill maybe, but at least the system was secured. Fat lot of good it did him now. "I've sacrificed enough for this job. I'm not going to pluck out my eye and lend it to Slade or Aiden."

"I wasn't going to suggest that." She held up both

hands, picking up on the irritation in his voice. "I'm just trying to figure a way out of this situation."

"You mean the situation I've apparently made a mess of."

"I didn't say that," she said. "Stop trying to start a fight."

"I'm not."

"Yes, you are." But instead of getting angry, she reached over and grabbed his hand. "I know it's been a while, but you need to remember what it's like to work with someone, Javi. To be part of a team again. You've got one. Me, and Aiden and Slade. We have your back. I promise. We'll figure a way out of this and make sure the last two years haven't been a complete waste of your time."

"All right." He said it mainly to appease her. He wanted to believe Regan. For so many reasons. "If we can't use the evidence I've already got—"

"We can't use it right now. In the meantime, we need new evidence." She gripped his hand tighter. "We've got the house to ourselves. You're in charge of security. What are we dealing with?"

"Security cameras in the front and back of the house. Nothing inside. He likes his privacy."

"Which means he trusts everyone in here. That's good news. How often does Marcus update his computer passwords?"

"Knowing him, not very often." When she simply looked at him, he caught on. "You're thinking maybe we can access the information my system's got stored."

She shrugged. "Couldn't hurt to check his files, either. He printed out the manifest for the incoming ship. If he's not a compulsive shredder—"

"He's not."

"Then that gives us a place to start." She stood up, held out her hand. "Come on. It's worth a shot."

It hadn't dawned on Regan until tonight just how hard it must have been for Javi to run an investigation like this alone. No backup, no one he could trust. No one he could bounce ideas off of or confide in. The mental solitude must have been excruciating.

It would also take time for him to readjust to how his real job was supposed to work. If he came back to it.

Polished wood furniture with walls of shelves filled with books that looked as if they'd never been touched, let alone read, took up most of the office. A showpiece more than a practical space. Who was Marcus trying to impress?

"There's nothing unusual in his files that I can see." Javi opened the third drawer on the filing cabinet and sorted through the folders. "Just paperwork on long-established clients."

"Nothing filed under Valeri or Caleb Flynn, then?" If she didn't joke about it, she might scream. Stalled by technology and red tape. Sometimes the lines they couldn't cross were downright irritating. "He used code words for the shipments? Why not his partners and clients?"

Javi shrugged. "Nothing's standing out."

"What about Vaya or Demchenko? Anything in there about them?"

"Won't be on paper," Javi said. "Their partnership is a sort of gentlemen's agreement and wasn't finalized until today. Handshakes do the trick."

"Awesome." Regan made her way around the room, trailing her finger across the spines of the books, along the edges of the picture frames. She glanced over her shoulder as Javi sat down at the desk, opened the laptop.

"All right, let's try this. Here we go." He tapped on a few keys. The screen flashed to life, casting Javi's face into shadow against its bright glow.

In the reflection of the window, she caught a quick blip of red. "What the—"

"What?" Javi asked absently as he continued typing. "Typical. He just rearranges his birthday numbers."

"Seems rather simple considering who he works with." Regan looked back to the window, then turned to the shelves by the door. A set of framed photos, including a number from Marcus and Celeste's wedding, sat there. She moved closer, wishing the light in the room was better.

She picked up the largest frame, examined it. Turned it over before setting it back down. She did the same with the rest, then stepped left to check out the next unit. An antique mirror sat amid a collection of candles. When she lifted it, something rattled inside.

"I think I've got something." Javi stopping typing. "This file was created in the last twenty-four hours. He named it Boat Registrations."

"That means something to you?" Regan flipped the mirror around, slid a nail beneath the back covering. It popped off.

"Marcus gets seasick. Ships he can handle, but he hates boats. What are you doing?"

"Not sure. What's in the file?"

More clicking sounds came from the keyboard. "Wire

transfer confirmations from a Swiss bank to one in the Cayman Islands."

"The home of illegal income." She stared down at the small, square plastic housing inside the mirror, which had a false front and a tiny, blinking red light. "You said Marcus doesn't like surveillance cameras in his home, didn't you?"

"I did. They freak him out."

"And you didn't plant any?"

"Waste of time considering I'm already getting everything on his computer." He went back to typing.

Regan stared at the light, considering. If Marcus hadn't put the camera in himself and Javi hadn't, then who…?

"I'm just going to print these—"

"Wait." She replaced the backing on the mirror and returned it to its spot. A mystery for another time. He had enough on his mind without adding another mystery to his full plate. "Don't print them. Email them."

"To who?" Javi's brow furrowed.

She walked across the room to join him, placing herself between the camera's sight and him. She lowered her voice. "Email them to me at the ATF."

He shook his head. "I don't under—"

"Backup plan." She remembered her earlier conversation with Slade. "This could compromise Antius. Give him a reason to flip on everyone, including Flynn. Marcus's computer, his documents, it would all be coded coming into an ATF account he'd only have if he had a personal connection with an agent. Your ex-partner. Lends some credibility to your statements, right? He wouldn't be able to explain it. Trust me," she said when he hesitated. "The higher-ups can't question my loyalty. And I can confirm chain of evidence. I'll forward the email to Slade and Aiden. They can run those numbers and accounts against the history of that ship coming in. If there's a connection there, they'll find it. And hopefully in time to get that search-and-seizure warrant for the *Deadlight Express*."

A lot of *ifs*, she told herself. But she couldn't lose hope now.

"That's a lot to pin on one file in this computer."

"If what you set in place with your storage program is still working, you've already got these documents. This is just a way around the forty-eight hours we need to get to your computer," she said. "If you've got another idea, I'm all ears."

He shook his head. "I don't." With the emails sent, he logged out of the computer, closed it down and retrieved the printouts from the printer. "I hope this works."

"It will." Regan followed him out of the room, cast a throwaway glance at the mirror as she left, wondering who was on the other end of that camera feed.

Chapter 13

Regan reached across Javi's bare chest to pluck her cell phone off the nightstand. They'd shaken things up this evening by choosing her room rather than his apartment. With the windows open and the summer breeze blowing past the curtains, this time with him felt almost otherworldly.

But seeing a "call me" message from Slade was a stark reminder of how much she didn't want to return to the real one.

"That Slade?"

"Yup." Regan set the phone back down. "He's still working on things." It wasn't a lie, exactly. "It's late."

"Mmm." He stroked his fingers up and down her arm. She was in her new favorite position, splayed over him like a blanket, shivering against the chills he sent coursing through her body. It was as if the last two years hadn't happened; that they'd never spent a moment apart. And yet those same two years loomed like a canyon between them. Neither of them had said the words "I love you." Considering what had happened the last time they'd fallen for one another, neither of them wanted to be first.

"They'll be home soon."

Regan sighed. "Back to work, then. What's the plan for tomorrow night?"

"Plan?"

"For the ship." She lifted her head. "I'm assuming Marcus expects to be at the dock when it comes in."

"You assume correctly. My presence has been requested, as well. He wants to put my law enforcement experience to work, looking for possible hiccups or surveillance."

"Huh." She frowned. "Is that usual?"

"No," Javi confirmed.

As he said the words, that anxious feeling descended once more in her.

Something had shifted with Marcus in the last twenty-four hours. Javi couldn't put his finger on it just yet but… "It only makes me more convinced of what's coming in on that ship." He let out a long breath, squeezed his eyes shut. "I really hope Slade finds something we can use so that we can have actual backup there. I've had my sights on Flynn, but the people on that ship—"

"If there's something there, Slade will find it." She pushed herself up and looked down at him. "Question. When you ran background checks on the staff, did anything come up on Natalia?"

"Not very much." His brow furrowed. "She arrived in the States last fall. Celeste met her through a volunteer program at a local church. I was able to confirm her visa status through back channels. Why do you ask?"

She debated yet again. "She's been through a lot. I wondered if there was something in her background that might shed some light on her situation."

"I can take another look," Javi said. "I'd rather not

ask. She wouldn't expect it, and it might spook her more than she already is."

"True." Similar to what Celeste had said. "I guess I'm thinking about what's going to happen to her and Chef Fred when we blow Marcus's world apart. I seriously doubt Celeste can keep this place on her own. His finances are going to be frozen and her reputation destroyed. There won't be any money unless she's got some of her own."

"She's comfortable, but not this-house comfortable," Javi confirmed. "Maybe we'll be in a position to help Natalia. Those friends of yours you told Ivan and his brother about perhaps?"

Regan nodded. "Possibly."

He heaved a sigh. "I should get dressed."

"Why?" She touched his tanned back. "It's not like they don't know we're sleeping together."

"Distract them with our relationship and they won't pay attention to anything else going on in this house," Javi said. "Hopefully this time tomorrow night, we'll be done with all of this. Then…" He leaned back and kissed her. "We can talk about what comes next."

She watched silently as he reached for his clothes. "It's probably best if I stay here tonight. We need to get some actual sleep."

He grinned, glanced over at her. "Sadly, I agree." He put on his shoes and socks, got up and headed to the door. "I'll wait to go down after I hear them at the door. You change your mind about needing sleep, just flash your phone in the window."

She rested her head in her hand and watched him leave. "Good night, Javi."

"Good night, Regan."

She jumped out of bed, retrieved her discarded T-shirt and pants and went to the door. She opened it slightly in time to hear the telltale sound of the front door. Marcus's and Celeste's voices echoed up the stairwell, quickly followed by Javi's.

Regan hurried back to the bed, snatched her phone up and called Slade. "What do you have?" she asked the second he answered.

"On which front?"

"The email I sent you. The financial documents. Are they going to be enough for a warrant?" She held her breath.

"It's better than it was. And we found a tenuous connection between one of the bank accounts and a shell company listed as the ship's owner. Aiden's talking to a contact at the DOJ as we speak. I'll know more in a little while. He said if there's a problem, he'll call you himself. Worst case, the surveillance will get approved even if we can't board the ship."

Her heart relaxed slightly. "Okay." That would have to be enough.

"Now for the not-so-good news," Slade told her. "I reached out to a former confidential informant of mine from back when I was in the bureau. Once upon a time she worked the strip clubs on the West Coast, places where trafficking victims were brought into the country. She recognized that bird tattoo. Says the group it belongs to has lost its standing in the last couple of years. They aren't as strong as they used to be, although rumor has it they're making a play for a comeback."

"Demchenko or the Valeris?" Regan asked.

"Your guess is as good as mine. There's a chance it's both. Demchenko is their kind of people. In that world, even saying the name *Valeri* is like invoking the devil. All I could get out of her was that the bird is still their mark and anyone who has it has been through hell. You going to tell me who has one?"

"Natalia. The Antius housekeeper."

Slade swore, echoing Regan's own thoughts. "When this is finished, I can put her in touch with my cousin Georgiana. She's a volunteer at a crisis center for victims of human trafficking."

Regan added Slade's cousin to her list of special contacts. "What about that guy I got a picture of, the one who met with Celeste at the park?"

"I'm still running that down, but I've got some new ideas. It'll take a while yet. In the meantime, be careful. One wrong step and you could end up on a boat going to nowhere."

"Okay. There's a cheery thought."

"Get some sleep, Regan," Slade said before he hung up.

Her mind was racing with everything that was coming at her. At them. She looked at the time. Twenty-four hours. That was all they needed.

All she wanted.

She touched a hand to the center of her chest. Unease had settled sometime in the last few minutes. An unease she couldn't target or tie to any one thing. But it was there.

That video camera in Marcus's office. Niko Demchenko could have planted that the other night after he'd left the dinner table. A man like that wouldn't just walk out after being humiliated. He'd have stuck around and tried for payback of some kind.

She flopped onto the bed, rolled over and tucked herself in under the covers.

And then there was that secret meeting between Celeste and the man at the food truck park. Was Celeste having an affair? Although, that conversation certainly hadn't been particularly intimate.

She pulled Javi's pillow into her arms, cuddled it close as she breathed in the spicy scent of his aftershave. Regan closed her eyes, dreaming of a new day. A better day. A safer one.

For all of them.

She'd sleep on her questions and doubts. Consider options and plays. Maybe, hopefully, her brain would work them out before she awakened.

"Sleep in tomorrow," Marcus called after Javi as he headed to the back door after leaving Regan's room.

"Yeah?" Javi pivoted as Celeste headed up the stairs, her four-inch stiletto sandals dangling from her fingertips. "Good night, Celeste."

"Good night, Javi." Her smile was tight and strained and she didn't give her husband a last look before disappearing down the hall.

"It's going to be a long day and an even longer night." Marcus followed him into the kitchen. "We should both be ready for it." He grabbed a bottle of beer out of the fridge, popped it open, then reached in for a second one. He handed it to Javi. "Join me."

"Sure." Javi could not remember a time when his boss offered him a drink. "Something on your mind?"

"A lot of somethings." He wandered to the window overlooking the solar-lit garden and pool. "That homeless guy is back. Was sound asleep right near the gate when we drove up."

Javi winced. "I'll take care of it in the morning. Give the guy one peaceful night at least."

Marcus glared for a moment, then shrugged, dismissing the man and the idea. "You haven't asked who we're meeting tomorrow in conjunction with the shipment."

"It's none of my business." Javi took a long pull of beer, considered his response. "Doesn't matter who it is. It doesn't change my job. Besides, you didn't hire me to ask questions."

"No," Marcus agreed. "I didn't. I didn't hire your girlfriend to, either. And yet she does."

Javi merely arched a brow, even as his stomach pitched like a trawler in a hurricane.

"Celeste says she's been curious about Natalia." Marcus sipped from his bottle. "Asking about what might have happened to the girl before she came to work for us. Celeste suspected Regan was following her yesterday when she left the house."

Javi shrugged. Regan hadn't mentioned any of those things. "I can't speak to Regan's actions yesterday after we got back, considering I was with you, but as far as Natalia goes, Regan strikes me as a caring woman. And Natalia is—"

"Skittish, yes." Marcus finally faced him again. "Still. I don't like questions being asked about my staff. Or for my wife to feel threatened. I made a mistake agreeing to Regan taking over as Celeste's assistant without you running a background check on her. I'd like to make up for that now."

"You mean tonight?"

"I mean before our meeting tomorrow." Marcus pinned him with a look Javi had rarely seen. The paranoia seemed to be working its way around the group. It wasn't surprising, if Marcus was gearing up to go into business with the Valeris. "I don't want any surprises and I don't want to be accused of not doing my due diligence. Get it done, Javi." He toasted him with his beer before he stalked away. "And get it done fast."

A rattling pulled Regan out of an awful sleep. She'd been tossing and turning for most of the night. She opened her eyes and stared at the wall. There it was again.

She sat up, threw the covers back and jumped out of bed, heading straight for the window. She pulled it open just as Javi made his way up the rose trellis on the side of the house.

"What are you doing down here?" she whispered and reached for him.

"I've only got a couple of minutes," Javi told her, shaking his head at her insistence he come in. "I put the outside security cameras on a loop so I could get to you." His dark eyes sparkled in the night. "Marcus told me to run a background check on you."

"He…" Regan stepped back. "He did? Why all of a sudden?" What had she done or said that raised suspicion?

Javi's eyes narrowed. "He said you've been asking

questions about Natalia and that you followed Celeste yesterday."

"Well, I…" She hugged her arms around her torso and squeezed. "I saw her driving past when I picked up the dry cleaning. She said she was going to the club, but she didn't. I was curious."

"They tell each other everything. Whatever your excuse was, she didn't buy it. What am I going to find in your backstory?"

"What Aiden built for me," she told him. "It's solid. It'll hold." That was the only thing she was certain of right now. Her brother would never leave her open to attack.

"Okay." He checked his watch. "Try to steer clear of Marcus tomorrow as much as you can. He's amped up and that's not a good mindset."

"If I avoid him he'll definitely think something's up," Regan countered. "I'll keep going as I have been."

He shook his head. "Regan—"

"I have faith in you, Javi. You can convince him I'm in the clear." He had to; otherwise they were both going to be in trouble.

Javi nodded. He mouthed the words *good night* and took a step down. But he popped right back up. "What were you asking about? About Natalia, I mean."

She shook her head. "I don't want to muddy the waters. Focus on Marcus and Caleb Flynn. We'll worry about the rest later."

"We?" He still looked dubious.

"Honestly, Javi. It can wait. I wouldn't lie to you. Not now." That in itself was a whopper. But he didn't need to know that.

"All right," he agreed, but he didn't look happy. "First things first. Be safe."

"You, too." She leaned out the window and watched him climb down, then dart across the lawn to his apartment.

Marcus being suspicious was not something she had had on her bingo card. She reached up and closed the window.

"Great," she muttered and returned to bed, any promise of sleep now gone.

It didn't make sense. Why would Celeste have told Marcus about them running into one another, considering where Celeste had gone and who she'd met?

She adjusted her pillows and grabbed her phone. Before she talked herself out of it, she dialed. "Aiden? It's me." She took a deep breath and plowed ahead. "I think we might have a problem."

"Regan's background is solid. Everything checks out." Javi handed Marcus the printed file he'd spent most of the morning compiling. It hadn't taken very long, but he'd drawn out the process to buy some time. Not that there was anything concerning about her backstory.

Regan was right about playing things cool and not changing her behavior. Some of the suspicion he'd seen on Marcus's face faded as she kept her perfect mask of pleasantries in place while she served.

There hadn't been a dent in the shield of armor Aiden had created for her. Javi had pulled every document he could find, including her fake community college degree and taxes for the past seven years. Aiden was thorough, but then he would be, especially since it involved protecting his sister.

"You look surprised," Javi said as Marcus flipped through the pages.

"Pleasantly," Marcus admitted before he closed the file and tossed it onto the desk. "I'm also relieved. This is one less thing for me to think about."

"Should I ask?"

"Ask what?" Marcus gave his attention to his computer.

"About who we're meeting with tonight."

"I doubt his name would mean anything to you," Marcus said with a nervous edge in his voice. Javi had the feeling the pressure was getting to him. "Be ready in an hour." Marcus continued, "We've got a stop to make at Sutton Airfield."

"Sutton?" The private landing strip was more than two hours away and in the opposite direction of the docks.

Marcus glanced up. "Problem?"

"No," Javi said quickly. "No problem."

Marcus waved him off.

Javi exited, closed the office door behind him and caught sight of Regan tidying up the new floral arrangement on the entry table. "Hey." He motioned for her to follow him away from the office and into a small alcove by the sitting room.

She glanced behind her before joining him. "Everything okay?"

"Yeah." He rubbed his hand down her arm to ease his own nerves. "Your story held up. We can stop worrying." About her cover being blown at least. As for the meeting tonight… "He's on edge about something. We're leaving in an hour. We have to head to Sutton Airfield first."

She shrugged. "Never heard of it."

"It's a private landing strip about ninety minutes south. Puts us farther away from Los Angeles port than I expected. But someplace secluded like that, it would make sense if Flynn is flying back into the country under the radar. What's the latest from Slade?"

She glanced away, caught his hand and squeezed. "Just roll with things. We're almost at the end, Javi. You're almost done."

He nodded. He sure hoped so.

"Celeste hasn't come out of her room this morning." Regan stepped away. "I should check on her."

"She seemed out of sorts when they got home last night."

"Must not have been a very successful gala, then." Regan rolled her eyes, caught herself, then stepped back to him, reached up and pressed her lips to his. "Be careful," she whispered. "Please."

"I will be." If only because he had her to come back to.

"He said they were going to Sutton Airfield." After getting waylaid by Natalia needing help moving a collection of Celeste's clothes from one closet to another, and then fixing Celeste some tea to help with her migraine that had kept her in bed all day, Regan finally managed to grab a free moment to call Slade late in the afternoon. "They're leaving in like fifteen minutes."

"Don't worry. We'll get someone there," Slade assured her. "We'll make sure he's safe."

She didn't just want Javi safe. She wanted this case

closed once and for all. She wanted Caleb Flynn in custody. Javi wasn't going to be able to move on until he was. "Has Aiden had any luck convincing the DOJ to—"

"Still working on it. It would help if we could give them whoever has been helping Javi at the ATF. If only to confirm Javi's story."

"Deputy Director Dunning." She didn't hesitate in sharing the information. "From what Javi's said, he's the only one who knows."

"Got it. I'll let Aiden know. And FYI, I'm on the brink of finding out who your mystery guy from the park is. Keep your phone close."

"Thanks." She hung up and continued along the main hallway just as she heard the front door close.

Something caught in her chest. A feeling. A vibration. She was unable to shake it.

Regan ran through the foyer and went straight to the front door. She caught herself before pulling it open and instead stepped to the side to look out the window. She touched her fingers against the glass.

"Javi," she whispered as her heart almost broke.

Marcus and Javi approached an unfamiliar dark SUV entering the gate. The vehicle approached slowly and parked behind Marcus's car. When the driver and passenger doors opened, Vaya and Demchenko stepped out, circled around and blocked them in.

"Hands up." Demchenko's order caught a normally prepared Javi off guard.

"What?" But he did as he was told after opening the button on his suit jacket. Demchenko pulled Javi's gun out of his hip holster, handed it off to Vaya before he patted him down from ankle to shoulder. It took every bit of energy he possessed to keep his cool. "What's going on? Watch it," he growled as Demchenko drew his hands down Javi's arms.

Demchenko ignored his protest. "Watch." He held out his hand, his cold, vacant eyes narrowed.

Javi glanced at Marcus, who didn't seem particularly bothered or surprised by the greeting. "Give it to him, Javi," his boss ordered.

Javi snapped off the band, dropped it into Demchenko's hand. He examined it, turned it over and back. If he started pushing buttons…

"GPS?"

"No." The truth, thankfully, followed by a lie. "It was my father's. It's sentimental."

Demchenko gave it back to him, then yanked open the rear passenger door. "Get in."

"I usually drive." Again, he looked to Marcus.

"Things change," Marcus said. "Get in, Javi." He stepped closer. "Get in or I'll ask your girlfriend to join us."

Two years of work coalesced in an instant. All the time, all the effort, the sleepless nights and compromising he'd had to do. It all landed on him as that alarm Javi had been trying to ignore struck hard and sharp.

It was that particular sickening sensation that happened when an undercover agent knew they'd been made.

"Please…" Javi looked around, considering his options and Vaya moved in. "Don't involve her in this." There was calm in Vaya's eyes. But also a terrifying warning.

Javi was out of options.

Marcus brushed past him to sit behind the driver's seat. Javi kept his arms raised and walked over to get in the back seat on the passenger side. He glanced at the mansion and saw Regan standing at the window. Or maybe he just wanted to so badly that he imagined she was there. Javi calmed his pulse and gave a very small, imperceptible shake of his head before he sat back.

Vaya slammed the door shut.

Moments later the four of them were secured inside and headed toward the front gate.

"Anyone want to clue me in?" Javi asked as they waited for the gate to open.

Just as they thought the way was clear, Demchenko snorted in disgust and pounded a hand on the steering wheel. "What is this?"

The homeless man, along with Lucky, his dog, had ambled by, waving and muttering to himself. Demchenko leaned on the horn. Rather than stopping or hurrying away, the man circled back and walked past them a second time.

"Run him down," Vaya said as if suggesting Demchenko swat a fly.

Demchenko reached behind him for his gun.

"You shoot him and this street will be filled with cops in seconds," Javi lied. "I can get rid of him. Without alerting the neighborhood."

Vaya looked back at Marcus, who shrugged. "Make it fast," Vaya ordered.

Javi shoved out of the SUV and approached the man. "Hey, again."

"My friend." The guy wore the same baggy clothes and his hair and beard, if possible, were even shaggier and more unkempt than the first time they'd spoken. "All is good. Just taking a walk before going that way." He pointed in the direction of the shelter, then spun and pointed in the other direction. Lucky jumped up once and barked.

"You should get moving, then," Javi stated and grabbed the man's shoulder to turn him around. "I don't want you getting hurt."

The horn blared. Javi's heart pounded so hard he couldn't hear himself think.

The man stumbled and fell against Javi, his arms tangling between him and his knee-length coat. The stranger's hand caught on Javi's pocket and nearly ripped it off.

Javi turned his head against the smell but managed to keep ahold of him to push him out of danger. Lucky barked again, not at Javi but at the car as it inched forward.

"You need to leave," Javi said more forcefully this time. "You aren't safe here."

"Ain't safe anywhere." The man shoved him back and had both hands waving in the air. "Ain't nowhere safe."

Wasn't that the truth. Javi pulled his wallet out, but instead of handing him the cash, gave him the entire thing. If he wasn't coming back, at least he could help someone on his way out.

"Be safe, friend." Javi climbed back into the car, closed the door and settled in. He took a deep breath, embraced the fear and let it out. "Let's go."

Chapter 14

Regan's heart stopped the second Javi's hands went up.

She grabbed for the doorknob, only stopping herself when reason seeped in around the fear. She was unarmed and outnumbered. The second she stepped foot outside, she and Javi would both be dead.

They patted him down, examined his watch, then motioned for him to get into the back seat.

She held her breath as she watched, prayed even as she hoped she was wrong.

When Javi looked at her, she saw the truth in his eyes. He'd been made.

Anger and panic clogged her throat. It didn't make sense! *Think!* The agent part of her had to take charge and override the woman who loved him. *Think!*

Marcus wasn't the world's best actor near as she could tell. If he'd suspected Javi before now, he wouldn't have been able to feign ignorance.

She pulled out her phone and called Slade, but she was immediately put through to voicemail. What? "Slade, it's Regan," she snapped. "Call me back. Javi's cover is blown. They've…taken him." What else was there to say? What other questions were there to ask?

Stop! She forced herself to stand still, clear her mind. If this was anyone other than Javi, she'd come up with a plan. She closed her eyes and gave herself a slow count of five to focus. To think.

A horn blared outside, jolting her out of her fear. Her questions could wait. They didn't matter right now. Only one thing did.

"What's going on?" Celeste called from the top of the staircase. Even from a distance, Regan could see the woman was pale and unsteady. She looked unlike herself in jeans and a plain white T-shirt, her hair pulled back into a tight, high ponytail. "Regan? What's all the noise?"

"I don't know. Go back to your room and stay there." ATF Regan McKenna took over and she threw open the door to Marcus's office. The dim light irritated her even more when she flicked on the lamps, then immediately snatched up the mirror off the shelf.

She carried it over to the desk, disassembled it again and pulled the video recorder free. She held it in her hand, resisting the urge to crush it out of frustration.

"It was you, wasn't it? This is your fault." She muttered as she turned the inch-square cube over in her hand, looking for some clue as to who it belonged to. She cracked the back off and gave thanks to her brothers' endless conversations on the modern marvels of electronic surveillance equipment.

She angled the casing under the lamp, brought it closer to her face to see the interior. A thin black wire curled around a small computer chip. As she pulled the two free, a red light blinked. The red light she'd seen last night.

"Regan? What are you doing in here?"

Regan glanced up at Celeste's timid voice. "I'll explain

later." She sat behind the desk, opened Marcus's laptop and, since Javi had shared the password when he'd accessed the documents, quickly gained access.

"Is something wrong?" Celeste asked desperately.

"Yes." There was no point in lying now. She clicked on Network Settings, brought up the list of WiFi networks in the area and…there!

The camera was running off its own mini-network. The question was…where did it go?

"Regan?"

Annoyed, Regan huffed, "Celeste, really, I don't have time to…"

Whatever else she'd been about to tell Mrs. Antius evaporated into the ether when she looked up at the Glock .45 aimed at her head. A gun outfitted with a silencer.

Regan waited for the shock to hit, but it didn't come. Instead, she remained completely still, watching as the timid, flirty, somewhat flighty cartoon of a woman vanished. Her eyes darkened and sharpened. Her shoulders straightened and she stood taller, as if filled with confidence.

Her hand was as steady as a summer lake as she kept it trained on Regan.

"Nothing to say?" Celeste's voice had changed, as well, the quintessential all-American tone falling away beneath a Slavic accent. "I expected more of a reaction."

"Sorry to disappoint you." Rage and anger tangled around one another, settling into an uncertainty Regan couldn't control. Time was ticking away. Every moment she sat in this office, the possibility she'd never see Javi again grew. "Is this yours?" She inclined her head toward the camera. "Do you and your husband have some kind of sexy camera games going on or—"

"You disappoint me, Regan." Celeste took another step closer, the glow of the desktop lamp reflecting against the bright white of her shirt. "I'd honestly thought you'd catch on sooner."

Regan blinked. She'd noticed Celeste's right shoulder and the dark shadow beneath the thin white fabric. The dark outlined image of a bird on Celeste's skin. "Your tattoo."

Celeste inclined her head, a spark of interest lighting her detached gaze.

"It's a bird, isn't it?" Memories surged. The hushed conversations between Celeste and Natalia. They hadn't been about work or consoling Natalia. They had been about something else. Something the two women had in common: tragedy. And trauma. "A bird with a broken wing."

Celeste smirked and tucked a finger into the V of her shirt, pulled it down so Regan saw clearly that it did match the one Natalia had on her wrist. "I was given this when I was seventeen years old. I was told I no longer had my own life to live. I was to live to work, for them."

As much as she wanted to know who exactly the "them" was, now wasn't the time. "I'm sorry." Regan winced against the sudden chill. "I can only imagine—"

"No," Celeste said with an eerie calm. "You cannot. I would not want anyone to imagine what we went through."

"You and Natalia," Regan clarified.

"Us and hundreds of others." There was no grief in her eyes, only rage and certainty.

"The Valeri syndicate trafficked you. Trafficked you all."

"We thought they were finished once Edik and Marko were dead." She clicked the safety on her gun. "We thought when they were gone, we could finally be free. That the world would be free of their evil."

"But they started to rebuild," Regan said quietly. "With someone new at the top. Caleb Flynn." The pieces fell into place. The pieces Javi had put together over the past few years. Except he hadn't seen Celeste. He'd only looked where he'd expected to find answers: with Marcus. "Who's *we*?"

"What?"

"You said 'we thought when they were gone.'" Regan paused. "Who is the *we*, Celeste?"

"None of your concern."

"It is my concern if your surveillance video camera is what blew Javi's cover."

"It did not." But her tone made it clear she wasn't surprised at Regan's revelation. "Marcus received a phone call yesterday before we left for the gala. Someone who said Javi was known to him and that he was not *former* ATF as he'd claimed. The truth was that he was still active and a plant in this house." She shrugged. "Who it was makes no difference to me."

"Javi's been working for years to end the Valeri organization," Regan told her. "For longer than he's been here. He's sacrificed almost everything to do it."

"And you would know this because…?" Celeste asked.

Regan's cell phone rang.

"Don't!" Celeste ordered when Regan reached into her pocket.

Regan didn't hesitate to come clean. "I'm ATF Agent Regan McKenna. That's my backup and handler calling. If I don't answer it, this house will be surrounded in minutes. You'll have nowhere to go. You'll be arrested and detained, questioned and possibly charged. Whatever inroads you've made in this country will have been for nothing. You'll be sent back."

Her words broke through Celeste's cool demeanor, but not by much.

"You're going to lose whoever you're after, Celeste." And that's where things fell into place. "It's not Marcus you want revenge on because you could have killed him at any time."

"He's a fool. A useful one, but a fool nonetheless."

Regan wasn't going to argue with that. "Is it Flynn you're after? Caleb Flynn?" She ran through the names. "Or Vaya or Dem…" Celeste's eyes narrowed. "Demchenko. *M'yasnyk*. The Butcher. That's who you want."

Celeste's hand trembled slightly as the past shadowed her gaze.

"Let me talk to my people." Regan's hand inched closer to the phone. "Just let me—"

Celeste stiffened, her jaw locking down as her finger twitched.

"I can help you, Celeste! Let me. Please. I promise. I'm on your side." It took another moment, a long moment, but Celeste nodded once, sharply. "Put it on Speaker."

Regan pulled out her phone, tapped the icon, keeping her gaze locked on Celeste's. She felt fairly sure the woman wasn't going to use the gun. But clearly she was prepared to if necessary. "Slade." She swallowed hard. "You got my message."

"Already notified Aiden. I'm on route to you guys. Listen, I got a tentative ID on the man Celeste met with in the park."

"Yeah?" Regan raised her brows at Celeste's guarded expression. "Tell me."

"Rafiq Koenig. German national, former military. He also worked for The Hague, investigating war crimes once upon a time. There's a rumor he's heading up ASTRA."

"ASTRA." Regan shook her head as Celeste, looking impressed, arched a brow. "Never heard of it."

"Not many have," Slade said. "It's a covert organization. Alliance for Suppression of Trafficking, Retribution and Atrocities."

"Catchy." And no doubt heavy on the retribution.

"They color outside the lines. Aiden's run into a few of their operatives over the years. Says he tries to steer clear of them whenever possible. He used the word *ruthless*."

Celeste's lips twitched.

Regan stared hard at Celeste's gun. "I can understand that. What about Celeste? Anything ping on her picture?"

Celeste glared.

"Not one hundred percent confirmed, but we think her real name is Darya Sarkasian. Albanian by birth. Parents and brother and sister all killed by traffickers. She escaped from a holding facility that was run by one of the Valeris' contacts. Three guesses who."

"Niko Demchenko," Regan replied.

Celeste's gaze went ice-cold.

"Demchenko's on the top of ASTRA's hit list," Slade went on. "I don't think I'd stand in their way when it comes to them getting their hands on him."

"Duly noted. See you when you get here." She quit

the call before Slade could comment further. "Nice to meet you, Darya."

"This means nothing." Darya moved in, but there was a waver in her voice. "I'll be gone before they get here."

"Or." Regan's mind raced for a mutually beneficial solution. "You could wait for them and come with us. We can get Javi, Flynn and Demchenko together."

"Miss Regan?" Natalia pushed open the office door and poked her head in. Her doe-wide eyes filled with the sheen of dismay that gave way to horror "What—what's going on?" She clutched the door in her hand and stared at Darya as she spoke in her native language, fast and emphatic.

"I know what I'm doing!" Darya spat.

"Do not hurt her." Natalia walked into the room and put herself between the gun and Regan. "You said she was here to do good. She wants to help me. Help us. She told me."

Darya shook her head as if she found that impossible to believe. "They never listen. No one ever listens. We've been screaming into the darkness for years and—"

"I'm offering to help," Regan said softly. "I'm on leave. I'm not here officially, but I have connections. Javi's been building a case. He has evidence to use against Marcus for trafficking and smuggling, and by extension Vaya and Demchenko. None of them will get out from under this, Darya. Your work and sacrifice won't be unnoticed. You've dedicated years of your life to this moment, to bring down these men. Don't give up now. I need your help."

"With what?" Darya didn't look convinced.

"Javi said they were going out to an airfield to pick up a friend. Do you know anything—"

"It's Flynn." Darya cut her off. "I have video of Marcus making the arrangements. But not at an airfield. In a canyon off a road in the wild. I could not understand the name."

Regan swallowed her panic. "A canyon. Okay." How many could there be in Southern California within driving distance?

Darya lowered the gun but kept it at her side, finger pressed against the trigger. "I want to trust you."

Regan could see it in her eyes, along with the bitterness of the past.

The intercom for the front gate buzzed, the sound echoing out in the entry alcove.

Natalia looked between them.

"Let them in," Regan told Natalia. She stepped forward and gently wrapped her fingers around Darya's hand that was clasping the weapon. Regan didn't try to take it but offered comfort and understanding. She squeezed Darya's fingers. "Let me help you both."

Darya's jaw worked. Her eyes narrowed as if fighting the impulse to agree. "He cannot get away." She turned her head, her eyes nearly dead with pain. "Promise me."

"I promise." It was one Regan planned to keep.

Darya pulled away, relaxed her hold on her weapon and walked out of the office, leaving Regan to follow.

"Can you give me access to the video footage you've got of Marcus?" she asked when she joined Darya in the foyer. Darya hesitated, so Regan added, "I came here to help Brandon and Avril's mother win back custody of her children." It was, she suspected, something Darya would understand.

"I will give you access." Her clipped answers seemed more normal for this woman. "He should not have his children. He is a danger to them." Funny how the facade she'd kept in place for so long had melted away completely. There was no hint of Celeste Antius in the woman who stood in front of her now.

She touched Darya's arm. "Thank you." She pulled open the front door and stepped outside.

"What the—" She balked at the homeless man who had been camping out in front of the house the past few days walking up the driveway. His gait, his stature. There was something familiar about—

The dog at his side, or rather his feet, barked once when he saw her looking at him.

The man reached up and pulled off the wig of scraggly gray hair, removed the full beard as he approached Slade's car. He scrubbed a hand into his dark hair in a way that had it falling over one eye in an all too recognizable way.

"Aiden." Regan shook her head in disbelief. How had she not realized it was her brother? "I thought you had a job back east?" He'd been here the entire time? She walked down the steps and into a warm hug. "I can't believe you— Wow." She jerked back almost immediately, her eyes watering. "You went all method, didn't you? You stink."

"Part of the cover." The charming smile appeared briefly before he focused on Slade, then the women in front of the house. "Darya Sarkasian." He shrugged out of his jacket, tossed it on the hood of Slade's car, walked over with his hand out. "Aiden McKenna. Minotaur Security." He looked down at the weapon in her hand. "Nice gun."

"I have heard of Minotaur," Darya said. "You have an acceptable and admirable reputation."

Aiden arched a brow. "Nice to hear. Slade, where are we with Javi?"

Slade emerged from the back of his SUV, laptop in hand. He set it on the hood, opened it and displayed a program on the screen. "Transmitter's working just fine. Follow the blinking red light."

"Transmitter?" Regan looked at her brother. "How—"

"I slipped it in his pocket when he tried to move me along. He didn't come close to recognizing me."

"He's not the only one," Regan muttered. Leave it to her big brother to make her feel off her game.

"Can you see where they might be heading?" Aiden asked Slade, who shook his head.

"Darya heard mention of a canyon." Regan moved in beside him to look closer at the online map and the red blipping dot moving farther and farther away from Newport Beach.

"Lots of canyons in Southern California," Slade said.

Darya moved in, peered over Slade's shoulder. "It started with a *T*. Talbuck? Tali—"

Slade zoomed out, pointed to a spot that could realistically be in the right direction. "Trabuco Canyon?"

"Yes." Darya nodded. "That is the name."

"Let's go." Regan raced around to the passenger seat, but Aiden held up a hand as he dug into the back of the SUV.

"Give me ten minutes to grab a shower and change."

He hefted a packed duffel bag out of the back. "Unless you want to make an hour drive with me smelling this bad."

"You have five," Regan warned him, feeling her anxiety ease when she saw Natalia holding a wiggly, affectionate Lucky in her arms. "Then so do you!" Aiden called. "You're not dressed for pursuit. Suit up, Agent."

She looked down at her black uniform dress. She'd totally forgotten. "Fine. Ten minutes. But be quick!"

Javi had spent enough time in Southern California by now to know where they were headed was nowhere good. Not for him, at least. Not that he'd been expecting a weekend at a fancy hotel.

They'd been driving in silence for almost an hour and judging by the GPS map on the dashboard screen, all he saw ahead was open, empty space. When Demchenko took the turnoff for Trabuco Canyon's main road Javi accepted the low odds that he would come out of this alive.

With its dense groves of oaks and sycamores, expansive outcropping of rocks and dry creek beds, the steep inclines had taken out countless hikers over the years. Unfortunately, they'd thought the rugged terrain an athletic challenge, which they eventually failed. Most times he'd appreciate the spooky atmosphere provided by the natural area, but right now he looked for a practical, possible escape route should he make it out of the car.

"How long have you known?" Javi was running out of time and before this was over, he wanted to know where he'd messed up.

"About you still being an active ATF agent?" Marcus asked without taking his eyes off the tablet computer in his lap. "I was notified of that yesterday afternoon." His jaw tensed visibly as the SUV bounced along the winding road.

So he'd almost gotten away with it.

"Someone sell me out?" Someone at the ATF who had learned about Javi's undercover assignment perhaps?

"You were recognized," Marcus said. "Your name was, anyway. Reggie mentioned the scuffle you and Niko got into to my new business partner. It was then he said he knew a Javi Perez from a few years back. Said there was no chance you'd ever walk away from your badge, let alone take any kind of payoff."

"Then I guess he got three things right." Whatever happened, he wasn't going without a fight. He'd taken enough survivalist courses that he could make it out of here alive, or hide well enough to evade a few individuals who hadn't come close to dressing for a romp in the woods. "How is Caleb?"

Now Marcus looked at Javi. Vaya glanced back, those snake eyes glinting against the growing darkness.

"You'll see for yourself soon enough," Demchenko said. He turned on the headlights and continued down the dirt road. The last of the light faded under the weight and heft of the trees.

Demchenko slowed, pulling to a stop at a small lay-by. He parked, turned off the car.

The road was narrow, far too narrow to make any kind of U-turn. Chances were, to get out, they'd have to keep going until the area widened. It was, Javi thought as a plan began to form, a start.

"Is he late?" Javi asked.

"He is not." Demchenko sat back, pulled the keys out

of the ignition and dropped them onto the center console. "It won't be long."

Silence pressed in on him inside the confines of the car.

"Can we at least open a window?" The air was getting a bit stale with all this testosterone. No one paid him any mind. "I'm curious, Marcus. What deal did the Valeri syndicate offer you that would have you agreeing to smuggle human beings in and out of the country?"

Marcus glanced at him and for the first time, Javi saw genuine fear on his face before he covered it with a thin veil of contempt.

"No more talking," Demchenko ordered.

Headlights flashed in the rearview mirror. Javi twisted around as a luxury SUV pulled up behind them and parked. Demchenko and Vaya both climbed out and opened the back doors.

"Out." Demchenko cocked his head to the side.

Javi unfolded himself from the back seat, rolled his shoulders and arms to try to work out the kinks. Demchenko shoved him forward. Javi caught his footing but righted himself, avoiding a face-plant into the rough dirt. At least they hadn't tied his wrists together.

His hands flexed. He still had a chance.

He walked beside Marcus into the gleam of the other car's high beams. Vaya and Demchenko stayed directly behind them. Reggie climbed out of the front passenger seat, came around to open the door behind the driver.

Even in the shadows, Javi recognized Caleb Flynn. Even a Caleb Flynn who had had serious work done on his face. It was the swagger, Javi thought. And the eyes.

There was no changing eyes that flashed so easily from good to evil and back.

Gone was the typical FBI suit with its questionable ironing job. The suit Flynn was wearing now was runway ready. Flynn quickly buttoned his jacket, his designer loafers crunching the gravel road.

"Sometimes I love being right." Caleb Flynn didn't look at anyone other than Javi. "ATF Agent Javier Perez. It's not particularly good to see you again."

What Javi wouldn't do to swipe that self-satisfied smirk off his face. "I've been looking for you, Caleb. It's taken a while to find you."

"You've gone to great lengths to do so, it would seem." He nodded to Demchenko, then Vaya, and cast an almost disparaging glance at Marcus. "You let him sneak past your defenses, Marcus. That's careless. And not behavior we approve of in the Valeri organization."

"I have a lot to make up for, I know," Marcus said in a low, submissive tone. "I'm hoping bringing Perez to you is a first step in that reconciliation."

Judging by the distasteful expression on Flynn's face, Javi wouldn't put money on that being the case. If anything, he had the distinct feeling that Javi wasn't the only one about to be chucked off a ravine down one of these paths.

Up until this moment, he hadn't really considered what might happen to Marcus Antius other than prison. But now? Knowing what Regan had gone through to protect his children, Javi couldn't help but think what Marcus's death might do to Avril and Brandon.

Losing a father, losing a parent in any fashion, left wounds that would never completely heal.

Javi knew that better than anyone.

He noted an opening between a grouping of trees and wondered how close he might be to one of those paths leading nowhere. There was hope, he told himself. Until there wasn't.

"The ship is scheduled to dock in a few hours." Reggie Bogart stepped out of the shadows of Flynn's car to join them. "We should get back sooner than later."

"Not just yet," Flynn said. "I have some questions that need answers. Kasimir?" He held out his hand, into which Vaya placed a polished blade. Flynn jabbed the air and then held it close to Javi so that he could see it. "About the ATF's knowledge of my business dealings."

Javi shook his head and laughed easily. A hearty, spontaneous belly laugh. "You and I both know you aren't one to get your hands dirty, Flynn. And in case you forgot how undercover assignments work, I'm not in the know about anything to do with the ATF. One of the benefits of being persona non grata, whether it's the truth or a lie."

"This might be the case. But we can't be sure, can we?" He held up his other hand. "You are right about one thing, however." He passed the blade to Demchenko. "I'd rather leave this up to someone who knows what they're doing."

Javi turned away from Flynn as Demchenko moved in, his expression unreadable. He gripped Javi's shoulder, drew him close and plunged the knife into his side.

"Pull over and kill the lights!"

Regan jumped at Slade's order. He closed the laptop. The interior of the SUV went dark. Behind the wheel,

Aiden glanced to where Slade sat beside Darya in the back. She held her weapon on her lap like a prized pet.

"They stopped fifty yards down this road," Slade said, pointing out the windshield. "No idea what we're walking into."

"Get out," Aiden said. "Quietly."

Once she was out of the car, Regan tried to walk as softly as possible to meet the others now gathered at the rear of the vehicle. Aiden dug into the metal suitcase he had stashed there and handed out tailored Kevlar vests.

Darya shook her head and offered a mild expression of disgust. "No."

"You're on my team, you suit up." Aiden shoved the vest into her chest. "Otherwise, you stay here."

She opened her mouth to argue, but Regan stepped in. "You want Demchenko, this is how it happens."

Darya grimaced before accepting the protection. Once they were suited up and armed—Regan with her own sidearm from the apartment—Aiden gave brief instructions. They would move fast and in sync, two on each side of the narrow road. Darya would follow Slade, Regan on Aiden's six.

Weapons raised and secured, they moved out. They stayed as far away as they could from the brush to avoid being detected or heard. Every footstep Regan took felt like another lifetime away from Javi. She hadn't heard any gunshots, so she'd take that as a good sign. Not that he couldn't have been killed before they got here. That tracker didn't identify life signs and Antius had had a good lead.

"I can hear you thinking this to death from all the

way up here." Aiden looked back at her, warning in his eyes. "Blank it out. If he's still alive, we'll get him out."

Hope grew, however thin. "Promise?"

He nodded once. "Promise."

Her brother never made promises he couldn't keep.

Across the road, Slade held up his arm. Darya froze. Aiden and Regan did the same. The glow of the headlights up ahead had her and Aiden moving to join Slade and Darya. Slade pointed up and to the right, then moved into the cover of the trees. He took the lead and they made their way as silently as they could through the woods.

They crouched down, peering through the thick brush. The group of men were gathered between two vehicles. Regan peered, breathed a sigh of relief at the sight of Javi, alive.

"Is that Flynn?" Aiden asked Slade.

"Maybe," Slade said. "Could be, if he's had surgery or procedures." He looked back to Darya, who nodded.

"It is him."

"We get Flynn," Regan told her. "You get Demchenko." When her brother frowned at her, she lifted her shoulders as if in surrender. "I made a promise."

It took a moment, but he nodded.

"Something's happening," Slade said and they turned their attention back to the men.

Regan assessed the situation. Marcus looked far more cowering than she anticipated. Even from this distance she could smell the fear on him. What did he think would happen, getting involved with Flynn and the syndicate?

She'd lay odds Reggie Bogart was a coward at heart.

Too much of a weasel to be a serious threat. Made him negligible at best.

Vaya would ride it out and act as if he were bullet-proof, while Demchenko might very well walk straight into the hail of bullets believing himself immune. But Flynn…

Flynn was the wild card.

A wild card with a knife, apparently. She winced as the blade he held glinted against the headlamp's glow. When he passed the blade to Demchenko, Regan rose up, fear lurching inside of her like a breaching whale.

"Down!" Aiden ordered on a whisper just as the knife flashed and was buried in Javi's side.

Regan's mouth opened in a silent scream. Her brother's hand locked on her arm and pulled her back before she'd even realized she'd moved.

"Wait," Aiden said under his breath. Javi stumbled but remained on his feet. He pressed a hand against the wound. Blood spilled over and through his fingers. "That cut is a start, not the end. We need to let Javi know we're here."

Aiden was right. Javi needed hope. It might be the only thing that could save him.

Regan's mind raced, ideas tumbling over one another. She touched a hand to the locket around her neck. "Donut."

"You're hungry?" Aiden balked.

"No, Donut." She pulled the locket free of her shirt. "His bark. Javi knows his bark."

Aiden pointed at her. "Do it."

She made the sound. Once. Two times. A third.

Vaya and Marcus looked around, confusion on their

faces. Flynn, Reggie and Demchenko didn't seem to hear it.

Javi straightened and then he froze before hunching over again. The pain on his face made Regan's heart hurt, but there was also a glimmer of a smile.

"They'll draw it out," Darya said from behind them. "They will want him to suffer. It's what they do."

"He won't suffer for long," Aiden said. "Flank the car behind Flynn. Same teams. Slade, you and Darya go right. We'll take left."

Closest to Javi, Regan thought. She nodded, released the safety on her weapon as the others did the same. Aiden held up one hand, counted down. *Three, two, one. Go!*

Regan kept her focus on Javi, but remained alert for any sudden movement. She followed in Aiden's steps as Slade and Darya made their way around the other side.

She knew the instant Demchenko caught sight of them. The temperature around them seemed to plummet.

A chill swept through the air as he pivoted, reached into his jacket for his gun. Javi threw himself into Demchenko, tackling him like a linebacker. They went down hard.

Flynn spun around but Aiden had advanced fast, weapon raised and trained on the traitor. Vaya remained where he was, staring at them, his gaze dark and lifeless.

Marcus dropped and crouched, digging his manicured fingers into the dirt and mud, acting like there was an escape route below.

"ATF!" Regan yelled as she moved in. "Caleb Flynn, you're under arrest!"

Flynn pivoted around the car and dived for the trees.

He came up short when Slade threw out one muscular arm and clotheslined him from the other side of the vehicle. Flynn nearly did a backflip before he landed with a thud on the ground.

Slade moved over him, aimed his weapon at his face. "Hey, Caleb." The smile he offered sent chills racing down Regan's spine. "Remember me?"

Flynn groaned and his head tipped back into the gravel.

"Don't move!" Regan ordered Marcus and Reggie. "I mean it!" She found immense pleasure knowing Dina would be getting her kids full-time from now on.

"I want a deal!" Reggie yelled. "I'll talk for a deal!"

Even for a turncoat he was despicable, Regan thought. But she wasn't about to give him another moment of thought. "Javi?"

"Over here." But he didn't sound good.

"Go," Aiden told her. "I've got them. Slade? Where's Vaya?"

"He is here." Darya shoved Vaya in front of her. He skidded before landing hard on his knees. Blood gushed from his nose and trickled out the side of his mouth as he clutched his ribs. "So much for the mighty Kasimir Vaya. You will pay for the suffering you caused."

Vaya sneered at her over his shoulder, blood gushing from his nose and mouth.

Regan locked down her gun, shoved it into the back waistband of her jeans. She dropped in front of Javi, hauling him forward.

"It's not bad," he said, his voice clearly weak. He pulled his hand away and winced at the amount of blood. "Okay, maybe a little bad. Do you really need a spleen?"

"You're joking." Regan muttered. "First you got shot, now knifed. Let's not go for a third lethal weapon, okay?"

He chuckled, then groaned. "Way ahead of you."

"Where is Demchenko?" Darya loomed over them, gun at her side. She had Vaya's blood on the backs of her arms and spattered across the front of her shirt.

"Celeste?" Javi blinked as if he were seeing things. "Is that…? What's going…?"

"I'll explain later," Regan told him. "You need a doctor."

"Where?" Darya demanded of Javi.

He pointed into the break in the woods. "He went in there."

"Wait!" Regan grabbed for her as Darya stalked past, but Darya slapped her hand aside, glared at her with such ferocity, Regan had no reply.

Darya walked into the trees and didn't look back.

"Think she'll find him?" Aiden asked as he maneuvered a restrained Reggie and then Vaya onto the ground in between the two cars.

"Yes," Regan said without doubt. "I do."

"I need a phone." Javi started to wheeze. "Need to call the ATF." He grabbed hold of Regan's hand, squeezed tight. "I'm done. With all of it. I'm officially declaring my intention to retire."

Regan pressed her mouth to his, reveling in the feel of his touch. He was alive. Alive! They both were. She tugged off her Kevlar and then her T-shirt, leaving her in a sports bra, but she didn't care. She pressed the wadded-up cloth against his side. "We need to get you to the hospital."

"Faster to take him ourselves. Slade?"

Even as Aiden said it, sirens blared in the distance.

"I texted my former FBI supervisor before we left the estate," Slade told them. "They're bringing an ambulance, too."

Relief surged through Regan and she breathed easier. When she saw Marcus looking at her, she took Javi's hand, and put it where hers had been, with the cloth. "Keep it tight," she ordered and got up to walk over to Marcus.

She bent down in front of him so she could look him in the eye. Confusion filled his gaze.

"Who are you?" He shook his head as if dazed.

"Dina sent me."

"No." Realization shone before his eyes went cold. "She can't have them. They're mine! I did all this to protect them! He was going to kill my kids unless I agreed to his terms."

"If that's true—" Regan clung onto her emotions and tried for calm "—then protect them from what's about to happen to you. You'll likely have a large bounty placed on your head, courtesy of whatever is left of the Valeri syndicate. Who do you think they're going to blame for this? Him?" She jutted a thumb at Flynn. "He's already a dead man. I give him a week, maybe less in prison. You either get to join him there or maybe take advantage of a plea deal. One that requires a prison sentence." Preferably a long one. "But one that will be a lot more kind than his."

"In case you need added incentive," Aiden said. "A search and seizure warrant is on its way to the LA harbor for the *Deadlight Express*. The harbormaster is already in custody and he hasn't stopped talking." Aiden smirked. "Whatever is on that ship, you're going to want to get out ahead of it. Plus, there's about eighteen months' worth of computer evidence about to be delivered to the authorities in what?" He looked at his watch. "About twenty-four hours. Clock's ticking."

"I want visitation," Marcus seethed.

"It all depends," Regan rasped, trying to stay cool when all she wanted was to see this guy pay for the hurt he'd caused. "They've earned themselves a couple of guardian angels. Whatever contact they have with you will be up to Dina. And the two of us." She indicated Javi. "Hope that makes you sleep better at night."

When she rose, it was with a feeling of relief and exhaustion. The buzz of adrenaline she'd been riding for days began to fade. Even now she could feel every cell in her body start to relax. Vehicles abruptly pulled to a stop. Clusters of people spilled out and headed in their direction.

Regan returned to Javi, pushed him back to the ground when he struggled to stand. "Stop, Javi." Regan put a hand to his chest. "Just stop. It's over." He reached out his free hand, wincing in pain. "You can come home now."

"Home." He forced a laugh. "Don't really know where that is."

"Yes, you do." She leaned down, pressed her forehead against his. "It's with me."

"I love you." He touched her face, squeezed his eyes shut. "Wasn't sure I was going to get the chance to tell you, but I love you."

Regan smiled. "I know."

He laughed again, then groaned as a pair of uniformed

EMTs made their way past Aiden. Regan moved away so Javi could be tended to.

Additional agents and officers from the ATF and FBI swarmed the site, gathering statements and suspects.

"You know what this means, don't you?" Aiden asked as the two of them stood amid the chaos. Regan looked into the woods where Demchenko and Darya had vanished. "What what means?"

"You and Javi." Aiden knocked his shoulder against hers. "I've been keeping Mom up to speed on your investigation. Your presence has been requested next week for dinner. In Boston. The whole family will be there," he added. "For both of you."

"Oh?" She couldn't stop the smile from spreading across her face. "Are you going to make it this time? You've been awfully busy lately."

"You're mistaking me for Howell." Boston, after all, was his home base. "You can confirm with Mom once Javi's out of the hospital." He slid his arm around her shoulders as they watched Javi's gurney being lifted and wheeled away.

"You hear that, Javi?" Regan called after him. "We've got a dinner date with my parents."

He lifted a hand and stuck his thumb in the air.

Regan beamed, rested her head on her brother's shoulder and closed her eyes. "Three McKenna siblings down, one to go." She laughed when Aiden groaned. When she looked up at him it was with gratitude and love. "Thanks for having my back, Aiden."

"Always, kid." He tightened his arm and hugged her again. "Always."

Epilogue

Six weeks later...

"**Y**ou finally kept your word." Regan stretched out her legs and arms, basking in the warm glow of the sun beating down on them. "You got me to the beach."

"I always get there," Javi chuckled. "Eventually."

She smiled up and into the sun.

She'd thought things had gone crazy after Javi's "disgrace," but that had been nothing compared with after the story broke about the capture of Caleb Flynn, the arrests of Reggie Bogart and Marcus Antius and the extradition of Kasimir Vaya back to his native France.

For weeks, video of the boarding of the *Deadlight Express* and the discovery of more than a hundred trafficked men, women and children had saturated the news. Javi's name had been mentioned numerous times as the lead investigator who had led to its capture.

As for Niko Demchenko, neither he nor Darya Sarkasian had been seen since that night in the woods. But Regan suspected she'd come across Darya at some point again. Women like that...they stayed on target until the job was done. And there was a lot of evil in the world to combat.

As for Javi, the ATF had welcomed him back not only with open arms, but with a retroactive promotion that gave him his choice of career moves.

Regan and Javi had traveled directly to Philadelphia for Dina, who got to welcome Avril and Brandon back home. Avril had even drawn Javi a special picture to thank him for the letter he'd written to the court. A letter that had brought tears to Regan's eyes.

Life had indeed shifted on its axis. For both her and Javi.

Not ten feet away, the ocean broke and tumbled over the shore of the private Hawaiian beach attached to one of Aiden's safe houses. They'd arrived only yesterday and spent most of their time since then in bed, until finally venturing out for the sun and sand that had been promised to her years before.

Javi lifted his arm when she sat up and touched the stitch marks in his side. "It's healing nicely." He caught her hand, brought it up to his lips and kissed her fingertips. "I'm fine."

"Yes, you are." She rolled into him, rested her head on his shoulder. The warm sand sank into the bare skin exposed by the bikini her sister Wren had helped to pick out. "You've got ten days here in paradise to change your mind, you know."

"Change my mind about what?"

She rolled her eyes. "Retiring."

He tucked his chin into his chest and looked down at her. "Do you want me to change my mind?"

"I want what you want." She'd miss working with him, but she'd be just as happy if he was safely out of law enforcement. If he stayed on the job, the fact was that there'd be no more chance of undercover work, given all the attention he and the case had gotten in the media. So yeah. Civilian life for him suited her just fine.

"So, I had a conversation with your brother last week."

She groaned and buried her face in his chest. "Nothing good ever follows that statement."

"No, this would be good for me, I think. He's looking to diversify Minotaur. Training classes for young people wanting to go into law enforcement for the right reasons. Working with boys' and girls' groups around the country. Giving opportunities to kids like I was. Kids who are looking for something…bigger, where they can make a positive difference. It would mean traveling, but also, I'd have a lot of flexibility with my schedule."

"I have to admit my brother is a very smart man who knows a good idea when he comes up with it. Don't tell him I said that, though," she quickly added, spotting a cheeky grin on his face. "You've earned the right to do whatever you want with the rest of your life, Javi."

"Yeah?" He threaded his fingers through hers. "'Cause I'd really like to make this thing between us official." He tilted her hand up. "I asked your father before we left. If he was okay with me asking you to marry me."

Regan half snorted and half laughed. "You did not." She sat up and brought him with her. It was so old-fashioned, not to mention unexpected. An action that didn't annoy her nearly as much as she thought it should. "What did he say?"

"Well, first he said that it wasn't any of his business if you wanted to marry me and second—" he kissed her again "—he gave his wholehearted approval."

"Uh-huh." She smiled against his lips, touched a hand to his cheek. "That sounds like my dad."

"Now Aiden on the other hand…" He laughed when she gently slugged him. "Kidding. I'm just kidding. So will you?"

"Marry you?" Every cell in her body sparked to life. "All right." She tried to hide her enthusiasm, tease him, as if he asked her this every day, and it wasn't the thing she wanted most in the world. "I think I'd like to do that. What do you say we stop in Vegas on the way home?"

* * * * *

For more great McKenna family romances from Anna J. Stewart and Harlequin Romantic Suspense, visit www.Harlequin.com today!

Get up to 4 Free Books!

We'll send you 2 free books from each series you try
PLUS a free Mystery Gift.

Both the **Harlequin Intrigue**® and **Harlequin**® **Romantic Suspense** series feature compelling novels filled with heart-racing action-packed romance that will keep you on the edge of your seat.

YES! Please send me 2 FREE novels from the Harlequin Intrigue or Harlequin Romantic Suspense series and my FREE gift (gift is worth about $10 retail). I may cancel anytime by emailing ReaderServiceInfo@Harlequin.com or by calling 1-800-873-8635. If I don't cancel, I will receive 6 brand-new Harlequin Intrigue Larger-Print books every month and be billed just $7.19 each in the U.S. or $7.99 each in Canada, or 4 brand-new Harlequin Romantic Suspense books every month and be billed just $6.39 each in the U.S. or $7.19 each in Canada, a savings of 20% off the cover price. It's quite a bargain! Shipping and handling is just 75¢ per book in the U.S. and $1.75 per book in Canada.* I understand that accepting the free books and gift places me under no obligation to buy anything—they are mine to keep for free no matter what I decide.

Choose one:

☐ **Harlequin Intrigue Larger-Print** (199/399 BPA G3CD)

☐ **Harlequin Romantic Suspense** (240/340 BPA G3CD)

☐ **Or Try Both!** (199/399 & 240/340 BPA G3CE)

Name (please print)

Address — Apt. #

City — State/Province — Zip/Postal Code

Email: Please check this box ☐ if you would like to receive newsletters and promotional emails from Harlequin Enterprises ULC and its affiliates. You can unsubscribe anytime.

Mail to the Harlequin Reader Service:

IN U.S.A.: P.O. Box 1341, Buffalo, NY 14240-8531

IN CANADA: P.O. Box 603, Fort Erie, Ontario L2A 5X3

Want to explore our other series or interested in ebooks? Visit www.ReaderService.com or call 1-800-873-8635.

*Terms and prices subject to change without notice. Prices do not include sales taxes, which will be charged (if applicable) based on your state or country of residence. Canadian residents will be charged applicable taxes. Offer not valid in Quebec. This offer is limited to one order per household. Books received may not be as shown. Not valid for current subscribers to the Harlequin Intrigue or Harlequin Romantic Suspense series. All orders subject to approval. Credit or debit balances in a customer's account(s) may be offset by any other outstanding balance owed by or to the customer. Please allow 4 to 6 weeks for delivery. Offer available while quantities last.

Your Privacy — Your information is being collected by Harlequin Enterprises ULC, operating as Harlequin Reader Service. For a complete summary of the information we collect, how we use this information and to whom it is disclosed, please visit our privacy notice located at https://corporate.harlequin.com/privacy-notice. Notice to California Residents—Under California law, you have specific rights to control and access your data. For more information on these rights and how to exercise them, visit https://corporate.harlequin.com/california-privacy. For additional information for residents of other U.S. states that provide their residents with certain rights with respect to personal data, visit https://corporate.harlequin.com/other-state-residents-privacy-rights.

HIHRS2603